SPIRIT, HEART, AND BACKBONE

"Why don't you cooperate with the United States Army, Mrs. Ames? As a citizen of the United States of America you must cooperate with us by answering our questions," the lieutenant said.

"Now, Mister Holmes, get one thing straight. Don't you go to threatening me with your Army stuff. The Apaches were here long before the United States become the United States. I happen to be friends with some Apaches. I consider them just as much citizens of the United States as I am."

"If you would just tell me where these friends of yours are living, it would make things much easier."

"Easier! You have no idea what it means to work for a living to survive in these parts. You spend all your time either riding around the mountains looking for Apaches who you can't find, or down in the parlours with the whores in Tombstone. You are on my property, Lieutenant Holmes. I am telling you to get on that horse and leave."

Holmes grabbed me by the shoulders and started shaking me, saying, "Why don't you listen to reason?"

Something snapped inside of me when he started with my shoulders. Without giving another thought to anything I kneed the lieutenant between his legs with all my strength. He dropped his hands from my shoulders, and moaning real loud, grabbed his privates as he sunk to the ground. All I heard was his sabre jingling as it hit the dirt.

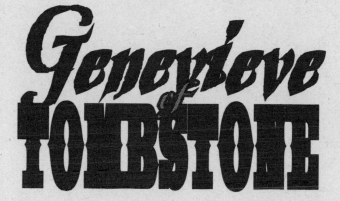

Genevieve of Tombstone

John Duncklee

LEISURE BOOKS NEW YORK CITY

To my wife, Penny, as always.

A LEISURE BOOK®

November 1999

Published by

Dorchester Publishing Co., Inc.
276 Fifth Avenue
New York, NY 10001

ISBN 0-8439-4628-8

Printed in the United States of America.

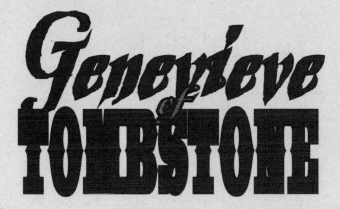

Prologue

The story of Genevieve is her own, told to me when I was doing field work for a doctoral dissertation. I started out investigating the evolution of cattle ranching in southern Arizona. Many of the old-time cattlemen around Tombstone and the Sulphur Springs Valley advised me to find Genevieve. Their advice proved valuable in several ways.

Most important for me was the friendship Genevieve and I struck together. When I interviewed her over a period of several months, she was always ready to tell me about her life as a whore and cattlewoman during the difficult times of the 1880s and 1890s.

Genevieve's reliable memory served me well. After cross-checking the events that she related to me, I found her story accurate beyond a doubt. Her opinions about the ways of husbanding cattle may not have been popular at the time she was managing the Quarter Circle L, but some of her theories were adopted by others at a later time.

The more I talked with Genevieve, the less important the doctoral dissertation became. When I began to organize Genevieve's story in order to begin writing it, I realized that I would not write a dull doctoral dissertation that few besides my committee would read. I had to write Genevieve's story.

Tucson, Arizona Territory, March 18, 1904

Chapter One

Hannah Turner came busting into the parlor all out of breath. A long lock of her brown, windblown hair fell down over her right eye. Dropping the hem of her flowered skirt to her ankles, she exclaimed, "Genevieve, come quick! Custis was shot! It happened on Fifth Street, right in front of the pawnshop. I didn't wait to see if he's dead or alive. I just came running to find you."

I jumped out of the chair, told Roland he was to stay with Paula, and tore out with Hannah toward the center of Tombstone. When I saw my husband lying in the street, I ran over, knelt down beside him, and took his head in my arms. I could see right off by the blank look in his eyes he was gone. Hannah told me later that I commenced to wail something awful. She come over and put her arm around my shoulders.

Marshal Phillips stepped up and told me that Custis had

got into it with Harry Dobbs and Luther Breeland. Then he told me that Dobbs had shot Custis in self-defense. I looked at the revolver in Custis's hand.

"Marshal, Custis never owned a revolver, only his Sharps carbine. Don't be telling me Dobbs shot him in self-defense. Find out who belongs to that revolver. I'll bet it's Dobbs."

I was still crying and could barely get the words out of my mouth. I was so angry, I felt like taking that revolver and killing everyone who was standing around gawking at me and Custis.

"Gunther Gorman, the undertaker, will be by shortly, ma'am," the marshal explained. "Why don't you let me take care of things here, and you go to the Palace."

"Marshal Phillips, I'll stay with my husband. Then I'll find out what happened. You don't seem to care about the truth."

I stayed there holding Custis while the crowd stood around in a circle watching. Hannah was there with me. She had seen most of what had happened, and promised she'd tell me everything once we were alone.

Paula pushed her way through the crowd and kneeled down next to me too. "My God, Gen" was all she could say. Then Paula commenced to crying with me. The three of us stayed there until Gorman pulled up with the hearse. We stood up and watched as the marshall, Gorman, and two of the onlookers lifted Custis into the back. Gorman told me he would take care of Custis and make all the necessary arrangements. I was too numb to say anything. Paula and Hannah helped me walk into the Crystal Palace, where we sat down at a table. Hannah got up and brought us some mescal.

"Genevieve," Hannah began. "I watched Custis come in

and order his usual mescal at the bar. He'd downed three shots before Dobbs and Breeland came in the door. Those two walked straight to the bar and ordered mescal too. One of them, I think it was Dobbs, said something to Custis about being too friendly with the Apaches."

"Did Custis talk back to them?"

"Custis stood there looking straight ahead and didn't say a word to either of them. They both needled Custis like they were wanting to start a fight with him, but Custis paid no attention to them."

"Did they force Custis out of the bar?"

"No. Custis left by the Fifth Street door. As he walked past Dobbs and Breeland, he paused and said, 'Who my friends are is my business, and nothing gives you cause to hair-brand my calves.' He walked out fine with no sign of being drunk. Those two ranchers got up and followed him out the same door. Not long after that, I heard a shot. I ran out to see what had happened. There was Custis lying in the street facedown with those cowmen leaning over him. That's when I ran to Paula's to get you, because I know that's where you go when you come to town. Dammit, Genevieve, I'm so sorry this had to happen to you."

"Thanks for your help, Hannah. I can't believe my Custis is dead."

Paula asked Hannah to see that my mules were put up for the night. Then Paula took my hand and helped me walk to her parlor house. Along the way I asked about Roland.

"Angie's taking care of him. Don't worry yourself. You're both spending the night, or as long as you want to."

"I reckon you're my best friend, Paula. What in the world am I going to do with Custis gone?"

"You'll find a way to handle everything, Gen. You're one of the strongest women I know."

11

I reckon the toughest thing I ever did was to tell little Roland his father was dead, and that he wouldn't ever see him again. When we got back to Paula's, she gave us a room. I took Roland in there with me alone. I tried to tell him without crying, but I couldn't. He commenced crying too, but I reckon it was because I was crying, not because he understood about Custis.

How I was tortured that night! Roland fell asleep pretty quick, but I just sat on the bed, sometimes with my head in my hands sobbing away like I'd never stop. Other times I sat there looking out the window or at the wall, wondering what to do. I was plumb sad, just completely sad. Then I'd get so angry I wanted to go get the Sharps and kill both Dobbs and Breeland in front of the entire town. Toward morning, I got to thinking about what a wonderful man Custis had been, and how much we loved each other. Then I'd cry some more.

Paula offered to go back to the ranch with me. That Paula, I don't know what I'd have done without her.

"I've got to figure some way to have Roland looked after while I ride the ranch," I told her.

"There should be some woman in town who would take good care of him."

"I'm not leaving my boy in town, Paula. I just need someone to go out to the ranch to watch him when I'm out somewhere checking cattle. I'm sure Custis would want that."

"Ranching is tough enough for a man, Gen. Why don't you consider selling out and moving to town?"

"Like I said, Custis would want me to raise Roland on the ranch. And besides, I like it there. It's my home."

"You're probably right. I'll have Angie look around and see if she can find someone."

I stepped to the washstand to rinse away the tears, and had a look at myself in the mirror. My green eyes didn't have their usual sparkle, and the whites was all red from crying. I brushed out my long black hair, braided it, and put it up in a bun at the back of my head. I stood there in front of the mirror wondering why life at the claim and ranch hadn't put more age on my face. I still had the same creamy skin I'd had back in Missoura. I straightened up all five foot seven of me. I was just too young to be a widow.

After breakfast, Paula and I went to the funeral parlor. Gunther Gorman met us at the front door, which had a wreath hung on it made of yellow-green desert broom branches. Gorman was dressed in a black suit and wore small, round spectacles that slid down his pudgy nose. His flabby cheeks had a pinkish shine to them. His bald head had a faded blond fringe, and his earlobes wiggled when he moved.

He took us to a room with some stuffed chairs to sit on. Gorman had his hands folded like a preacher as he stood facing us.

"Mrs. Ames, I can't tell you how deeply sorry I am that your husband, Custis, has met such a sad fate. I know that you want the very best for him, so I am doing everything possible for him and for you."

I was wondering when he was going to get down to business. All I wanted to do was pick up Custis and get out of town as fast as I could.

"I will have Custis laid out by early afternoon. You may come by for a viewing after one o'clock. In the meantime, if you have a church preference, I will be happy to make funeral arrangements, or I can arrange for the services to be held here."

13

"Mr. Gorman, I don't think Custis cared about churches and all that, so I reckon I'll just come by and pick him up."

"In that case, I will arrange for burial in the cemetery."

"Mr. Gorman, I don't think you understand. I said I'll come by and pick up my husband. He ain't going to be buried in no boot-hill cemetery."

"In that case, I will have everything in order by one o'clock, Mrs. Ames. I will also have your husband's personal belongings for you at that time."

Paula and I left the funeral parlor as soon as we could get up from the chairs. That Gorman was real spooky. Paula said I handled everything just fine. She also told me that those funeral fellers take advantage of upset people, especially widows. It was then that I fully realized that I was now a widow. Genevieve Ames, widow of Custis Ames. Tears flooded my eyes again as we walked back to Paula's.

Angie had found a Mexican woman, Sofía Sanchez, who agreed to come out to the ranch and take care of Roland while I was riding. Sofía was waiting for me at her house, because she didn't want to be seen going into Paula's parlor house.

Angie took me and Roland over to make arrangements. Sofía was smiling and seemed glad to see us. Her husband had been killed in the Tough-Nut mine shaft, like so many other miners. She had raised her only daughter, who had married and gone to Tucson. Roland seemed to like Sofía right off, so I told her what the job would be, and she said she'd be ready by afternoon.

Along about noon, I went over to the livery stable to get the mules and hitch them up to the buckboard. I paid the old former cowboy, and he helped me with the mules even though I didn't ask. I thanked him and drove the buckboard back to Paula's to pick up Roland. The little feller didn't seem no different than always, so I reckoned he didn't realize his father was dead. After all, he was only a little more than a year old. Paula come with us to the funeral parlor.

Gunther Gorman met us at the door again, and we saw the coffin setting there in the middle of the room. Gorman was all business, took my arm, and led me over for the viewing. Paula had Roland by the hand and was entertaining him as best she could. The coffin lid was open, and when I looked in, there was my Custis. But it wasn't Custis.

He was all dressed up in a suit and necktie, with his hair all slicked down like some kind of dandy. I was plumb shocked. I was angry to see what Gorman had done to my Custis.

"Mr. Gorman, that ain't the way Custis was. He never wore no necktie since I met him, and he never owned a suit of clothes like that."

"Mrs. Ames, I have only done what is customary. The suit, shirt, and necktie comes to only twenty-two dollars."

"Well, Mr. Gorman, you just take that suit, shirt, and necktie off my Custis and put his own clothes back on him. For one thing, Custis would not feel good in all that fancy stuff. And, for another thing, I'm not paying twenty-two dollars for something that's going under six foot of dirt."

"Mrs. Ames, this is highly out of the ordinary."

"Whatever it is, it is. Now get about getting my man back in his own clothes so's I can get him back to the ranch."

Paula, Roland, and me drove over and picked up Sofía. Then we went to Paula's to get her spend-the-night things because she had decided to come to the ranch with us. When we got back to the funeral parlor I made sure Custis was dressed in his own clothes. Gorman and some other feller loaded the pine coffin into the buckboard.

Gorman gave me his bill. I looked at it for a minute, then handed it back. "Send the bill to Harry Dobbs and Luther Breeland."

Gorman's long earlobes jiggled as he shook his head. "Mrs. Ames, I must insist on your honoring this account."

"I didn't open this account to begin with."

With that, I slapped the lines on the backs of the mules and we headed out of town. Before we got past Allen Street, Marshal Phillips strode out into the street and held up his hand for me to stop. I reined up the mules, and the marshal, with his hat pulled down low and his badge sparkling in the sun, waddled up to the buckboard.

"Mrs. Ames, I understand that you're taking your husband back to your ranch for burial, and I'd like to offer to help you."

My anger rose real quick. "Marshal Phillips, instead of coming out to help bury my husband, why don't you corral Dobbs and Breeland, and see to justice. They murdered my Custis in cold blood, and you know it."

I didn't wait for an answer. I turned my head and slapped the lines on the mules' rumps. They kind of jumped, and we were again headed out of Tombstone.

Paula patted me on the arm when we left the marshal in our dust. "I swear, Gen, you tell it just like it is."

The trip back was good for me. I didn't say much to anybody. Sofía and Roland were sitting in back on the grain sacks, getting to know each other. Paula sat next to me on the seat. She seemed to know I didn't want to talk. When we pulled into the barnyard, I reined the mules around to leave the buckboard under a big shade tree until I could get the grave dug. I unhitched the mules, drove them to the barn, and unharnessed them. After carrying the pick and shovel that Custis had brought from the claim to the spot next to the shade tree, I proceeded to the house.

Before I commenced to dig I had to change clothes. Sofía was already building a fire in the stove. Paula was playing with Roland. I could see everything was taken care of, so I went out and began doing what I needed to do.

Before I commenced with the pick and shovel I climbed up on the buckboard to have a look at Custis. I opened the lid on the coffin and there he was in the same clothes I last saw him alive in. I wondered why there wasn't any sign of a bullet hole, so I reached down and managed to turn him over on his side. That's when I saw the hole in his shirt with a big splotch of dried blood around it. Shot in the back! I turned him so he was lying on his back again, and shut the lid. Again my anger rose. I wanted to scream.

It was easier digging than I had expected. When Paula come out to tell me supper was ready, I had got down about two foot. We all sat down to the table, and I suddenly missed Custis something terrible. I got up from the table and went out to where the buckboard stood. I commenced crying again and talking to Custis through the coffin. I wondered if I'd ever get over him being gone. Then the anger come on me again, and I started pounding my fists on the coffin. The next thing I knew, Paula had put her arm around my shoulders and was holding me tight. I told her about Custis being shot in the back. She reached around and pulled my head to her. We stood there together, me crying again, and her stroking and patting my head.

I commenced digging again before sunup. I'd got down another foot or so when Paula come out and offered to spell me.

"This is something I must do by myself," I told her. "I reckon it's me trying to get done with all the hurt."

After eating breakfast I played with Roland for a little while, then went back to digging. I got to thinking while I was picking and shoveling. I remembered when my pa and ma were burned up in the house back in Missoura, and how bad I felt not being able to say good-bye to them. I knew Roland didn't seem to know what was happening or what had happened to Custis. I decided that he should see his father dead in the coffin, and watch him being buried. It might not mean much to Roland now, but someday it might.

I figured I had dug down six foot about midafternoon. I went into the house, changed into my town clothes, and we all went out to the grave. Paula and me unloaded the coffin from the buckboard and set it next to the grave. I opened the top of the coffin and took Roland by the hand.

"This is your daddy, son," I told him. "Your daddy has left us for another place, so we have to bury him here under this tree. But he'll always live in our hearts. Never forget your daddy."

Roland pulled his hand out of mine. He stepped over next to the coffin and reached his little hand over. He turned once to look at me, and then put his hand on Custis's cold cheek. I commenced to cry. Roland turned and come into my arms crying too. I held him close there and patted his back. I heard Paula crying behind me, but I didn't look at her.

Chapter Two

I wasn't one of them famous women in old Tombstone. I was just a common whore what was trying to make a living from the oldest profession in the world. But I wasn't one of the crib girls, either. They had a tough life in those little boxlike shanties. The Chinese, Negroes, and Indians made 25 cents for their services. The Mexican gals got 50 cents, the Frenchies, 75, and the Americans a dollar. I worked in a parlor house, where ten dollars was standard and an all-night went for thirty. I did all right as far as making a living, because there was always plenty of men wanting what might be called recreation in that old mining town. I bedded a bunch of them, made them happy for a spell, earned my keep and then some, but I'll never forget one old boy who kept coming back.

He was a cowboy turned prospector. He had an old burro, and was out in the hills more than he was in town.

But when he come to town he was raring for excitement and he come over to my place to find what all he was looking for. Well, I did my best to give Custis Ames what was in his dreams while he was out a-digging in the hills beyond where the strikes had already been made.

Custis would come over to Paula's place first thing when he got to town. He'd ask for me, and I'd come into the sitting room to palaver awhile. He always began by telling me the color he'd found and how much he thought it would assay for. Then he'd get to telling yarns about when he was cowboying in New Mexico way north of Silver City. He liked telling about how he come to be friends with some Apache Indians at his line camp. I'd heard tell that Apaches wasn't likely to be friends with whites, but I believed what Custis told me. I reckon I wanted to believe everything that man said. He'd often mention that what he wanted most was to strike a rich vein of ore, sell the claim, and buy a cow ranch.

Damned if I didn't hope his dreams would come true to his expectations, because Custis was a fine gentleman, always took his old scruffy hat off and put it in front of his belly to show respect to me, because I was a woman. Custis never thought of me as a whore. He respected me as a woman, and that's probably why I fell in love with him. He was the reason I quit whoring in Tombstone. There was something about Custis that was different than the run-of-the-mill blokes that I generally serviced.

He was gentle, kind, and had a loving streak in him that turned me real crazy when we was bedded down. I come to look forward to Custis coming to town. I knew he'd be coming over for a night or two before going back to the hills with that old burro to pick away at those rocks to see if there was some color in them. Durned gold and silver keeps a man looking no matter what he might have left behind.

Well, it was one of those times when Custis come to town for supplies and a little fun with me that my entire life come around to a drastic change. Gollies, why I ever let that Custis talk me into leaving a good-paying profession like I was in to become the wife of a dreaming prospector, I'll never know. But the rascal sure did a number on this gal, who should have known better.

He come into the parlor and asked for me. I had to hurry to get ready, because I'd already turned a trick with the mayor. I come on down the stairs and there was Custis waiting for me as was his usual way, with his ole scruffy hat at his belly.

"Miss Genevieve," he said as he rose up from the chair. "I come into town for supplies today, an' I come over here to see you, as usual. But, Miss Genevieve, I would like to take you out on the town for supper, if you'd care to come with me."

"Well, Custis, I'd like nothing better than to go out on the town with you, but I have to check with the establishment first," I replied.

"Well, do your checking so's we can be gone, lady."

He referring to me as "lady" just did me in. Hell's fire, the way Custis treated me did me in anyways. I hustled back, told Paula that I was fixing to go out on the town with Custis, and she said for me to have a good time.

Custis took me by the arm and escorted me to the Crystal Palace. "We can have us a drink before we go to supper," he told me.

He pulled a chair out from a table for me to sit in, and I was so durned startled at that kind of attention that I near missed setting down. The bar gal, Hannah Turner—I knew her from when she spent a couple months at my place of employment—come over. Custis ordered some kind of French brandy I'd never heard of.

Hannah come back and set the two little glasses in front of us. When Hannah left, Custis took a hold of his glass and raised it up, waiting for me to do the same. Hell's fire, I had no idea what that man had on his mind, so I took ahold of my glass and raised it up to his. We both took a sip of the brandy. It was a lot smoother going down than the mescal I was used to drinking.

"Genevieve, I've been thinking lately that we oughta get married. Every time I go back to the claim I can't think about nothing else but you, lady. Now, that gets dangerous when I'm trying to concentrate on how long a fuse to cut on a charge. The other day I was thinking about how nice it was going to be seeing you, and I cut the fuse too short. I didn't even notice how short it was until I lit it off."

"What happened when you figured it out?"

"I scampered out of that shaft. Damn near didn't make it out in time before the blast went off. I sat down at the entrance plumb out of breath and shaking."

"Is that the only reason you want to get married, Custis?"

"I'm trying to tell you I love you, lady. I started building a house for us out on the claim."

"Sounds like you're pretty sure that I'll say yes."

I had to needle Custis a bit.

"I been thinking about asking you for quite a spell."

"Then I reckon I better say yes before you change your notion."

"Then you're saying that you'll marry me, Genevieve?"

"That's what I just said, Custis. When do you figure you want to do it?"

"I oughta get the house built first. I don't want you having to live in a tent."

"Custis Ames, I've lived in a tent before. I can live in a tent again. And besides, I can help build the house."

"Well then, lady, I reckon I best be looking for a saddle horse for you."

We clinked our little glasses together again.

"Here's to us, lady," he said, and drank the glass dry.

I sipped my brandy little by little as we talked.

We said our vows on April 4, 1882. I didn't have any idea what I was getting myself into, marrying Custis and going out to that durned claim of his. He bought me a little zebra dun mare to ride. That made me feel even more like a lady, to be able to ride while Custis walked the entire way, leading his old burro loaded with supplies.

I had no notion of how much the claim was worth or how much ore he could dig out to pay our living. I didn't really care. I just loved the old coot. Actually, Custis wasn't old. He had just turned thirty-two when we married. I was two months shy of twenty. But I was an old twenty in lots of ways. After all, whoring does seem to pile age on a woman faster than other ways of life might.

When we finally got there I saw the start he'd made on the house. The walls were made from rocks, because most of the country thereabouts was nothing much more than rocks. I took one look and knew what I'd be doing for quite a spell. Hauling rocks and putting them in place on the walls. I was correct in assuming that, but Custis helped a lot, especially after he'd blasted and had to wait for the smoke and dust to clear from the shaft.

I went down the shaft only twice. He took me down there first off when we got there after tending to the zebra dun and unloading the burro. Custis couldn't wait until morning to show me where he thought the vein of gold would show. He explained all his theory, but I didn't listen much because I was feeling closed in down there. All I wanted to do was get back out in the air. The second time was when he flat insisted that I had to look at the vein when he finally found it. That was seven months after we married.

I worked hard building the house. When we had the walls pretty much up, Custis bought some poles from Jimmy Carr, who was freighting timbers off the Huachuca Mountains and selling them to the Tombstone mines. I always thought Jimmy was smarter than the miners because what he was selling was something a feller could see growing on the mountain. Of course, he had to work hard cutting the timber and dragging it down the mountain slope with his sixteen white mules.

When Jimmy come by with the roof poles I could tell he recognized me, but he didn't say anything. I remembered him from my former place of employment. He never asked for me, so I didn't know him that way. Angie was his favorite. Angie was good friends with me and she told me that she liked Jimmy Carr better than the miners.

Custis and I lifted the poles up onto the walls, wedging them in with rocks and mud. We made the roof out of ocotillos lashed together with rawhide and covered them with almost a foot of mud mixed with dried-out sacaton grass. We gathered the grass from the banks of the big arroyo near the trail to the claim. It was sure nice to have a cool place to live and sleep in during the hot summer. The roof didn't leak either. That Custis was good at doing a lot of things. But he was best at loving me when he wasn't too tuckered out from drilling powder holes with his single-jack hammer and star drills.

The day Custis dragged me down the shaft to see his vein of gold was another turning point in our lives. He had set the charges the morning before, and set them off about midafternoon. I remember it was a Wednesday, because I marked it on the calendar. I marked down all sorts of things on the calendar. The next morning he didn't wait for all the smoke to clear. He was in too much of a hurry to see what the blast might have uncovered.

I was cutting up some venison for a stew when he come out of the shaft and into the house with a chunk of ore that sparkled in the sunlight. He wore a grin from ear to ear. When he turned it over I saw why. Gollies, the durned rock had a nugget in it as big as an apricot!

Then I had to go down in that shaft to look at the vein. I must admit I was impressed with it, and I gave him a big hug to show how proud of him I was.

"Lady, this claim is worth a bundle of money. I'm hankering to sell it and buy us a cow ranch. I'll build a big house on it at headquarters so's you'll have plenty of room to move around in."

Custis had grown up on a cow ranch in Texas. He would have stayed cow ranching, but he was the youngest of four brothers. The ranch wasn't big enough to support them all, so Custis headed for New Mexico to find cow work. He cowboyed for a spell, then drifted to Tombstone when word got out about the boomtown. By the time he arrived, most of the country had already been claimed up, so he bought his old burro and headed farther out, looking for gold or silver.

The claim come about when he found an outcrop of sil-

ver covered by a bunch of catclaw. He filed on it and commenced digging the shaft, following the color. It was first
off silver, but when he got down thirty feet or so, he began
to see streaks of yellow in the quartz.

Custis had always apologized for the house on the claim
being too small for us. The day after he found the gold, he
left for Tombstone riding the zebra dun mare and leading
the old burro, loaded with the ore he had hurriedly high-
graded. I stayed at the claim guarding. All of a sudden
Custis was scared somebody might show up and steal his
pile of high-grade ore even though we had never yet had
visitors.

There was a bunch of bad-assed varmints around Tombstone in those days. It wasn't long after Paula and I arrived.
It was October, late. A Texas cowboy, Curly Bill Brocius,
shot Marshal Fred White. Then a year later the gunfight at
OK Corral between the Earps and Clantons shook up the
town a mite. Nobody seemed to know what happened. I
didn't pay much attention to all that sort of goings-on.
Tombstone was silver, and that's what we thought about.
The rowdy stuff just happened along the way. Then Custis
and me went to the claim.

It felt nice being alone for a few days. I hadn't been
alone since I was seventeen when my ma and pa burned up
in the house fire. I had always slept in the barn, because
there wasn't room in the house on that little farm back in
Missoura. Otherwise, I'd have burned up too. I had no kin,
so the Gillians, a neighbor family, took me in for a spell. I
did a heap of crying.

I was just getting used to the new surroundings when
one night Mrs. Gillian was off midwifing and I was cleaning up after supper. Mr. Gillian come up behind me of a
sudden and clamped his big, callused, hairy hands over my

bosoms. It scared me so much, I just froze up and stood stiff as a statue.

He commenced sweet-talking me, but I didn't say nothing. I stood there facing the sink until he took his hands off my bosoms and turned me around to where I was facing him. I wanted to break away and run out of there, but Gillian was strong and had me by my shoulders so's I could hardly move. I couldn't look him in the face. All I could see was the buttons on his overall straps. Then he took one hand, grabbed my chin, and pulled my head up to where I had to look at his face. There was a big grin on his mouth and a queer look in his eyes. His nose was twitching and the smell of that big farmer's breath was as sour and rank as a slop bucket that's been in the sun for a day or two. Behind his silly-looking grin was his four tobacco-stained snaggled teeth. At that moment I thought he was the ugliest man I'd ever looked at.

When he grabbed my waist and pulled me into him I could feel that swollen member push against my belly. I thought about screaming out, but he must have figured what was on my mind, because he clapped one of those big, hairy hands over my mouth and told me to shut up.

It was right after that when I decided it wasn't no use to fight the bastard. He must have figured my mind again, because he picked me up and carried me to my bed. He had my dress off over my head in seconds, and I remember just lying there as he stepped out of his overalls. I don't remember much after that except hurting bad when he entered my virginity. Some time or other I must have passed out. When I woke up, I tiptoed around, looking. Gillian wasn't in the house. Suddenly, I knew what I had to do. I cleaned up as quickly as I could, got dressed, stuffed what few clothes I had into an empty flour sack, and slipped out the back door. I saw the light from his lantern down in the barn as I lit out for the road to town. I hoped with all my hopes that the bastard would stay in the barn a spell. The only thing I thought about was getting myself away from there.

The first light of morning was slipping in from the east when I reached town, sore-footed, leg-weary, and eyes all puffed up from crying. I didn't want to see nobody I knew, because I felt dirty all over from what Gillian had done to me.

I had some money in old man Duffy's bank from the sale of what was left of the farm. I figured it would last until I got myself to Saint Joe and found a job doing something. I was alone in a world I didn't know anything about.

While I waited for old man Duffy to open his bank I went to the small restaurant by the stage station. By this time I was so hungry, I thought the sides of my stomach was sticking together. The biscuits and gravy, washed down by inky black coffee, did wonders for my general feeling, but I was impatient to get myself farther away from that ugly Gillian.

Old man Duffy asked me a passel of questions about what I intended to do with the money. I told him a bunch of lies so's he'd hand over what was coming to me. Then I went straight to the stage office and bought me a one-way ticket to Saint Joe just as the four horses pulled the stage around the corner onto Main Street, blowing dust all over the fronts of the buildings.

Downing wasn't a stop where they changed teams, but they stopped long enough to rest the horses a bit. There was only one passenger in the stage that morning. I watched her climb down and go into the restaurant. She was dressed up in pretty traveling clothes and fancy hat.

There I was standing by the stage wearing my old dress, a pair of scuffed-up shoes, and no hat at all. At least I'd taken time to comb out my hair before I reached town. I was always proud of my long black hair. About that time, I wondered if my eyes were still puffed up from crying.

I reckon they was, because when we was settled in the stage and heading out of Downing, the lady kept looking at me and smiling. I thought she was the prettiest lady I'd ever seen. She had shiny, copper-colored hair stuffed up under her black velvet hat except for ringlets that hung down in front of her ears. Her blue eyes sparkled, and her face was like nice, soft white clouds just at the start of sunrise. The pearl necklace, around the high collar of her maroon velvet dress, matched her skin.

"It looks like we're the only passengers, so we might as well know each other. I'm Paula Glover from Philadelphia."

"I'm Genevieve Roland. I'm from Downing, where I got on."

"Where are you going, Genevieve?"

"Saint Joe. How about you?"

"Tombstone, out in Arizona."

Paula Glover soon seemed like an old friend. I reckon she come along just at the right time. By the time the stage got to Saint Joe I had told her about the fire, and even about what Gillian had done to me. I cried a bit when I told her about it, but she calmed me down and said she understood my feelings.

I had never been on a stagecoach before. The closest thing I'd ridden on was a slow-moving buckboard, so I wasn't really too well prepared for the bumping and jostling over the rutted roads that seemed like they'd never end.

We stayed two nights in Saint Joe. Paula Glover talked me, Genevieve Roland, into going to Tombstone, Arizona

Territory, where she was planning to start her house of joy for the miners. She told all about whoring and how easy the money was if a girl looked at it as a business. I listened close as she told me all about Tombstone, and how there was a passel of money to be made there.

You'd think by the time I got to Saint Joe I would have been used to riding in a stagecoach. The food at the stage stations tasted half rotten, and what wasn't was so greasy that I wondered what happened to the rest of the hog. And the dust! And the heat! By the time we stopped for overnights we was so hot and sweaty that the dust caked on us like an extra hide. I got to thinking that I should have stayed in Saint Joe.

When we got to bumping and jostling through West Texas I commenced to wonder if I was heading to the end of the earth. I had never seen such desolate, dried-up country. The country looked like God plumb forgot to finish the job. The sage and prickly-looking shrubs were everywhere. I was used to seeing green fields, tall trees, and streams with running water.

Every so often there was more passengers got on. Then we was crowded all scrunched up next to each other. A big sloppy fat man got aboard in El Paso and sat next to me by the window. His whole insides must have been filled with garlic, because I never smelled a ranker-smelling breath in my life. Even Gillian's was sweet compared to that man's. I forgot about the rough-riding stage until he got off somewhere in New Mexico. Paula never complained a bit the entire trip, but I could tell she was glad when the fat man left the stage and the driver tossed his luggage down from the top.

New Mexico didn't look any better to me than West Texas, but I could see mountains in the distance, taller than

I'd ever seen before. I hoped Arizona would be greener and nicer.

We arrived in Tombstone on July 14, 1880. What a lively place way out in the middle of nowhere! The mines was vomiting silver, and the town was booming. It was no wonder to me why Paula decided to set up her business in Tombstone. There was other bawdy houses in town, but Paula's was the best.

It wasn't long before I knew more about life than most seventeen-year-old girls. Paula taught me a bunch. Whoring ain't a bad way to make a living, just as long as a woman's careful. And I'll say one thing, it's a bunch easier than scrubbing floors or slopping hogs.

It wasn't all roses for Paula. She hustled around and bought the house. I don't know where she found all the other girls, but I remember a couple came from the cribs. Within a month, Paula had the place fixed up right pretty, and we went to work. Some of the miners were customers, but most couldn't afford us at Paula's and stayed with the crib girls. After all, the hard-rock boys were only making three dollars a day. Most of our customers made good money with businesses of their own.

The first fire that swept through Tombstone started in the Arcade Saloon by Fifth and Allen Streets on June 22, 1881, less than a year after Paula and I arrived from Saint Joe. The proprietors had a barrel of whiskey they had condemned, and were fixing to ship it back. They knocked the bung out, and one of them dropped the rod they were measuring with into the barrel. So old Hazelton, the bartender, got a piece of wire to fish out the rod. He had a lighted cigar in his mouth, and when he was fishing for the rod, the fumes from the barrel got touched off by the lighted cigar and exploded.

The fire spread fast, because the wooden buildings was dry and close together. The fire wagon got there, but there wasn't enough water pressure to get the flames out quick. People was putting wet blankets on their buildings, tearing down porches, and throwing buckets of water on the flames when they could get close enough. Lucky for us, the fire got put out before it took Paula's house. The *Epitaph* reported that there was $175,000 in damages, and only $25,000 was insured.

Paula told us that if her place had burned, she had fire insurance. Paula knew what she was doing. As it turned out, we had more business than ever, because three houses of joy burned to the ground and only one was insured. Paula was some kind of woman. She went to the madams of the two houses what weren't insured and offered to lend them money to rebuild. One of the women said she could handle the expense herself, but the other accepted Paula's generosity.

The town built back in no time. Two months after the fire, everything seemed back to normal. Then, a little less than a month after Custis and me was married and out at the claim, another fire commenced in a water closet in the rear of the Tivoli Saloon. That one burned the entire heart out of Tombstone. Paula's place burned to the ground, but she had tents pitched to use while she had the place rebuilt with her insurance money. Custis and me had just finished the roof on our house at the claim. Six months later, Custis found the vein and his nugget and went to town, riding the zebra dun mare, leading the burro with the load of ore.

Custis come back a week later. He was riding a big bay gelding and leading my zebra dun mare and the burro. Another man, dressed up fancy, was with him, riding a chestnut sorrel mare. Custis introduced the man as Wilbur

Burnsides, an agent for some mining company by the name of Gleeson.

I unloaded the supplies from the burro while Custis and the agent feller went down the shaft. I had supper on the table when they come out a while later. Wilbur Burnsides was polite and thanked me for the supper before he sat down with Custis at the table. I had already eaten, so I sat down on the bench outside the door and listened.

"There is no doubt about your mine's potential. But, Mr. Ames, I have to consider the costs of hauling the ore to the stamp mill, and the labor involved with the mining."

"Mr. Burnsides, you're not talking to a three-dollar-a-day miner. I done all the work on this shaft and I found the silver and the gold. You just looked at it with your own eyes and know damn well it ain't salted."

"Oh, I am not questioning the validity of your mine. I am saying that the costs of mining the ore are considerable. I must keep all these items in mind in order to represent my clients properly."

"Well, you can tell your clients that Custis Ames's price for his mine stays at eight thousand dollars cash until somebody comes up with the money. Until someone does, I'll keep blasting and digging even though my druthers is to get me and the missus a cow ranch."

Damned if I wasn't proud of my Custis for standing up against that city dandy. Hell's fire, Custis had a bunch of sweat, time, and powder invested in that hole in the ground.

"I should ride back to town, and telegraph my clients about this situation. I must tell you, I will have to point out the costs that I have estimated."

"I'll ride back with you, Mr. Burnsides. A feller can get all turned around in this country after dark."

"I would be much obliged, Mr. Ames."

I come close to laughing out loud listening to all that "Mr. this" and "Mr. that." Custis said he'd be back as soon as he could. I got the feeling Custis had sold the mine in spite of all the Burnsides feller kept going on about expenses.

A week later, Custis come riding home on the big bay. I could see the big grin on his face a hundred yards down the trail. I got up off the bench and walked out to meet him. He dismounted and gave me a big hug.

"Got your price, didn't you, Custis?"

"Shore as hell. It was like when I used to watch Pa in a horse trade. He never budged a dollar once he put a price on one. But, lady, I've got more'n that to tell you. We're going to pack up and move to our cow ranch."

"You been busy in town."

"Remember me talking about Tom Smalley's outfit, on the west slope of the Dragoons?"

"I remember you saying it was good grass, and Tom has a good bunch of cows."

"Well, lady, I saw Tom in town. Seems he's having to move into Tucson. His wife is sickly, and he wants to be close to a doctor in case she needs one bad. We had a good palaver about the ranch, and I ended up buying him out, cattle and all."

"I'll be damned" was all I could say. Things were happening faster than I could keep up with.

We packed up everything we could get on the old burro, made the trip to the Quarter Circle L, and unloaded the stuff into the biggest house I'd ever been in except Paula's in Tombstone. But this was different. It was just for us, me and Custis. I stayed there, messing around arranging things four or five times, waiting for Custis to get back with the rest of the stuff. A team of mules and a buckboard come with the ranch. He drove it back to the claim to get all the high grade he'd blasted out. That was for what he called "just in case." He unloaded it behind the barn.

It didn't take us long to settle in at the ranch. I took care of what I could around headquarters, and Custis was out getting acquainted with his cows. The headquarters consisted of the house, the barn, and the corrals. The house was made of adobe with walls two foot thick. The front door opened into the big living room, which had a stone fireplace that could easy hold three four-foot logs. The cooking room was bigger than the whole rock house at the claim. There was three rooms for sleeping, with a hallway to get to them.

The barn was not much of a building size-wise, but it kept the saddles and other tack dry, and was a good place to hang deer, antelope, or beef carcasses to cure. The barn's walls was of adobe, same as the house. The corrals was made from mesquite, *estacada* style, which means there was pairs of mesquite posts sunk in the ground next to each other every six foot. Mesquite poles laid down inside the posts up to six foot high made a tight corral that held most any critter a feller put inside.

Now, I said "most" any critter, because we had one tall, wild, maverick bull in there one time. Custis had drove him in with a bunch of cows. Since a maverick ain't branded, Custis wanted to put the Quarter Circle L on that big feller's hip, so I went out to help get that big devil tied down. He was kind of beautiful in his way. Must have been eight year old by the look of his shaggy forelock hanging down between those two long, curved horns with rings where they come out of his head. He was most all dark brown with speckles of white here and there, and he had that wild look in his eyes that told a feller not to mess with him unless he was dead serious.

I caught up the big bay gelding and saddled him. Custis was aboard a stocky gray horse that'd come with the ranch. I led the bay through the gate into the largest corral, where Custis had put the old bull and the cows. I shut the gate and mounted the bay. I was shaking out a loop in my manila throw rope when Custis rode over to tell me what he planned to do to catch the maverick. We was to ride slow and try to get him away from the cows in a corner. Then Custis was going to try and rope the critter around the horns. I was then supposed to rope his hind legs. Custis had spent a bunch of time teaching me how to throw a catch rope, and I must say I enjoyed cow work.

If all went well up to that point, we'd stretch the old bull out and get him tied up good to get him branded.

A leggy, wild-eyed, man-shy critter like that can spoil the best of plans, and that bull wasn't about to get roped. That's probably why he was a maverick to begin with. Custis and me rode over slow like with our loops shook out and ready. The cows seemed to know we wasn't after them and moved out of the way until we were facing our target in the far corner of the corral. I watched Custis and I watched the bull. Custis was easing the gray around to where he'd have a good shot at the horns. The maverick bull pawed the ground and lowered his head, never taking his eyes off Custis. He shook his head and snorted at the same time. Now, I'll tell you, that Custis was a good hand with a throw rope, but when he took one fast swing and let the loop fly toward the maverick's horns the bull dodged his head so quick it was like a streak of lightning. And at the same time he come charging straight at me and the bay.

That bay horse jumped sidewards so fast that I durn near

flew out of the saddle. I grabbed the saddle horn and some-how stayed aboard. The next thing I saw was that old maverick taking a flying leap plumb over the six-foot-high corral fence. We rode over and looked. That bull was high-tailing it straight toward the mountains with nary a look back.

"I reckon that old son of a bitch deserves to stay maverick," Custis muttered, and rode over to open the corral gate. "Might as well give the old devil his cows back."

The cows was pretty spooked by all that rodeoing in the corrals, and they was chasing after the maverick when we last seen them.

Every once in a while, after Custis come back from a few days' riding in the mountain country, he'd tell me about seeing that maverick bull. We could spot his calves easy. They was all leggy with some pattern of dark brown and white. Custis kept all the maverick's heifer calves to grow into cows. He allowed that a leggy cow'd walk far-ther to water and cover more country rustling for feed.

Our cow herd was a mixed bunch. Their bloodlines stemmed from the old Spanish cattle that had come in with the Spanish explorers and Jesuit missionaries. So we had cows all colors of the rainbow with long horns and rock-hard hooves.

The rangeland run from the grassed slopes and foothills near the Río San Pedro up to the high country in the south-ern half of the Dragoon Mountains. Custis always said it was ideal cow country because the cattle had free migrat-ing with the seasons.

There was a well at headquarters that furnished water for the house and the livestock. Tom Smalley had it dug and told Custis that the Mexicans who had dug it said they'd hit an underground stream. It must have been something like that, because it's never gone dry. Smalley had also built a bunch of represos along the washes that come down from the mountains. These dirt dams caught water during the rainy seasons and held it most of the year. There was several springs in the mountain country. Custis built troughs next to a few so the cows could get water easier.

We spent a lot of riding time keeping strays out and getting our strays back where they belonged. Roundups was spring and fall, and all the neighbors worked together on roundups. That way a feller seen to branding his own calves as well as the neighbors'. After fall roundups we trail-drove all the three-year-olds to the railroad at Willcox. It took several days to get them there and Custis'd come home with stories about how the whiskey would flow once the cattle was all loaded. It all sounded like those cowboys had quite a time, but I was glad to stay home at the ranch to tend things.

Right after the maverick bull jumped the corral fence and we'd let the cows loose, we was unsaddling the horses. "Custis, I got something I need to speak with you about," I said as casually as I could.

"What's that, lady?"

"I'm with child, Custis."

The way his lower jaw dropped near to his chest and his eyes popped out was kind of comical. "You're what?"

"You're going to be a father, Custis."

"Well, I'll be damned."

He took his hat off and scratched the right side of his head.

"What do I have to do, lady?"

"You've already done it, Custis."

"When do you reckon this is going to happen?"

"Should be in the neighborhood of the new year."

"Well, I'll be damned."

My announcement sent Custis into a spell of some sort. He had always been gentle with me in all respects, but after I told him I was going to have a baby, he treated me like I was about to break. I had to run him out of the cooking room when I was making vittles, because he hung around wanting to help all the time. I can't recall how many mornings I'd tell him to get out and look for strays. Down deep I appreciated his concerns, but I didn't want him getting all stirred up just because I was going to have a baby.

We had a few visitors from time to time. Mostly folks passing through heading for Tombstone or headed back out from Tombstone. Some stopped for a meal, some just to water their horses, and then there were a few who come in around dark and spent the night. I always kept a pot of beans on the stove, and usually some kind of stew would be simmering. I made biscuits most evenings, but once in a while in the winter I baked bread.

One evening shortly after I had told Custis about me being with child, I heard voices out in the barnyard. I went to the door and opened it to look out. What I saw gave me a start. Custis was out talking with four Indian men.

I thought I knew most stuff about Custis, but when I heard him jabbering away in Indian to those four, and them jabbering back, I commenced to wonder if I'd ever know all about that husband of mine. He must have spent more time cowboying in New Mexico than he'd let on.

One of the Indians had on an Army sergeant's jacket with the buttons all undone, and a yellow neckerchief around his head. Another had what had once been a cavalry officer's wide-brimmed hat. The other two were just dressed like Indians with buckskin leggings and shirts made of different materials.

I saw Custis point to the corrals. Then he turned and

walked toward the house as the Indians slid off their horses and led them into the nearest corral.

"We got company tonight, lady. Is there plenty on the stove for these men?"

"I got a pot of beans, and that venison stew has been slow cooking since morning."

"Good gal. They'll be spending the night in the barn."

"Custis Ames, the longer I'm married to you, it seems the less I know about you. I didn't have any idea you knew Indian lingo."

"I told you about the spell I spent punchin' cows north of Silver City. It was before I hit for Tombstone. I lived alone in a line camp up Mule Creek way. Five Apache rode in one day just as I was fixing to eat supper. I knew a little Spanish, but I didn't have no idea about Apache. I kind of used a little Spanish, a little sign language, and some English. They was about the same as me except they, of course, spoke their Apache."

"How come they didn't just kill you, Custis?"

"Well, to tell the truth I was a mite scared when they rode up. All I could do was smile and say howdy. They pointed to their mouths like they was hungry, so I signed them to git down off their horses and share my meal. I had a fresh deer carcass hanging inside the cabin, so I went on in and cut off enough steaks what I thought would fill their bellies. Then I tossed them on the coals and broiled them up good with salt and pepper. I also sprinkled a little red chili on the steaks."

"Why didn't they just kill you and take your deer carcass along with your saddle horses?"

"I reckon they could've easy if they had wanted to. But my pa always told us boys that with most folks if you treat them right, they'll most likely treat you right. I reckon when they seen me smile when they rode up, they must have figured I'd treat them right."

"I understand all that, Custis, but if they was Apaches, Apaches just as soon kill a white man as look at him."

"Now, Genevieve, I reckon your mind's been made up by white folks that consider these people savages. I got to know those Apaches because they kept coming back to visit and share meals. They brought venison and even packed in an elk one time. That time they stayed four days, 'til we ate up most of it. I jerked the rest. I learned a bunch of their lingo, and made some damn fine friends. When I left there they give me the eagle feather with beads around it. They said if I ever was to run up to any Apache to show them the feather. Then I would have another Apache friend."

"Is that feather on top of the mantel what you're talking about?"

"Shore is, lady. When these Apaches come in for supper, you'll see how they look when they see my eagle feather."

Well, when those Apaches come in through the door and stood there waiting for some kind of invite, I looked at them all straight standing there. They wasn't tall, but they was straight standing. And they smiled at me when I come out of the cooking room to join my Custis making them feel welcome to our house.

Custis was jabbering with them again, and then I saw the one in the sergeant's jacket looking at the eagle feather on the mantel. He walked over and picked it up real gentle like, turning it around like he was reading the beads. He carried it over and showed it to the others. They jabbered away for a spell, and then he took the feather back and put it back in its place on the mantel. Then they all took hold of Custis's hands, and come over to me and done the same, all the time jabbering away in their lingo. I didn't understand a durned thing they was saying, but by the look on their faces I knew they were friends. It was quite heartwarming for me to be in that moment after all I'd been told about Apaches.

For their size those Apache fellers had the biggest appetites I ever did see. For a spell I thought maybe the stew pot was going to run out before they got filled up. Custis followed them out to the barn when they got done palavering.

When he come back to the house we talked a bit about how he was glad that the Apaches was friends. Custis also told me more about the times he was cowboying up north of Silver City. Some of the white people around there lost their ears or hair to the Apaches, but they never bothered Custis, because they considered him a friend. I asked Custis to teach me their lingo so I could understand what all was being talked about. He gave me my first lesson that evening.

The following morning, I didn't get a chance at using the few words I remembered. The Apaches had left, probably long before the sun was even thinking about rising.

Chapter Three

I reckon our friendship with the Apaches was real important to understand what all went on, and why a lot of things happened. The first four, what come to the ranch, ate near all the stew, then left before morning, were part of a band living in the mountains.

The one in the sergeant's jacket was called "Hiding Fox." He was kind of the leader; leastways the others seemed to give him more palaver time. The one who wore the cavalry officer's hat went by "Mountain Thunder." The tallest of the other two, and when I say tallest, he was maybe an inch taller, was "Fast Bear." The shortest of them went by "Running Horse." They all had their Apache names, but I'm translating them because the names don't make sense in Apache unless you're Apache.

Hiding Fox was the one of them what wanted to learn

English from Custis and me. I learned a bunch of Apache from him while I was teaching him English.

The Indians didn't have any kind of schedule about coming to the ranch. They just appeared whenever they felt like it. And they weren't grub-liners. They contributed. We was never hurting for meat.

Custis always kept a bottle or two of mescal around. The Apaches enjoyed sitting around after supper sipping mescal with Custis. I took a bit myself on occasion. They never got drunk on mescal, but I could tell that when they commenced to laugh more than usual the fiery liquid was having its effect on them.

One day, after the Apaches had spent the night, Custis said he was going up in the mountains with them and would be back in a day or two. I was seven months along, and didn't feel like riding up into the mountain country. Besides, someone needed to keep the water trough full for the livestock.

Three days later, Custis come riding back close to sunset. I walked out to the corrals and waited while he unsaddled the big bay. He come over wearing a big grin on his face and gave me a hug.

"I'll bet this ranch and all the cattle that there ain't many white men been where I just come from, lady."

"Well, I got supper ready, so you can tell me all about it as you're eating."

"I can't wait that long. The Apaches taken me right smack dab to their headquarters. I felt like someone real important the way they all treated me. The headman was all questions about what I thought about all kinds of things. He's real serious and didn't smile much except when I told him that I understood how the Indians felt about white men coming in on their country."

Custis had taken my arm as we strolled back to the house. I sensed that he had done a heap of thinking about all the stuff he was talking about. He kept on jawing away as I put supper on the table.

"Hiding Fox is close with the headman. Toward the end of our first meal and palaver he told the headman you was with child. The headman agreed that Hiding Fox should bring his wife to you when you come due to birthing."

"I've been wondering about that lately, Custis. As far from town as we are, I been wondering what I'd do when my time comes."

"Well, you needn't wonder anymore. Blue Humming Bird, that's Hiding Fox's wife, is a birthing woman. She knows all there is to know about bringing babies into the world."

"A year ago I'd never have thought I'd be midwifed by an Indian."

"I reckon we've got real friends up there on the mountain. I feel like I can trust them a helluva lot further than my own kind. I'll tell you something else, lady, they made us members of their band."

"What on earth do you mean by that, Custis?"

"Hiding Fox got into a long palaver with the headman, and told him how we were friends. He went on about how you and me are different than other whites and can be trusted. Then Hiding Fox asked me if I would be one of them. He explained that it was an honor for them if I would. I told him it would be an honor for us also."

"What does all this mean? We don't have to go live with them, do we?"

"Nothing like that, lady. It means we're kind of honorary members of their band. They had a ceremony. Me and Hiding Fox became blood brothers. Here's the scratch where we mixed our blood with our hands gripped together."

Custis showed me the scratch made by a knife on the palm of his hand. "What does that make me?"

"Because you're my wife, you're like a sister-in-law to Hiding Fox and Blue Humming Bird."

"But I don't know Blue Humming Bird."

"You will. She's beautiful, and they have a son and daughter."

"Does this mean we're an uncle and aunt?"

"I expect it's like that. They also gave us Apache names. You're White Summer Cloud. I'm Man of Good Heart."

We talked about the Apaches until late that night. After we was to bed, Custis kept on telling me about every detail and how the headman pledged the friendship of the band. I must admit that I felt safer knowing the Apaches was our friends than if I had to depend on the Army for protection against them.

Custis went off on roundup two weeks later. It was November and commencing to get cold at night. I had plenty of firewood stacked up, and we had the buckboard I could use to go to town.

I was running low on flour, so I used that to justify me going in to visit Paula. A week after Custis left for roundup, I harnessed the mules and hitched them to the buckboard. There was a chill in the air, so I grabbed a blanket to bundle up with. The sun was just peeking its way to morning when I climbed aboard, took the lines, and clucked the mules to get moving toward Tombstone. That cold November morning felt good, and the mules seemed to feel good, too, as they slow-trotted the buckboard over the road to town.

I always went to visit Paula when Custis and me went to

town together. After we got the buying done, I'd go over to Paula's while Custis headed for the Crystal Palace to catch up on the news. This was the first I'd come to town alone, and I stopped the mules in front of Paula's before I went to get the flour.

As usual, Paula was glad to see me, and she had coffee brought into her private parlor. She gave me a big hug and patted my belly.

"Genevieve, you look wonderful. Being with child must agree with you."

"I reckon I feel as good as ever. But I have to tell you, I'm just plumb happy being married to my Custis and living out there on our ranch."

Paula raised her eyebrows a bit and pushed at her hair with her right hand. "You're lucky, Gen. Looking at you, your belly full of child and your eyes all lit up, makes me wonder if I should have come out here to start this business. If that worthless husband of mine had stayed home instead of smelling every hussy that came his way, I probably would have stayed in Philadelphia."

"You're still young enough to find the right man, Paula."

"You were lucky, Gen. Custis is totally different than most of the men who come here for their pleasure. All the time I've been here, there have been only two men whom I've invited to this parlor."

"Try Tucson. There's supposed to be a lot of men there, and I reckon they're a different sort than they are here in this here mining town."

"I don't know if I'd like living in Tucson. Here I'm a queen. In Tucson, I'd be just another woman."

There come a knock on the door. Paula got up and opened the door to see who it was. "Angie, come in. Genevieve is visiting."

Angie kind of squealed when she saw me, and come over and gave me a hug. "Genevieve," she said, patting my belly, "what are you growing in there, a punkin?"

"I'm hoping it's a little Custis, but it might be a little girl."

We laughed. Paula told Angie to help herself to coffee. When she had sat down she got serious of a sudden. "Genevieve, that agent feller, Burnsides, come in a couple nights past. Damn, I hope he never asks for me again. What a fuddy-duddy. Wouldn't take his shirt and necktie off. He wouldn't take off his trousers until he got under the covers. Afterwards he was telling me that he'd lost his job with some mining company all on account a Custis's and your claim."

"He told Custis he's the agent for Gleeson Mining Company."

"Past tense. When they started mining your claim the gold petered out real quick, and the silver don't amount to much, according to fuddy-duddy Burnsides. Seems Burnsides was putting himself across as a geologist, so the company figured he shoulda knowed what he was doing."

"Well, I'm glad Custis had brains enough to sell out when he did. I'd rather be cow ranching than mining anyway."

"I just thought I'd tell you what Burnsides was saying after I bedded the old fuddy-duddy."

We sat there in Paula's parlor for near two hours. Angie finally said she had to "get ready for the Tombstone Romeos," and left. I said good-bye to Paula and told her I thought she ought to take a trip to Tucson and look it over. I never said anything about our friends the Apaches. Custis had told me that some white folks might not appreciate us being friends with Indians.

It was way after dark before I pulled up the mules by the

house to unload the flour. I had bought three sacks of oats for the mules and horses too. I had just lugged the flour into the house and lit the lamp when I heard someone outside. I grabbed the Sharps and the coal-oil lamp and went to the door. It was Hiding Fox, so I told him to come in and went to put down the carbine and the lamp. Behind him come a pretty woman smiling at me in a shy kind of way. I knew it was Blue Humming Bird, and I welcomed her. I told Hiding Fox that I had to get the oats unloaded and the mules put up. He raised his hand and told me to stay and talk to his wife. He went out, and I heard the mules and the buckboard start for the barn.

Blue Humming Bird sat down at the table while I got the fire going to make some coffee. It was obvious to me that she didn't speak English. That sure enough tested me in what little Apache I had managed to learn. But, between signing and me using my sparse Apache, I learned that she'd come to meet me to see how far along I was.

Like I said, she was a real pretty woman. Her face was round like most Apaches', but she had a brightness in her eyes that made her glow with beauty. Her nose was thinner than those of the Apache men I'd seen, and I could see a few wrinkles coming in on her forehead. Her black hair was long like mine. I remember folks back in Missoura calling me "raven haired." Blue Humming Bird's hair had more of a bluish tinge to it than mine, and the beaded buckskin thong she tied it all back with made her look like a princess. In spite of her shyness, she was regal. I reckon that's the word to use for someone what carries theirself the way Blue Humming Bird did.

After putting up the mules, Hiding Fox come back to the house. By that time the coffee was ready, so they drank theirs while I saw to the stew I had put on the hot part of the Old Majestic stove.

Hiding Fox told me what I had already learned from his wife, but I reckon he wanted to make sure I understood. When we finished eating he told me to take Blue Humming Bird to my sleeping room because she needed to see me alone.

I led her to the room, where she signed me to lie down on the bed. I watched as she took a beaded deer-tail pendant from her neck and placed it on my belly. Her hands were a lot like mine, showing she wasn't afraid of work. She put her hands on my belly and felt around as she kind of chanted. When she was done, she left the pendant with its buckskin thong on my belly and told me to wear it. She explained that the deer's tail come from a strong, healthy buck, and that I was to wear it to help my baby grow to be strong and healthy.

I had never heard about such. I'd heard tell that some midwives had their special ways. Well, this one was special, and she made me feel happy and safe in her care.

I slept like a baby that night. The trip to town and all had tuckered me some. By the time I got myself out of bed in the morning and got the fire in the stove going, they was gone. Just like always, they just kind of melted away into the mountain.

Custis rode in several days later and announced that the roundup crew was about to start our country. I knew what that meant. I would have three days of cooking beans, biscuits, and beef for the men. The chuck wagon cook would be of some help. Leastaways I wouldn't have to furnish plates.

I told him about Blue Humming Bird and Hiding Fox

coming to visit, and I showed him the pendant she had told me to wear and what for.

"Now, lady, when the crew's here grubbing down, don't be wearing that deer's tail to where they can see it."

"I'll make sure I be wearing a high collar, because I'm keeping it on like Blue Humming Bird said to."

Custis smiled. I knew what he was thinking; he was happy to know that I had taken to the Apache midwife.

The day the crew arrived, cold winter weather pushed in from the west. Custis worried about getting the cattle off the mountain in a storm, but the rain held off for two days. About noon the third day a slow drizzle commenced, but the men didn't stop work. They put on their yellow slickers as they gathered the last bunch from the south range. I was disappointed not being able to go out to the gather and see the cattle, but Custis told me he thought they were in good shape and the market seemed to be holding.

I asked him if they'd turned up the wild, leggy corral-jumper.

"I spotted the rascal way high. There was no cows with him, so I just left him be. Good thing it was me who saw him, otherwise we'd have spent an extra day trying to get him off the mountain."

"How do his calves look this year?"

"They're a good bunch. I figured we branded close to twenty of his calves, and there was eight good heifers I'll keep back."

I was glad when the roundup crew was gone. Custis, of course, went with them to trail the sale cattle to Willcox. He come back in six days, happy with the money he'd got for the cattle, and glad to be home again.

I was springing out quite a ways, and I felt like I was

51

carrying a sack of oats in my belly. Whatever it was, it was a kicker. Custis liked to feel it, and said he thought it'd be a boy since it kicked so much.

Just before Christmas, Hiding Fox and Blue Humming Bird come in one morning. I was sure enough glad to see my midwife, because I didn't know but what I was going to birth out any day.

She went to the sleeping room with me and felt around my belly. When she finished feeling she put her ear down on my belly. I reckon everything was in good order, because she lifted her head up and smiled a big grin at me. She signed me that the birthing would be soon. I could feel my bosoms getting full up and swollen.

We went back to the table, and I sat down. Custis listened as Blue Humming Bird spoke. He told me that she had decided to stay until the birth because it could happen soon. Hiding Fox would stay too, and go hunting with Custis.

We was all eating venison steaks when the dogs commenced barking out in the barnyard. Custis got up and went to the door. Wilbur Burnsides, the agent we'd sold the claim to, rode right up to the house and got off his horse. He didn't look a bit different than when he come out to the claim to look at the vein. He was still dressed up with a necktie and wore the stupid-looking round hat that would nary keep the sun out of his eyes. He walked right up to the door like he owned the place.

"Mr. Ames, you and I have some business to attend to."

"I seem to remember we finished our business quite some time past."

"In some ways we did, but in other ways we didn't. Now, if I may come in, we can talk these matters over."

I reckon Custis didn't think about Hiding Fox and Blue

Humming Bird sitting at the table. Either that or he'd quit caring who knew who his friends was, because he stepped aside and held the door open for that fuddy-duddy.

Burnsides's eyes liked to have bugged plumb out of their sockets when he saw the two Apaches sitting at our table. He cleared his throat several times. "I didn't realize you had company," he said, his nervousness obvious.

"This is Hiding Fox and his wife, Blue Humming Bird. She's here to midwife Genevieve."

"Well, I suppose it's none of my business, but couldn't you have found a midwife in Tombstone?"

"I didn't bother to look, Mr. Burnsides. Now, suppose you spit out whatever you come out here for."

"I came out to inform you that you owe me a considerable amount of money."

"Now, how could you possibly figure that, Mr. Burnsides?"

"When my company started mining the claim which they purchased from you, the gold vein ran out after the first blasting. They dug the shaft deeper, and to their complete disappointment the silver ore was very low grade. Therefore, you must return a good portion of the purchase price, Mr. Ames."

"Now, that's about the most comical thing I ever heard, Mr. Burnsides. For one thing, I bought this ranch with the money your company paid me for my claim. When you buy something you buy it, Mr. Burnsides. If I was to buy a horse from you and when I got the devil home his teeth fell out, I'd be stuck with a toothless horse. You saw the vein and the shaft, and you bought my claim. Whatever happened after you commenced mining it seems like your misfortune, but it shore ain't mine."

53

John Duncklee

"Well, Mr. Ames, since you don't seem to understand ethics, you will be taken to court on the charges of salting your mine."

"Now, I'll tell you another thing, Mr. Burnsides. I shore didn't salt my mine. You just take me into court, charge me with anything you want. But right now get your arse out of my house, mount that nag of your'n and beat it back to Tombstone, or I'll turn this Apache loose on your ears."

Custis slammed the door and turned to face us. "I've played some poker in my travels, and I'm pretty good at figuring a bluff. I'm reckoning that Mr. Wilbur Burnsides is trying to go for a bluff, threatening to take me to court."

Burnsides couldn't have rode a mile down the road back to Tombstone before I felt the first labor pain. I call it a labor pain, but it was more a squeezing. I'd had them before, and I didn't know but what this was going to be another. But it was sure enough the start, because I had another one an hour later. That's when I told Blue Humming Bird that I thought things were starting to happen.

She didn't seem worried, but signed me to go into the sleeping room and lie down so's she could feel around again. She stayed there with me with her hands on my belly. The next one come along, and she smiled. We went back to the men and told them what was about to happen. Custis got all excited, but Hiding Fox just sat where he was without any expression on his face.

Custis went out to the wood box and brought in an armful of short pieces of mesquite to keep the fire in the sleeping-room stove burning. He come back and sat down at the table. "What should I do now?"

"Nothing to do but wait," I told him.

"Well, there oughta be something."

54

"Just relax, Custis. The baby will get here when it's ready, and not a minute before."

We sat there saying nothing for a spell. I reckon I taken Custis aback when I snapped at him. After a while I suggested he and Hiding Fox go out and tend the horses because Blue Humming Bird and me had everything under control.

Custis grumbled a little, but they went out to the corrals. My labor was getting on faster. Blue Humming Bird signed me to go back to the sleeping room. I taken off my clothes and got myself under the covers to wait. Blue Humming Bird had carried a buckskin bag into the room, and she started taking stuff out of it and putting it all on the table. When she was done doing that, she sat down next to me and smiled her pretty smile at me. I felt real good, and I wasn't in no way scared of what was about to happen.

Thoughts about raising a child come to my mind between the pains. I couldn't help think that I was heading for a long time of taking care of the baby along with Custis. If it was going to be a boy, I knew Custis would have a good time teaching him about cows and horses. I'd have my hands full with a girl, getting her all prettied up for going to town and such. I'd teach her cooking and sewing, but I'd let Custis take over about all the ranch stuff. Whichever the baby was, boy or girl, there was bound to be a change in our lives.

The pains kept getting harder and closer together. She took my hand and held it every time I commenced to close my eyes and wince.

The men come back and I told Blue Humming Bird to get herself something to eat. She didn't want to leave me alone, but I insisted. It was nice to be alone for a few minutes. I took my mind off the labor by thinking about when I was little and Pa put me up on Midnight, his black mare. I learned how to ride with Midnight. One evening, I watched her birth a little sorrel filly, so I knew a little about what was going on with me.

Blue Humming Bird come back from her supper and sat down again next to me. About a half an hour went by before my water broke and everything down there was warm and wet. She had me get up on my knees and spread them apart. Then she commenced to chant, and I kept on trying to push the baby out. All of a sudden she signed me to lay back down.

I don't remember much after that except I could hear her chanting. The next thing that comes to mind is opening my eyes and seeing that baby lying between my swollen bosoms. I raised my right arm up and softly stroked the baby's head. Blue Humming Bird reached down and picked it up to show me that I had birthed a son. I smiled back at her and signed her to go tell Custis.

The look on Custis's face when he saw his boy was priceless. He was one big grin. I'll bet if he didn't have a shirt on, his belly button was grinning too. He come over to the bedside, leaned over, and kissed me.

"You done yourself proud, lady," he whispered.

He didn't want to pick up the boy, especially after the little feller began to whimper. Blue Humming Bird propped me up a bit so I could nurse easier. "What about naming our son Roland, after my maiden name?"

"Sounds like a right good name for the boy," Custis replied.

Hiding Fox told Custis that the boy needed his Apache name. Custis thought for a spell. "Since we're brothers I'd like you to name my son," he told Hiding Fox.

"He must be named for his future. I give him Man With Strength of Cougar," Hiding Fox said.

Hiding Fox and Blue Humming Bird stayed with us another three days. She was good help with everything while I got back to doing what I had to do. The men went out riding, checking the cattle and all. Little Roland was a good feller. He always told me when he was hungry, and I was always ready to pop my nipples into his little mouth. Nursing him gave me a wonderful sense of motherhood, something that I suspect don't come to a barren woman. I enjoyed every minute caring for his needs.

I had come to love Blue Humming Bird real strong. When they left for the mountain I had a tear or two in my eyes. I could tell Custis and Hiding Fox got along like brothers, and it was good for Custis to have such a close friend.

I wondered about why the whites and the Apaches couldn't just be friends, and quit all the fussing. Though, I could see why the Apaches felt intruded upon, and getting their whole lives disrupted.

I could understand the whites wanting land to farm and ranch. But I couldn't understand why everybody couldn't sit down and palaver it all out and live with one another instead of trying to kill each other off. I thought Custis and I was real lucky to have our Apache friends. Little did I know that being friends with the Indians would create a great big bunch of hell.

A week after our Apache friends left there come two of our neighbors riding into the barnyard. Custis had rode in, and was unsaddling over by the barn. The dogs raised a ruckus when the two riders approached. Custis walked over to where they had reined up their horses. I had just finished nursing Little Roland and put him down to sleep. I put on my coat and went outside to stand by the door to see what was going on, and invite them in for supper.

It was Harry Dobbs and Luther Breeland. I heard Custis invite them to get down off their horses and come out of the cold, but Dobbs said, "What we have to say, we can say right here, Ames."

I didn't like the sound of his voice, so I just stood by the door and listened.

"What's on your mind, neighbors?" Custis asked, standing there with his hands stuffed into the pockets of his jacket.

"There's talk in town that you have some Apaches in your house."

"What if I do have Apaches in my house? It's my house."

"We don't cotton to Apache scoundrels around here, Ames. We've worked roundups together, and you seem a helluva lot smarter than to get friendly with them savages."

"I reckon I'll be friends with whoever I choose to be friends with," Custis replied, shifting his weight from one leg to the other.

"Ames, you're talking like a fool," Breeland added. "You'd be a helluva lot better off with us as friends than to be taking up with those goddam Injuns."

"I figure I can be friends with anybody what wants to be friends, including you fellers."

Dobbs raised his right arm up and shook his fist at Custis. "A friend of those heathen bastards is no friend of ours. You'd best think this out more, Custis Ames."

"If you fellers don't have anything more to say, I reckon I'll be going in the house and see what the missus has for supper. You're welcome to share with us."

Custis turned and started for the house. Breeland raised his voice. "We don't share nothing with Injun lovers."

Custis didn't answer, and kept on walking. I opened the door and we went in, shutting the door behind us.

"I reckon we got trouble brewing, lady."

"Sounds to me like you might be right."

We didn't say much during supper, but both of us knew what was on the other's mind. The baby slept through it all, but as usual, started squalling in the middle of the night. Custis rolled over, and went back to sleep once I had a nipple in Roland's little mouth. I didn't mind getting woke up, because it gave me some nice time with my baby.

It was the day after the neighbors had come over that Hiding Fox and Blue Humming Bird come in just about dark. She had brought a cradle board with her to give to me. There was beadwork on it and buckskin thongs to tie the baby in. She showed me how to use it, and explained that Apache women carried their babies in their cradle boards while they went about their work. Little Roland sure enough looked cute all tied in on it.

Neither Custis nor me said anything about what the neighbors had said. The Indians left early the next morning.

Another winter storm eased in by noon the day they left. We was glad for the rain. There ain't a cow rancher nowheres what ain't glad for rain anytime. But in this country, where rain can be temperamental, we welcomed every drop. It looked like it might be snowing up on the mountains, and I hoped our Indian friends would make it back to their home before it got bad traveling.

The storm lasted six days, drizzling all the time. The ground was plumb full and running off. The arroyos filled up and the represos caught water. Custis was beside himself, happy with the prospects of good spring feed for the cattle.

It commenced to warming along about March. The

weeds sprouted like hair on a dog's back, and the grasses greened up at their bases. By April the cattle had slicked off real pretty, and the calves seemed to grow as fast as the weeds. I must have been a good milker, because Roland was getting all filled out, looking more like a person every day. He was a good baby, and healthy as a young bull on green feed. There must be something to wearing the deer tail that Blue Humming Bird had given me.

Along about the last week in April, Custis got into a mood where he didn't talk near as much as usual. I decided to ask what was bothering him.

"Roundup's coming up, and I don't hanker to work with my neighbors after them coming over that night and getting uppity about us being friends with the Apaches."

Chapter Four

Custis rode off for roundup, still not happy with the prospects of working with the neighbors. I felt sorry seeing him riding off as I was standing in the barnyard with Roland strapped onto the cradle board. I hoped with all my hopes that he wouldn't come to any harm just on account he was friendly with Apache folks.

I was nursing Roland when Custis rode in ten days later. I thought he'd come to tell me when the crew would be working our country so that I could get the grub ready.

"The crew won't be eating here," he mumbled after he swung down off the bay. "And I'm done working with the bastards."

"What happened?"

"Well, lady, they was so cold to me that they only talked when they had to. And then it was 'Ames this' or 'Ames that.' Before, they'd call me Custis. When I'd sit down to a

61

meal, I found myself eating alone because those fellers would move away from where I was."

"Did all our calves get branded?"

"I saw to that. If we missed any, I can pick them up as I find them."

I put my arms around that dear husband of mine and commenced to cry, I felt so bad for him. He patted me gently on my back and told me not to bother myself with such. When I got done crying I got mad, especially when he told me that Dobbs had told him to send a representative to work in the fall roundup.

Custis said he'd like to send Hiding Fox and twenty of his brother Apaches to work the fall roundup as his reps. "That'd give those bastards something to think about."

We both calmed down some after he took care of the bay and sat down at the table to eat supper. "I'm kind of glad they didn't want to stay here and grub down. I don't hanker to have them near our home, lady."

A few days later, Custis harnessed the mules and hitched them to the buckboard. He needed horseshoes and grain, and I needed to get some cotton cloth to make Roland some summer clothes. It was the first time I'd gone off to town since before the birthing, and I was looking forward to seeing Paula.

Being how it was well into May, the country had dried up some, and it was getting on to hot days. I had Roland tied onto the cradle board and held it across my lap as Custis drove the mules.

As the mules pulled the buckboard toward town, I saw where range fires had burned patches of the grassland between arroyos. The patches was blackened by the fires, but the bases had tinges of green where the new stems was already pushing up.

"The range fires seem to help the grass," I mentioned.

"I always figured range fires was natural. They keep the brush off the hills. It's same as up on the mountain. Natural. Thins things out."

When we reached town, Custis left me and Roland off at Paula's while he went about buying what he was in need of. Paula and all the girls had fits over Roland. I was real proud of my boy. He took to all the attention and smiled up at everybody. When they all had their fill of holding Roland we went with Paula into her private parlor. Paula poured us coffee and sat down to have a talk.

She told me about how that sorry Wilbur Burnsides had told everyone he saw about us having Apaches in our house. Paula also told me how Burnsides had taken to drinking too much and she had to tell him to go elsewhere for his excitement.

"I didn't like what he was saying about you and Custis anyway, so when he come over here drunk one night, it was a good excuse to tell him to leave and not come back."

"He threatened Custis about taking him to court on charges he salted the claim," I told her.

"I wouldn't worry about Mr. Burnsides. He came to Tombstone claming to be a geologist. I guess he figured it would be easier work than using a double-jack and drill. After your claim disappointed the Gleeson bunch, they discovered that Burnsides had never been a geologist. He had left New York just ahead of the police. It seems he was a bookkeeper, and was found to have sticky fingers."

"What does he do for money now that the Gleesons fired him?"

"That's a question a lot of people are asking."

Paula went on about Burnsides, and how he was catching all kinds of hell from the town.

"He was walking down Allen Street a week or so ago," Paula continued. "The wind was blowing up the dust. It was gusty, and all of a sudden Burnsides's little round hat flew off his head. The wind took it down the middle of Allen Street, and it bounced along like a ball. Burnsides chased after that hat, but every time he was close to grabbing it, a gust of wind blew it out of his reach."

Paula started laughing as she told the story. She had been there to see it all.

"When the little derby went bouncing toward Fifth and Allen Streets, a group of miners were just leaving the Crystal Palace. They saw the bouncing derby and the balding Burnsides chasing it. One of the miners jumped out into Allen Street and kicked the bouncing hat clear up on top of the Crystal Palace roof."

"What did Burnsides do then?"

"He stood there and told the miner he didn't think kicking his hat onto the roof was very gentlemanly. Of course, that made the miners laugh more than ever."

Custis come back to Paula's quicker than I thought he would. Angie come back to the parlor to tell me he was waiting for me. I said good-bye to Paula and took Roland back out to the buckboard. I could see Custis was flared up. As I was settling onto the seat a couple was passing by. I heard the woman say, "Look, Charles, she even carries that poor little baby on a Indian cradle board."

Custis heard it too, but he didn't say anything. He was too intent on telling me what had happened to him.

"I got all my buying done and went to have a drink at the Crystal Palace. When I reached the bar I saw that worthless Wilbur Burnsides standing down a ways, drunker than hell. He had his funny round hat on, but it looked like a herd of cows had run over it. His necktie was undid and hanging down his dirty shirt. Except for the stupid-looking hat I 'most didn't recognize him."

"Who else was there?"

"A couple of miners, but they were sitting down at a table. I ordered a mescal, and when the bartender brought me the glass and bottle, Burnsides looked over and recognized me. 'Well,' he slurred. 'If it isn't Ames, the Indian lover.' "

"The man was real drunk, so I didn't pay no mind to him. I just filled my glass and tossed the mescal down like always. Right after I filled the glass a second time, Burnsides kind of half staggers over and starts accusing me of salting my claim. Well, lady, you know I'm not a fighting man, but I just up and knocked that bastard on his arse, paid for my drinks, and went back to the buckboard."

"I reckon I had best get the material for Roland's clothes so we can get on back to the ranch."

"I'd appreciate you getting a move on with it, because I don't feel too good around here. Some people turned their backs to me."

I hurried up getting the cotton cloth. If I hadn't been in such a hurry I'd have looked around more, but I thought Custis was right about getting gone out of town as soon as we could.

Hiding Fox and Blue Humming Bird come out of the barn when Custis reined up the mules. It was the first time I'd seen Custis smile big since before the roundup. I was real happy to see our friends again, too. Blue Humming Bird picked up the cradle board, with Roland still asleep in it, and carried him into the house. I left him sleeping while I got supper started. Hiding Fox had brought half a venison with him, so I cut off some steaks to broil as soon as the fire went to coals.

Roland woke up as I was just about to cook the steaks, so I untied the thongs and got some milk going into him. When I was done nursing him, Blue Humming Bird took him while I put the steaks on to broil. Roland took to her right off, and squealed with delight when she tickled his belly. She opened her buckskin bag, took out a doll carved out of wood, and handed it to Roland. He looked at it for a while, then let it go so he could look at Blue Humming Bird. She signed me that the figure was for good luck and a strong body.

Custis and Hiding Fox come in after they got through tending the mules and unloading the buckboard.

After supper we sat around the table. I listened mostly while Custis and Hiding Fox talked back and forth. I learned some more Apache just by listening. I felt real lucky to have friends like those. They stayed three days with us. Custis and Hiding Fox went riding, checking the cattle while Blue Humming Bird and I had a good time talking. I was getting pretty good at understanding her lingo, and she was learning English little by little.

As usual they slipped away from the ranch early one morning. I was feeling sorry to see them gone. Custis told me that Hiding Fox and his brothers was getting a little spooked by what looked like more cavalry out on patrols.

The summer clouds started flying in high around the first of July. The wind from the southwest kept those big, billowing, white clouds moving fast, but we saw more and more every day. Most mornings the sky was clear, but by midday the thunderheads rolled in from the south. About a week into July the wind calmed down enough so that the clouds didn't look like they was flying. By late morning they commenced to bunch up and get darker. I was out in the barnyard collecting hen's eggs when I looked up and saw a huge cloud, black and boiling. Suddenly, out of nowhere, a bolt of lightning come flashing down, the thunderclap with it. I lit for the house, because I don't hanker to be caught outside when the lightning is striking around.

I barely got inside the door when the rain come down out of that cloud like someone had tipped it over and dumped it. I looked out the window and it was pouring rain so hard that I couldn't see the barn or corrals. I reckon the thunder had woke up Roland, so I left the window to nurse him. When he had his fill the storm had mostly passed, but the rain went on for a half hour. I wondered if Custis was getting rained on up in the mountains, because he'd gone riding early, still looking for calves that needed branding.

I carried Roland outside when the rain quit, and we found the rest of the eggs in the barn. The ground was all soaked and everything smelled clean. The air was cooled off, and the sky was still full of thunderheads.

Custis rode in along about sunset. I had a big pot of venison stew waiting for him. He tended his horse and come in from the corrals. There was a big grin on his face.

"That was one helluva storm. I was a way up in the piñon country when it hit. The lightning struck all 'round me, and I lit out for some boulders to get as far away from it as I could."

"It rained a big hunk down here. I'm glad I was near the house."

"Well, if the storms keep coming we'll have good feed. As I was riding back I passed by Turkey Tank, and it caught some water. That's kind of rare for the first summer storm to run off extra."

"How's everything on the mountain?"

"I almost forgot. I spotted the old, leggy, longhorn bull up in that boulder country. What a sight he was. I didn't get too close, but I saw where he'd broke one horn and there was a lot of dried blood on his head and shoulders."

"What in the world happened?"

"Like I say, I didn't get too close because the old feller was standing there stomping his hooves at me. It looked like he mighta had an eye gouged, too. I thought about pulling out the Sharps and putting him out of his misery, but I got to figuring if he's still ornery enough to stand there and stomp his hooves and snort at me, he'll fare all right."

Custis took a couple of sips of the coffee I'd handed him before he continued his story.

"I rode around him and was fixing to see if there were any cows up higher. Then I saw what had happened. A big she-cougar was dead in between two large boulders. I looked her over and saw where that leggy bull had gored her with a horn. He must have broke the horn on a boulder, because there was dried blood where the boulder looked scraped. I reckon it was a helluva fight. I'm sure enough glad the old bull won."

"We'll probably have more calves to brand without that cougar roaming the high country."

"She most likely has some young'uns ready to hunt."

I felt sorry for the old bull, and wondered if Custis was right in not putting him out of his misery. My head felt strange when I thought about that broken horn.

The storms come in most every day well into August. The grass greened up, grew tall, putting out seed heads and lots of leaves around the bases. The trees and brush growing along the arroyos got greener with all their new leaves. The mesquite and catclaw had a good crop of beans. Custis reported that all the represos were plumb full, and he reckoned we were in for a good winter with the water in the tanks and the hills covered with all that good grama grass.

Along the middle of September the storms quit. We knew there would be a dry spell before any winter storms set in. But winter storms were not always on time. We had gone to town only once since the day Custis had got into it with Burnsides.

It was about sundown, the last day of September, that three men rode in. The dogs were barking something furious because the men had rode up faster than most visitors. I went to the window, and saw Custis come out of the barn to see what the strangers were wanting. I went back to the cooking room to fill the coffeepot because I reckoned Custis would have them come in and sit a spell.

Both the stew and bean pots were full, because I'd started both that morning. Good thing, too, because when Custis opened the door and the three cowboys came in, I knew they had rode in for supper. They had a certain look to them that told me they were not out for a pleasure ride. First off, I noticed they all brought their guns into the house with them. I filled their plates with stew and beans. They were three hungry men, and ate two helpings apiece.

Custis didn't introduce me to them, and I didn't ask who they were. They had a few snorts out of the mescal jug when they finished. Custis told them they were welcome to spend the night, but the one what seemed like the leader said they had to be putting miles between them and Tombstone.

"We've got a cow trade a-going, and hafta git there by morning," the leader feller said.

He didn't say where they had to get to by morning, and neither Custis nor I asked. They thanked Custis and me for the supper, telling us that they might stop by some other time to spend the night. I followed Custis and the cowboys out the door. We watched them mount up and ride out, heading up toward the mountain.

"They're rustlers," Custis remarked when they were gone. "They didn't say who they were when they rode in, and I didn't ask them. But lady, the one feller, who was boss, has got to be Zwing Hunt. He used to be a freighter, but found it was easier to make a living rustling cattle."

"He said they were in a hurry to get to a cow trade."

"I've a notion they're running from the sheriff, because there ain't nobody to trade cows with up on that mountain."

"Do you reckon they'll rustle our cows?"

"If they do, I'll know about it, but I doubt they bother us any. Treat people right and they tend to treat you right. We fed them and didn't ask questions. They probably won't take from us because they know they can stop by for food another time."

"I hope you're right, Custis. We've got enough worries with the neighbors without having to deal with the likes of rustlers."

One morning Custis hung around the house later than usual. I knew he had something on his mind by the way he kept filling his coffee cup and kind of milling around the house. Finally he sat back down at the table while I was nursing Roland.

"Lady, I've been thinkin' about the fall roundup."

"I knew there must have been something squirming around up in your head."

"You remember I told you Dobbs said I should send a representative to the fall roundup instead of working it myself? Well, I've done a heap of pondering about all that, and I reckon I've decided to go to town and look for a good cowboy to hire."

"Suppose Dobbs and Breeland have got everyone against us?"

"I'll have to take that chance. I'm not looking for trouble with anyone, and I figure it's best to send a rep to the roundup. There's something else I haven't talked about that's boogering me."

Custis scratched his head in back of his ears. When he did that, I knew he was trying to get the words together to tell me something.

"I've found six calves on our cows that were earmarked and hair-branded. All six had Harry Dobbs's earmark and hair-branded with the slash diamond."

"I'm not following you, Custis."

"It's a way to steal calves. They find an unbranded calf sucking one of our cows. They catch it, earmark it, and then hair-brand it. Then they turn the calf loose so's the mama raises it. When the calf is ready to wean, they go out and drive it back to their corrals, where they put their brand through the hair to the hide. As long as the calf wears their brand, and not sucking our cow, the calf belongs to the one what stole it."

"Why would Dobbs do that sort of thing when he's got three times the cows we have?"

"Both Dobbs and Breeland would like us out of the country because we have Apache friends. Shortening our calf crop is just one way to discourage us."

"What did you do with the calves you found hair-branded?"

"I roped them and branded the Quarter Circle L on their hides."

"Back to hiring a hand to be your rep during roundup.

How do you know that Dobbs and Breeland won't steal from you and pay off your rep?"

"I don't. I just have to be careful who I hire."

"I reckon you best get to town and start looking."

Custis went out and wrangled in the mules, because he would need the buckboard to pick up grain, flour, and beans, besides hiring a cowboy. I decided it was best to stay home to look after things here, even though I would like to have seen Paula. He harnessed and hitched up the mules to the buckboard early the next morning. I gave him a kiss good-bye and told him to stay away from bad hombres.

By this time Roland was crawling all over. He was probably the happiest young'un I'd ever seen. I talked to him a lot. He liked crawling while he carried the carved wooden figure that Blue Humming Bird had given him. He also liked the old tin cup I let him play with, and he was delighted with the noise it made when he banged it on the floor.

I was wishing our Apache friends might show up for a visit, but I knew it wouldn't do to have them here if Custis found a cowboy to hire. The cowboy might not take to Indians and head back to town. I still didn't understand why white folks was so turned against Indian people.

Custis didn't come back until late the following day. I went out of the house when he pulled into the barnyard. The buckboard was loaded with supplies and an old saddle was perched on top of the grain sacks. A Mexican sat on the seat next to Custis.

"Lady, I want you to meet Luis Huerta. He's our vaquero."

"I'm happy to meet you, Luis."

"El gusto es mío."

Custis and Luis unloaded the supplies for the house, then drove the buckboard to the barn to unload the grain and Luis's saddle. When Luis stepped down off the buck-board, I was impressed that he was taller than most Mexicans I had seen. His blue eyes were clear against his dark brown face. The thinness of his nose and the slight curve in it made me think he must have broken it some time or other. I could see by his callused, gnarled hands that he was no stranger to work.

I rounded up some bedding and carried it out to the barn. Custis had a couple of straw mattresses out there for when Hiding Fox and Blue Humming Bird visited. Custis come back to the house after he got Luis located.

"I was lucky to find Luis. He's worked up here a lot, but mostly south and a little north of Tucson. He's on his way home to Arispe, down in Sonora, but wants a few months' work. I think he'll make a good hand for us."

"He seems all right. Does he speak any English?"

"He speaks quite a bit, but like most of those fellers, he'd rather talk Mexican."

"You won't have to worry about fall roundup now."

"I'm glad of that. He seems like he's been around up here a lot. I have the notion I can trust him to be loyal to us. He seemed happy as all get-out to find a job after just getting to Tombstone this morning."

"As long as you feel good about him is all that matters. He might be good at breaking the two three-year-old colts you've been trying to get to."

"I was thinking the same thing."

Custis changed his mood. It was good to see him happy again. Luis took his meals with us, and I got to know him better. He played with Roland after suppers were over, and seemed to fit right in with us. Custis decided to begin working our three-year-old steers off the mountain before the rest of the neighbors started fall roundup. With Luis to

73

help, it wasn't too difficult to find the steers and drive them down to the hills. There was plenty of feed and plenty of water. By the time fall roundup begun, they had all the steers we figured to drive to Willcox off the mountain. Custis and Luis got all the calves branded, too.

The evening before Luis was to ride over to Breeland's to start roundup, Custis told him part of what was going on so's he'd know if the neighbors come up with any remarks. Luis rode out on the bay in the morning, leading one of the three-year-olds that he had made a lot of progress with. Luis was good with horses, too.

Custis rode out every day to keep the steers from drifting back to the mountain country. Hiding Fox and Fast Bear showed up with Custis about a week into roundup. I was surprised at how I could understand what was being said as they were palavering after supper.

Hiding Fox had seen Luis and Custis riding the mountain country but didn't want to intrude. Custis told the Apaches about the neighbors so's he could explain about Luis being hired on. I could see that Hiding Fox was angry. He told Custis that he had seen both the neighbors in the mountains but they had never seen him. "We can look like trees or rocks when we want to," Hiding Fox remarked.

They were gone when Custis went to the barn the next morning to grain the horses.

Luis returned when the crew was ready to drive all the steers to Willcox. Custis and Luis gathered the steers easily and drove them over to join the rest. Custis had to go along to get our steers sold. When he and Luis rode in after the trail drive, Custis seemed like his mind was somewhere besides on the ranch.

"Well, Custis Ames, what's bothering?"

"I reckon I shouldn't be bothered. The steers sold well,

and we don't have money problems. But, lady, the way the neighbors treated me was embarrassing in front of Luis. They barely spoke to me the whole drive to Willcox, and when we got done with everything they rode off without us."

"What did Luis have to say?"

"He doesn't like them. He even told me he thought they were coyotes."

"Luis seems to have good eyes and ears."

Custis got over the glooms in a day or two, but when Luis said he was ready to leave for Arispe, Custis seemed sad again. They had become good friends while they was working together.

Custis told Luis to take one of the three-year-old colts to ride home, and that he would look for him come spring. Luis thanked Custis, and thanked me for feeding him so well. He promised he'd be back as soon as the spring weeds sprouted.

By the middle of November the first chilly spell hit. Then it warmed up again, and clouds, long, gray clouds, begun coming in from the west. The first rain come in one night, and it was still drizzling the next morning. I liked the rain. Of course, all cow people like rain, but I liked watching it come down, sink into the ground, and then start little rivulets once the ground was full. I liked listening to it hit the roof, even when it woke me up in the middle of the night.

There was about four winter storms that year. Roland commenced walking, so I had my hands full making sure he didn't scamper off somewhere and get lost. Custis reported a lot of snow on the mountain most of the time in January.

One evening he rode in late. The sun had already sunk down behind the Huachuca Mountains. When he come in the house he looked sad.

"I found the old maverick bull dead today."

"Where was he?"

"Up there near the boulders close to where he'd fought that she-lion."

"What happened? Did he find another cougar to fight?"

"I don't think so. There weren't signs of any fight. I reckon it was just his time. The broke horn was still dangling, but it looked all healed up. He'd lost the one eye that the she-lion had clawed out."

"I reckon there's a time for living and a time for dying. That old feller done a heap of living, I'd say."

"I reckon you've about said what I was thinking, lady."

It's funny how you get attached to some animals. I hadn't seen that old, leggy bull in a long time. I just heard Custis tell about seeing him and such. But when I heard he was dead, I had a sad feeling, even though he was an old one and had come to the end in his own way.

I was getting kind of antsy being stuck in the house, watching and taking care of Roland. I was wishing I could go out riding again with Custis. I wanted to go to town and see Paula, too. Ranch life is fine in most respects, but there's times when I wanted to get away and talk to somebody else besides Roland and Custis. I told him about hankering for a trip to town. He said we would make the trip the following week because he had some cow work to get done.

Two days later, he rode in driving three bulls into the corral. He hollered for me to come look at them. I took Roland by the hand, and we made our way to the corrals.

"See these three," Custis said, still mounted. "These are sons of Old Maverick."

The three bulls in the corral looked like the old one. They had long horns like their daddy, and all three had long legs. The largest of the three had almost identical markings as Old Maverick.

"I saved these fellers to replace their daddy," Custis said, beaming. "I've got a bunch of his daughters, too."

I was real happy about seeing those bulls. Losing Old Maverick didn't seem so sad anymore. Roland wanted to see over the corral, so I lifted him up. Custis rode close, lifted him over, and plunked our son down in front of him on the saddle. The little feller had a quizzical look on his face when he sat down, but squealed with delight when Custis made the horse walk slowly around the corral. The bulls stayed out of the way, and didn't seem to be nearly as wild as their father had been.

Custis drove the young bulls back up the mountain the following day. We went to town two days later. We didn't get as early a start as usual, and as we got close I could see that Custis was getting nervous.

"Just go about your business," I told him. "Make no never mind about what folks say. Just ignore them."

"You make it sound easy, lady, but it ain't. I get riled when I hear them saying stuff toward you."

"I appreciate your concerning yourself, dear man, but just let them be. Make like you're hard of hearing."

We didn't get to town until midafternoon. Custis left Roland and me at Paula's and went about his business. I was glad to see Paula and the girls. Roland made a big hit with them all, scampering up and down the hallway. I felt real lucky that Custis had come into my life, and then little Roland. I hoped the same thing would happen to Angie and the others. The girls played with Roland while I went back to Paula's parlor to have coffee and palaver.

That brings me back to where I commenced my story.

Chapter Five

It was quite a job lowering the coffin into the grave. I had two ropes underneath, and Paula took ahold of one, me the other. We got it to the bottom without dumping it, then we commenced filling in the grave.

We were scraping the last of the dirt over the top when I heard Sofía scream. I looked up and saw her running toward the house as fast as she could. Then I looked toward the barn and saw what had scared the poor woman. Hiding Fox and Blue Humming Bird were standing by the corrals.

I raised my hand in greeting. Roland saw them too, and went running toward Blue Humming Bird. Paula gasped, but I turned to her and told her everything was all right. Blue Humming Bird lifted Roland up and gave him a big hug. I told Paula I needed to talk to the Apaches, so she went back to the house to calm down Sofía.

My Apache friends smiled at me as I approached them.

When they saw that I wasn't smiling in return, their faces turned to a wondering look. I told them about what had happened to Custis, and that I'd just finished burying him under the shade tree. Tears come to their eyes, and I commenced sobbing a bit. Blue Humming Bird handed Roland to Hiding Fox and come over to take me in her arms.

I managed to calm myself before I let my anger take over. Hiding Fox asked me who the murderers were. I told him Dobbs had done the shooting but Breeland was with him. He warned me that they might cause more trouble, since I knew they done it in cold blood and not in self-defense. Hiding Fox seemed wise as ever.

After I explained everything, I thought it might be a good idea to have them come to the house so Sofía could see they were good people. With Paula, we sat down at the table. I introduced the Indians to my friend, but Sofía wouldn't come out of the cooking room. Paula didn't know Apache, so I was kind of an interpreter. All the while, Roland sat on Blue Humming Bird's lap.

I got up to ask Sofía to heat up some stew. She was in the far corner of the cooking room, getting as far away from my Apache friends as she could. I stirred up the coals in the stove, put some wood in the firebox, and set the stew pot on the hot spot. Sofía seemed frozen in the corner. Plumb scared, I reckoned. She had the look of a dog that had been beaten. Cowering. I went about getting the food ready for my friends.

After our meal, Hiding Fox and Blue Humming Bird went out to the barn for the night. In the morning, of course, they were gone. I looked at the grave and saw a stick holding a small buckskin pouch standing in the middle. I reached down and felt the outside of the pouch. There was something in it that felt like stones, but I didn't open it to find out. I figured it was their way, and I wasn't going to do anything that might be wrong in their eyes.

Sofía had calmed down, so I thought everything had smoothed out, but after breakfast I learned that I was mistaken. She told me that she wanted to go back to Tombstone that same day. It's a shame what fear does to some people. I talked it all over with Paula, then asked her to take Sofía back to town, because I felt I needed to get out riding to check the cattle.

"What will you do with Roland while you're riding?" Paula asked.

"I'll put him up in front of me. I'm only going to check things, not do any cow work."

"I'll be back tomorrow, Gen."

I saddled up the zebra dun mare, lifted up Roland, and mounted, myself. It was too late to get into the high country, but I managed to cover most of the foothill range, especially over near Dobbs's country. I didn't see any hair-branded calves, but I did notice quite a few Slash Diamond cattle watering at one of our represos. If Roland hadn't been along, I'd have pushed them back into their own country. As it was, I let them be, but knew what I would do once I was riding alone.

Roland got to fussing, so I unbuttoned my shirt and nursed him. I figured that would hold him until we got back. I headed the mare back about midafternoon. The range looked good. There was plenty of feed left over from summer, and the grasses were beginning to green up from the winter storms. I saw filaree sprouting here and there. Custis had told me that filaree in the spring was good to lay fat on the cattle to hold them through the dry months of May and June, even into July if the summer rains come late.

I was one happy girl to see Luis sitting on the bench outside the barn when I rode in. Of course, when I got to telling him about Custis I got sad again. Luis was sad too, and walked over to Custis's grave, taken his hat off, and crossed himself.

"I come back like I promised, señora. The sorrel is a good cowhorse. I used him a lot at the rancho near Arispe."

Roland commenced fussing again, so I unsaddled the mare and we all went to the house for some beans.

"I'm sure glad you're here, Luis. I got left with Roland, and he ain't big enough to be riding a horse by himself yet. I had a woman from Tombstone come to watch him while I was riding, but Hiding Fox and Blue Humming Bird scared the woman bad, and she went back to town."

"I was scared the first time I saw them, but Custis told me they were friends. I didn't worry after that."

"They're still friends, and always will be as far as I'm concerned."

"*Bueno.*"

Next morning Luis saddled the bay after breakfast and rode off for the mountain country. About noon Paula arrived, driving the buckboard, trailing a saddle horse hitched behind.

"Gen, I can't stay. I wish I could, but there was a fight at the house between a couple of drunk miners, and Angie couldn't handle them. They tore up the place."

"I thought there was a marshal to keep order in town."

"I never could count on the marshal much, and now that he knows I'm sympathetic to you, I guess I can never count on him."

"Luis come back yesterday, Paula, so don't worry about me. He'll take care of the cattle just fine."

"I'm glad he's back. I was thinking I should look around for a cowboy to come out and help."

"Come inside, and we'll get something to eat. Then you can go on back to the lawless town of Tombstone."

We had a good talk. Paula told me that Sofía wouldn't have lasted long anyway, because she kept talking about her boyfriend all the way to town. When we were done, I told Paula I'd take care of the mules and she could ride on back to town.

I'd never seen Paula ride before. I wondered how the horse would take to her skirts flapping. I held his head while Paula got herself up in the saddle. I could tell the horse was kind of spooked. He jumped a little when I turned loose of the bridle, but Paula kept his head up like a bronc buster. We said good-bye, and I watched as she headed off down the road. I wished she could have stayed longer, but I knew what drunks were capable of doing to a place.

The following afternoon, while I was getting things ready to feed Luis when he come in from the high country, I heard the dogs barking. I grabbed the Sharps and went to the door to see who had ridden up. Just as bold as could be, Sheriff Brauley, Harry Dobbs, and Luther Breeland was riding in like they owned the place.

As I stepped out into the barnyard, I held the Sharps in front of me, ready. They reined up their horses when they saw me standing there. I had a strong desire to pull down on those varmints and start shooting, but I stood my ground to hear them out. Brauley held up his right arm as if he was reading my thoughts.

"Mrs. Ames, we aren't here to do you any harm, so put that rifle down."

"Sheriff, I'll stay put. Say what you come out here to say, and then get off my ranch."

"Mrs. Ames, we have reason to believe you're harboring Apaches, and that you even talk their lingo."

"What I talk and who I talk to is none of your business."

Then Dobbs spoke up. "I won't be having a Injun lover for a neighbor. Those bastards come down an' help themselves to my beef."

"I'd suggest you might be more friendly to them instead of shooting at them every time you think they're stealing."

"What are you doing, beddin' down Apache bucks like you done Tombstone miners?" Breeland asked.

"Mr. Breeland, I'd sooner bed down Apaches than cowards that shot my husband in the back."

I thought that'd make them mad enough to draw on me so I'd have the excuse to send some Sharps slugs their way. Brauley held up his arm again.

"Mrs. Ames, you can't blame these men for being upset with you having Apache friends when they lose cattle."

"Well, Sheriff, those two killed my Custis in cold blood, made it look like self-defense, and bought off the marshal. I'll be friendly to anyone I choose to be friendly to, but I'll guarantee I won't be friends with those murderers. Now, I think you might better get off this ranch."

Chapter Six

I stood there watching as they reined around their horses and rode off down the road. Something about it all made me swell up with pride. I wished Custis could have seen me. Maybe somehow he did.

I got to thinking when I'd put the Sharps back and was going to look in on Roland. There was something about the entire situation that made me believe I hadn't seen the last of Dobbs and Breeland. They were mean. But they were cowards underneath all the talk. I didn't enjoy wondering what they would try to do to me next.

Running the ranch was a heavy burden on my shoulders. I had Luis to do most of the riding, but driving the steers to Willcox and getting them sold was something I'd never done. With neighbors like Dobbs and Breeland, I was forced to the drive with only Luis. But I had to figure out something to do with little Roland. I thought about asking

Paula to care for him while I was gone. I also wondered about asking Hiding Fox and Blue Humming Bird if they could take him for the while.

When Luis rode in from the high country that evening, I quit thinking about the fall roundup and shipping. He told me that we should start branding calves, because he knew about the neighbors' habit of hair-branding. Here I'd been trying to figure out how to care for Roland, but when Luis talked about branding it suddenly come to me that if I hired another cowboy, I could take care of Roland.

Early next morning, I got the mules hitched to the buckboard and Roland and me headed for Tombstone to hire us a cowboy to help Luis. I stopped by Paula's to leave Roland off while I looked around town for an out-of-work cowboy.

Angie overheard our conversation and told me about a feller from Texas what had drifted in a couple days before. He'd spent some of his money at the house with one of the girls. I listened to her description of the cowboy as a sandy-haired, tall and lanky man, about six foot with his boots on, and wearing a black hat with a wide brim.

My first stop was the Crystal Palace to see if Hannah might have an idea where I could find him. Hannah greeted me with a hug, and I saw my cowboy standing at the far end of the bar. I asked Hannah to introduce me to him, so we passed around two other customers, and I met Ben Newsom.

"I'm looking for a cowboy that knows what he's doing and can work mountain country," I explained.

"Well, ma'am, I could be just the right cowboy for y'all. I've worked mountain country and desert. I'm good with a rope, and if y'all have any green horses what needs broke, I can do that to boot."

"When can you start?"

"I'll start soon as I get out to your ranch."

"Throw your rig in my buckboard, and we'll be going soon as I pick up my boy."

My new cowboy went to the Grand Hotel to gather his belongings and was back at the Palace in half an hour. Meanwhile, Hannah and me had a good palaver. She told me all about Dobbs, Breeland, and Sheriff Brauley coming back from their visit to me. They were madder than wet cats, telling everyone in the bar that I was running a whorehouse for Apaches.

We picked up Roland at Paula's on the way out of town. Ben wondered why I had left the boy at a bawdy house. I leveled with him about once working there, because I figured he'd hear about it sometime.

"Y'all mean that I'm working for a lady of the night?"

"Was a lady of the night. Not anymore. You're working for the Quarter Circle L Ranch."

I hadn't said anything about Luis, just that he would be working with another man. We made good time going back to the ranch, and arrived before Luis had finished whatever he was doing. I told Ben to put his gear in the barn, and that there was a spare bed in there for him to bunk in.

I started making biscuits and warming up some chili con carne. Ben come over to the house just before Luis rode into the barn. I poured him a cup of coffee and talked to him while I worked. I found out he had come to Arizona on account of he'd heard that a lot of Texans had come over here after Mr. Gadsden bought out Mexico.

"That was quite a spell ago, wasn't it?"

"Yeah, but the word around Texas is that there's more grass in Arizona, even if there's Indians to worry about."

"I don't worry about Indians. I've got good friends who

are Apaches. You'll probably meet them one of these days."

"Well, ma'am, I don't hanker to meet no Apaches. That ain't why I come out here."

I decided to let the matter of my Apache friends drop, and went about getting supper ready. I knew Luis would be riding in directly. I hoped this Ben would work out all right so's the calves would be all branded before Dobbs and Breeland got to riding on fast horses and throwing long ropes.

Luis arrived close to sunset. I saw him from the window as he led the bay into the corral and come ambling toward the house. I introduced him to Ben after he knocked on the door and I let him in. Neither man smiled, and I wondered what was going on in their heads. We all sat down to the evening meal, and I tried to start some sort of conversation. There was a tense sort of atmosphere all the time we was eating.

Luis finished first, thanked me for supper, and went out to the barn. Ben sat there, sipping at his coffee.

"Mrs. Ames, we need to get something straight here right off."

"What's on your mind?"

"I didn't know you was working a Mex when I hired on. Now, I don't mind working cows with a Mex long as he don't try bossing. But back in Texas we don't eat or sleep with them."

"Well, Ben, you're in Arizona, not Texas. If you don't want to eat your meals with Luis, you can take your plate outside. If you don't want to sleep in the barn, take your bed somewhere else."

"I reckon the Mex oughta be the one to eat and sleep outside."

"Your reckon is dead wrong on this outfit. Luis is a fine man, and a top hand with cattle and horses. The fact him being Mexican makes no never mind to me. If you can't sort out all that business in your head, you can throw your gear in the buckboard, and I'll drive you to town in the morning."

"That don't leave me much of a choice, ma'am."

"The way I see it, Ben, you've got two. I'd like to have you stay on, but it's got to be on my terms."

"I reckon I'll take the trip back to town."

I was a mite upset that I'd have to hitch up the mules again in the morning, but I figured it was better than having a Texas cowboy what thought he was better than Luis because he was lighter-skinned.

The trip to town was mostly in silence. I talked to Roland mostly. I let Ben off by the Grand Hotel, and wished him luck. Neither Paula nor Angie had any ideas where I could find me another cowboy. I asked them to send out anyone they might meet who wanted cow work and didn't mind working for a woman or with a top-hand Mexican vaquero. On the way home I found myself wishing Roland was old enough to ride.

That evening, I explained to Luis about Ben Newson. Luis understood, and thanked me for my loyalty. He also offered to ride to Arispe to bring his oldest daughter to take care of Roland while I was out branding. Since the trip to Arispe and back would have taken a couple weeks, I thanked him but told him I needed him to keep working the high country to get all the calves branded he could.

About a week later I was surprised when I went out to see what was upsetting the dogs and saw a man riding in on a shiny black gelding. I looked hard to recognize him, but he wasn't in any way familiar. When he dismounted, I saw he was tall, well-dressed, and steely-gray-haired under his black, wide-brimmed hat. His ruddy face was clean shaved, and his green eyes had a sparkle to them.

"Howdy, Mrs. Ames, I'm Tom Smalley. I heard about Custis, and would like to express my sympathy to you."

"Thank you, Mr. Smalley. Custis told me about you when he bought the ranch."

"I hated to sell out, but Ellen, that was my wife, was sickly, and needed a doctor's care in Tucson. Ellen passed on three months ago."

"I'm right sorry to hear that, Mr. Smalley. I reckon we've both lost someone dear to us. Put up your horse and come in the house for coffee."

Smalley put the black in the corral while I heated up the coffee. Like Custis had told me, Tom Smalley seemed like a good sort. However, I was wondering what he'd come plumb back to the ranch for. After we small-talked for a spell, I found out.

"Mrs. Ames, you're overdue on Custis's note on the ranch, and I'd like to know what you intend to do."

"I'm sorry, I don't know what you're talkin' about, Mr. Smalley."

"I'm sure Custis must have told you that he paid me cash for the cattle, as is customary, and six thousand on the ranch. He signed this note for a thousand, which was due last month."

While he was telling me all this, Smalley took the papers out of his pocket and handed them over to me. I looked at the note, the date that the thousand come due, and wished Custis had explained it all.

"This comes as quite a surprise, Mr. Smalley. Custis never made mention of owing money on the ranch. I reckoned he had paid for everything."

"I assure you that what I'm telling you is correct."

"Oh, I'm not questioning you at all, Mr. Smalley. I can see Custis's signature, and all the figures. It's just a big surprise."

"I can see that it is, but I have to ask you how you intend to take care of this."

"I need to think a bit, because I won't have a thousand dollars until I ship the steers in the fall."

"Now that we've met each other, Mrs. Ames, there might be a way we can work all this out."

"What are you meaning to say?"

"You're a real pretty woman, and you seem like a real nice sort. With Ellen gone, I wouldn't mind coming back to the Quarter Circle L and be partners with you."

"What are you meaning, partners?"

"You probably need a man in just the way I feel the need for a woman. Besides, a woman running a cow ranch alone is fighting a tough battle."

"Mr. Smalley, I plumb forgot about men when they killed my Custis. I've got thieving neighbors, a son to raise, and a cow ranch to run. I may be a woman, but I'm a determined woman. It may take a day or two, but you'll get your thousand dollars."

"Mrs. Ames, I happen to know what you did for a living before you met your husband. Why don't you make life easier for yourself?"

"Mr. Smalley, I reckon you best get out to the corral, climb on that black gelding, and leave me be here. I'll meet you at the bank in one week. Somehow, I'll have your thousand dollars."

I was commencing to feel he wasn't going to leave, but after I said what I did, he left without saying another word. I kind of felt sorry for Tom Smalley, but I sure didn't hanker to pay for the ranch by bedding him. Then I commenced figuring how I was going to scare up that thousand-dollar surprise.

The thought of paying the thousand dollars with my body crossed my mind. I even looked myself over in the long mirror on the door as I was getting ready for bed. My long, raven-black hair was still shiny. I was still proud of my bosoms, even though they wasn't as firm as before I nursed Roland. My belly had gone back, and my hips hadn't spread out much. I was more muscled up in my arms and legs, but that come from the hard work I had been doing since I married Custis. All in all, I figured I could go back to Paula's and make a thousand dollars easy, but it would take longer than a week. The last thing I wanted to do was to have that Tom Smalley living with me and Roland at the ranch. That wouldn't have been fair to my Custis.

Behind the barn, I knew there were the sacks full of high grade that Custis had brought over from the claim on the old burro. I had no notion of what the ore might assay at, or sell for. The next morning, Luis helped load the sacks into the buckboard. After breakfast, I caught up the mules, harnessed them, hitched them up, and drove to Tombstone.

By midafternoon I had three hundred dollars. I drove the buckboard to Paula's. We sat in her parlor, and I told her about Smalley's visit.

"I need to borrow seven hundred dollars, Paula. I'll get it back to you with interest when I ship the steers in the fall."

"I'm happy to lend you the money. After all, you're my best friend, and I'd hate to see you lose the ranch."

I got out of the chair and gave her a hug. "Thanks, best friend."

As I was driving the buckboard down Allen Street

toward the bank, I noticed Smalley's black gelding tied up in front of the Crystal Palace. I turned the mules onto Fifth Street and pulled up in front of the pawnshop, right where Custis was gunned down. Roland was still with Paula where I had left him.

Smalley was standing at the bar talking with Hannah. I went up to them, greeted Hannah, then turned to face him.

"I have your thousand dollars, Mr. Smalley. If you will please give me a receipt, I'll pay what I owe."

"Well, Mrs. Ames, that didn't take long."

"I told you I was a determined woman."

"Let me buy you a drink."

"I'd just as soon get our business took care of. As it is, time I get back to the ranch it'll be dark."

I turned over the money to Smalley and he gave me a receipt. I drove the buckboard back to Paula's to pick up Roland.

"Why don't you leave Roland with me for a week or so. Then you and your cowboy can get some work done without your having to try and hire someone else," Paula suggested.

"I think I'll take you up on that. Once we get the calves all branded, Luis can take care of everything that needs riding."

I rode with Luis every day, looking for unbranded calves sucking Quarter Circle L cows. When that was done, we started driving the old cows without calves down out of the high country. I figured to sell those old Nellies in Tombstone to the butcher. They wouldn't bring much, but I'd get them off the grass. Custis had explained all that. I remember him saying, "A cow that don't give a calf is worse than no cow at all, because she'll eat just as much grass and give nothing back."

We gathered about thirty head of old cows. There was two or three what looked liked they was carrying calves, but they had so many rings on their horns, broad noses, and eyes slanting downward, all signs of old age, that we drove them into town with the rest.

I stopped by Paula's to see Roland when I'd finished with the butcher. He was getting along fine, and Paula said he was no bother. I told Paula I'd be in to fetch him home in a couple of days. Luis and I rode back to the ranch.

Roundup for the other cowmen started. I sent Luis over to help, even though we had our calves branded. There was always the chance that we'd missed some. I drove to town and picked up Roland. By this time he was starting to talk a lot more words, and I started thinking about how I was going to school him.

With Luis out on roundup, I looked forward to some time alone with my son. Book learning was something I had had little of, but my ma taught me how to read and write a bit. At least I could read the papers Smalley had set in front of me. Of course, Roland wasn't old enough to learn reading and writing, but I had it in mind to make sure he got what I didn't. Angie had given me an old book of fairy tales, so I sat down with Roland every day and read to him until he fell asleep.

Several days after we got back from town, Hiding Fox rode in with Mountain Thunder, Fast Bear, and three other Apache men. He left his friends at the barn and said he wanted to palaver with me alone. We went to the house. I was glad Roland was taking his afternoon nap so me and Hiding Fox could talk without him bothering.

I asked about Blue Humming Bird. Hiding Fox said she was back at their place in the mountains with the children. He commenced asking me all about how Custis was killed, who had shot him, and everything I knew about it. I told him best I could, since all I knew was what Hannah had told me and what I'd figured out myself. Hiding Fox seemed real serious about me telling every detail, and I was wondering what was going on in his mind. He had me describe Harry Dobbs twice.

He seemed anxious to leave when we finished our palaver. I walked back to the barn with him, and it was then that Fast Bear gave me a quarter of venison. I thanked him and the others, said my good-byes, and carried the meat back to the house. I must say, I was glad to have the venison, because I was running low and we was eating mostly beans.

Luis come back from the roundup two weeks later. He said they had branded five Quarter Circle L calves that he and I had missed, and that the neighbors had treated him all right in spite of him being my rep. He had noticed quite a few Slash Diamond calves that looked like they was sired by one of our leggy bulls.

"You might as well ride their country once in a while and drive back any of our bulls or cows you find."

The heat of late May got more intense in June. By the middle of June I looked for clouds every morning, but the sky was blue and clear. But pretty soon the big, white, cotton looking clouds commenced flying high in from the south. On San Juan's Day, the twenty-fourth of June, there was a bunch of clouds rolled in early, and by noon they had slowed, building up into dark masses. It wasn't long before I heard a clap of thunder. I looked up and saw streaks of lightning followed by more thunder. Then I saw the smoke.

I reckoned it was about a mile or so north of headquarters. It commenced as a sort of grayish-white plume. As I stood in the barnyard watching, it got bigger and turned a yellowish brown. I knew I had me a grass fire.

We'd had them before, and there just ain't nothing to do but watch. I was glad when I felt the first raindrops on my hat and looked down to see the ground getting speckled. If the wind changed, the fire might head my way.

Custis never got upset with range fires, even though they sometimes burnt up a lot of grass. "Come the summer storms, the grass will come back stronger than ever," he would say. If he was still here, he'd probably ride out to the fire to watch it.

The black, boiling clouds overhead spilled out a good shower, and when it quit I looked out to where the fire had been, and saw just a few wisps of smoke. San Juan's Day had lived up to the Mexican tradition by raining.

At two years old, Roland was getting big enough to start learning how to ride. The next time I went to town I bought him a small saddle and some straps to hold him on. The zebra dun mare was dog gentle, so I saddled her up, lifted Roland into the saddle, and tied him on with the straps. He was giggling the whole time. I led the mare around the corral a few times so Roland could get the feel of being alone on top of her. Then I opened the gate and led her out into the barnyard. Roland did fine. I'd handed him the reins so's he could get used to them right off. I led the mare with a halter rope. The zebra dun was as good as gold. She knew there was a little feller on her back, and she stepped real careful and slow. I was proud of them both.

I led her back to the corral and turned her loose with Roland in control. I showed him how to neck-rein her and how to pull back so she'd stop. After twenty minutes or so, I thought it best to end the first lesson. I reckon Roland had learned a lot before from riding in front of me.

Luis spent several days in the high country, and when he come back he told me he needed to get back to Arispe to tend to his own place and his family now that it was summer. I was sorry to see him go, and was glad he promised to come back in the fall to help roundup and ship the steers. I let him take the sorrel gelding for his trip south.

Within a week I had Roland riding alone out in the barnyard. I watched the mare and knew she was going to be just right for the boy. I didn't feel so left alone to run the ranch. Now I could take Roland with me to check on the cattle.

The clouds had quit spilling rain after the one storm on San Juan's Day. The country had dried up real quick, and toward the end of July I could tell we were in for a dry spell.

Living way out where we were, I didn't hear much about what was going on, especially since the neighbors never visited because of the way they held me as an Indian lover and a whore to boot. Town trips were few, and the last time I'd hitched up the mules was before San Juan's Day. I hadn't seen hide nor hair of my Apache friends, and wondered what was keeping them from coming by.

The last week in August, I found out why. The dogs went out of the barnyard barking like there was a whole pack of coyotes coming in to steal their food. I had just come in from unsaddling after riding out to check the represos to the north. The blue uniforms told me that I was being visited by the U.S. Cavalry. There was six of them led by a young-looking lieutenant with blond hair and a flimsy-looking blond mustache to match. The rest were black Buffalo Soldiers, every one of them looking real serious.

The lieutenant raised his gloved hand after they entered the barnyard. The troop come to a halt. The lieutenant dismounted, handed the the reins to one of the troopers, and, pulling off the glove from his right hand, come toward me with his saber jingling.

"Mrs. Ames, I am Lieutenant Evan Holmes, U.S. Cavalry, stationed at Fort Huachuca. I am under orders to investigate the murder of Harry Dobbs and the wounding of Luther Breeland by a band of Apache Indians two weeks ago."

You could have knocked me over with a feather. Dobbs killed, and Breeland wounded. Now I knew why I hadn't seen Hiding Fox and Blue Humming Bird.

"This is the first I've heard this news, Lieutenant. I haven't been off the ranch in quite a spell."

"Would it be asking too much to go inside in order to talk this over?"

"Of course not. Let's go in the house, and I'll warm some coffee. Why don't you tell your men they can water their horses in the big corral."

The lieutenant turned toward the troopers and ordered the corporal to have the troop dismount and water their horses.

He sat at the table while I poured the coffee. All the time I was wondering what had gone on. I sat down across from him.

"Well, Lieutenant, I'm real curious as to what happened."

"According to Mr. Breeland, he and Mr. Dobbs were riding together, as they often did. They were looking for a good location for a represo near the base of the mountains. They had tied their horses to a tree to inspect a potential site on an arroyo. Suddenly, seemingly from out of nowhere, eight Apache warriors surrounded them. The two ranchers were helpless. Mr. Dobbs drew his revolver, was promptly shot in the chest, and fell to the ground. The Indians then quickly overpowered Mr. Breeland, disarmed him, and tied his hands behind him with rawhide thongs."

"Was Dobbs dead?"

"Not dead, but dying. The savages picked him up from the ground and propped him up against a tree. They first cut off both the poor man's ears. Lucky for Mr. Dobbs, he was near death, because the next atrocity the savages committed was to remove his trousers, sever Mr. Dobbs's private parts, and stuff them in his mouth."

"Was Dobbs dead then?"

"According to Mr. Breeland, who was witness to the entire horrible affair, Mr. Dobbs slumped into death as his blood flowed from his genital area."

"If the Apaches had Breeland tied up, how did he get away from them?"

"Mr. Breeland thought he was about to have the same treatment, but the savage who had mutilated Dobbs walked over to him and cut his right ear off. Mr. Breeland said that this particular Apache wore a U.S. Cavalry sergeant's jacket and yellow neckerchief around his head. After that, the Apaches untied Mr. Breeland and motioned for him to leave on foot. Mr. Breeland walked out of there as quickly as he could. He heard the savages *kiyi*ing. He glanced over his shoulder and saw them starting up the mountain, leading the two horses they had stolen. They left Mr. Dobbs propped against the tree."

The description of the Apache wearing the sergeant's jacket fit Hiding Fox. I had a sudden feeling of joy, even though what he done to Dobbs was mighty gruesome. Somehow I looked forward to seeing Breeland with only one ear. I didn't exactly know what to say, but I reckoned I ought to sound all surprised and horrified. Just before I commenced to speak, something inside my mind snapped.

"Lieutenant Holmes, your story is interesting," I replied. "But I don't know why you're here investigating. This is the first I've heard all this, but I can't say I'm sad about what happened. That feller, Dobbs, killed my Custis in cold blood, shot 'm in the back."

"Mr. Breeland told Sheriff Phillips that he thought he heard the name 'Custis' coming from the savage who mutilated Mr. Dobbs, mixed with all the jabbering going on."

"Are you done with your investigation, Lieutenant?"

"Not quite, Mrs. Ames. It is common knowledge in and around Tombstone that you are friendly with the Apaches, and that you even speak their language."

"What's wrong with being friends with people who are friendly to you? I'd sooner have Apaches as friends than those thieving, murdering neighbors."

"Since we are at war with the Apaches you may be considered as one aiding and abetting the enemy, a serious crime."

"That does sound a mite complicated, Lieutenant, but I'm just friends with some Apaches, and that don't seem like aiding or whatever."

"Then you should be willing to tell me where these Apaches stay in the mountains."

"I can't tell that, because I don't know. But if I did know, I don't reckon I'd tell you. That wouldn't be friendly to them. Then I'd be aiding and whatever you fellers. Besides, for all you know it might have been the Apache Kid that done the deed on Dobbs."

The lieutenant didn't seem to know what to say to me, but I could tell he had more on his mind. I decided to sit still and say nothing just to make the poor devil suffer a bit. He tipped up the tin coffee mug and took a sip.

"Mrs. Ames, if you don't mind, I would appreciate your

permission to bivouac my patrol here for the night before we proceed to the mountains in the morning."

"That's fine with me, Lieutenant. You can put your horses up in the big corral where there's water. The cattle won't come in until morning. All I've got is some stew, and there ain't enough to feed all your men, but I can have some venison steaks broiled up pretty quick."

"Thank you, Mrs. Ames, I might enjoy a venison steak, but the men have field rations. I do appreciate the use of your corral for our mounts."

"I have plenty of venison steaks for your troopers, so if it's all the same to you, if I'm cooking one for you, I'll cook for them too."

"That really isn't necessary, Mrs. Ames."

"You might not think it's necessary, but this is a hospitable outfit. I treat all guests the same. If you was Apaches, you'd get fed too."

"Thank you, Mrs. Ames. Let me know when you are ready, and I'll have the men bring their mess kits."

The lieutenant left the house. I commenced getting the fire in the Old Majestic ready for the steaks. Gollies, he seemed like such a stuck-up sort. Roland was out with the troopers. I went out to cut some venison off the quarter in the barn. I could tell the troopers were having fun with my boy. As I passed by, they took off their hats and smiled at me. Roland followed me out to the barn.

I heard the lieutenant ordering the troopers to unsaddle their horses, which he called "mounts," and put them in the big corral. I got the steaks cut and went back to the house with Roland to commence cooking.

I made a big pot of coffee and broiled the steaks with ground red chili. The bean pot looked like it had enough in it to go around. I kept thinking about how the white officer would have eaten one of my steaks without offering any to his men. I didn't know whether it was because the lieutenant was white and the men black, or that because he was an officer, he thought he was better than they was. I reckon it was a bit of both. I also wondered what Hiding Fox would say if he knew I was feeding the cavalry what was hunting him.

When everything was ready, I went outside and told them to come over for their supper. They brought their tin plates and cups, and I had them come to the cooking room so I could fill their plates with steaks and beans, and their cups with coffee. They was all nice and polite, thanking me for the supper. I let Roland go outside and eat his beans with them. The lieutenant sort of hinted 'round that he'd like to join me in the house for supper, but I didn't invite him. He ate outside, but apart from his men.

Roland wandered back to the house with his bowl as I was getting things cleaned up in the cooking room. It was dusk by then, so I read him a story. It wasn't long before he got sleepy. I turned in about an hour after I put him to bed.

Chapter Seven

I don't recollect when the yelling commenced, but it woke
me up. I lit the coal-oil lamp and put on my clothes as fast
as I could. I grabbed the Sharps as I went out the door. The
lieutenant and his troops were all up by the corrals talking
as fast as they could in what I would call total confusion.
When I got there they was all standing around one of the
Buffalo Soldiers who was lying on the ground. Two of the
troopers was bent over, looking at him.

"What's all the ruckus about?" I asked.

The lieutenant quickly turned toward me.

"Our mounts have been stolen!"

"Are you sure you closed the gate to the corral?"

"Certainly, Mrs. Ames. Corporal Johnson posted a sentry. As you can see, he is lying on the ground unconscious.
It must have been those murdering Apaches."

"Is there anything I can do for him?"

"He was struck on the head. Perhaps if we carried him to the house."

"I'll get back and get some more lamps lit. Bring him in."

I scurried back to the house, all the time thinking it must have been Hiding Fox and the rest who done the stealing. I thought it was pretty durned comical until I realized I'd probably end up taking the soldiers into Tombstone. I also wondered why I was volunteering to look at the unconscious man. I wasn't a nurse. I reckoned it was because I was the only woman around, and men seem to count on women to know how to nurse.

I had them carry the unconscious soldier into my sleeping room and lay him down on my bed, where I could get a better look at him. I put two lighted lamps on the table next to my bed so I could see. I had the two troopers what had carried him in turn him over because I couldn't see nothing wrong in front. There was a swollen lump, with some dried blood around it, on the back of the poor devil's head. By the looks, he'd been unconscious for quite a spell.

I went into the cooking room and got a pot of water and a clean flour sack. Then I washed away the dried blood. All the while the lieutenant stayed sitting at the table with a blank look on his face. We turned the unconscious man back over and I washed his face off, hoping the coolness would bring him back into the world. I must have done this for half an hour before the man let out a low groan. The two other troopers just stood there and watched.

Pretty soon after that first low groan his eyes flickered open. Then a look of pain come over his face, and he closed his eyes at the same time. I kept putting the cool, wet flour sacks on his forehead. "You're going to be fine," I told him several times.

Finally he blinked for a while, and then his eyes stayed open. "You're going to be fine," I told him again, and he looked at me.

"Thank you, ma'am. My head hurts real bad."

"You've got a big knot on the back of it, is why it hurts."

I folded a fresh, cool, wet flour sack, lifted him up far enough to slide it behind his head, and let him back down.

"I'm gonna leave you be with your two friends while I get some coffee hot for you."

I brought him some coffee, and we propped him up so's he could sip it. I left him there with the other two and went back in the cooking room to get breakfast ready. The lieutenant didn't say anything. He seemed deep in thought, and I figured he must be wondering about what he'd say to his captain after losing the horses. It was probably like a cowboy getting bucked off and coming back to the bunkhouse afoot.

Breakfast was 'most ready when he come into the cooking room and stood leaning against the wall. "Mrs. Ames, would it be asking too much of you to borrow your horses?"

"I don't have enough horses to carry all your troopers, but I figured to hitch up the mules to the buckboard and take you and your troopers to Tombstone."

"That's mighty nice of you, Mrs. Ames. I would personally appreciate the use of one of your horses for myself."

He was sure enough trying his best to keep himself above his troops. I wondered what those soldiers thought about the lieutenant's snobby attitude. "You can saddle the gray gelding if you like. He'll follow the buckboard back from town, all right."

"I was hoping you could find it possible to take us back to Fort Huachuca, Mrs. Ames."

"I reckon I could if I had somebody here to take care of the cattle and all, but Tombstone's as far as I can help you with, Lieutenant Holmes. I'm sure you can telegraph the fort or borrow horses from the livery."

Two of the troopers came in after breakfast and cleaned up the cooking room while I got Roland ready for the trip to town. Three of the troopers came up to the barn and offered to help with the mules, so I let them give me a hand. They knew mules, I could tell by the way they hitched them up to the buckboard. Then they loaded their saddles and other tack into the bed of the buckboard. I wondered if Hiding Fox might be hiding behind a juniper tree, watching everything that was going on.

The lieutenant ordered one of the troopers to catch the gray gelding, then he put his McClelland saddle on the gray's back. I watched him out of the corner of my eye to see what the gray would do with a stranger in the saddle. I was hoping there might be some excitement, but the horse didn't mind the lieutenant or the McClelland saddle.

The troopers climbed aboard the buckboard. I told the one with the knot on his head to sit next to me and Roland. On the way into town I learned his name was Matthew Cooper and he was from Mississippi. His head still hurt some, but I knew that sitting on the seat was more comfortable than bouncing around in back with the other troopers.

The lieutenant rode the gray up front of the mules like he felt that position was better for an officer than taking up the rear. When we got to town, I pulled up the mules in front of the livery. I said good-bye to Matthew. He shook hands with me and Roland and thanked me for taking care of him. The other troopers came by and thanked me too. I got down and handed the lieutenant a halter to put on the gray. He thanked me for my hospitality and offered to have the disbursement officer at the fort send me a voucher. I told him that wouldn't be necessary.

I tied the gray's halter rope to the back of the buckboard, climbed back on the seat, and drove over to Paula's to tell her all that had happened. It was close to dark when we got back to the ranch.

Finally, I put the mules and the gray up and got us fed. When Roland was to bed I ambled out to Custis's grave with a lit candle. I set the candle down in the middle of the mound of rocks and stood there for a few minutes thinking about what a gruesome end Dobbs had come to. Then I smiled down at the flickering light dancing over the rocks. "I reckon justice comes along somehow, dear man. But I'll never stop missing you, Custis Ames."

I didn't sleep good that night. I kept thinking about Mrs. Dobbs. Having her husband killed the way he was must have been terrible for her, and I couldn't get it out of my mind. I reckon I must have spent half the night pondering if I should go over to the Dobbs place and talk to her, widow to widow. I must have fallen asleep after I had decided to ride over to see if there was anything I could do for her.

When the rains had begun again during the middle of July I was glad. Later on, with September coming up, the rains had commenced to slow down some. The summer heat was still with us, but I figured it wouldn't hurt Roland none to ride with me over to the Slash Diamond to look in on Mrs. Dobbs. Besides, we could check the cattle at two represos on the way.

I had never been over there because of the way the situation was, but I knew the way all right from riding close to their country. We rode out after breakfast. The cattle were just starting to gather at Coyote Tank when we were letting the bay and the zebra dun drink. We rode around, checking to see if the cattle needed any attention. The calves looked fine and slick from their mothers' milk, rich from all the green feed they were getting.

We rode out toward Cebolla Tank and did the same. I saw one two-year-old heifer coming close to calving. I made a note of her in my mind so I could come back in a couple of days to check on her. Every once in a while, first-calf heifers have trouble birthing. Custis always tried to keep an eye out for them.

By the sun, it was close to midday when we arrived at the Slash Diamond headquarters. The house looked bigger than ours and the barn was three times as big as the adobe one, even with the addition Custis had put on. The *estacada* corrals looked like they could hold a thousand head of cows at one time. Four dogs come running out to see who we were, barking like they was about to eat us alive until a gray-haired woman come out into the barnyard and called them off. I figured the woman must be Mrs. Dobbs. I reined in the bay when we were about ten yards from where she was standing. Her gray hair was neatly combed, and by the the wrinkles in her face I judged she was to be somewheres in her forties. She was still of good figure, and wore a black mourning dress.

"I'm Genevieve Ames, Mrs. Dobbs. This is my son, Roland. We rode over to tell you how sorry we are about what happened to your husband."

"Mrs. Ames, I must say you have a lot of nerve coming over here. How can you possibly think you are welcome after what your savage friends did to my Harry?"

I felt real uneasy. I glanced over to Roland. I could see

he was feeling uncomfortable, but I had to say something to Mrs. Dobbs. I was just about to speak again when she held up her right hand to stop me.

"I would appreciate your leaving immediately, Mrs. Ames. I find absolutely nothing in common with you."

She turned around abruptly and headed for the door.

"Mrs. Dobbs, we're both widows. That's what we have in common," I said to her back. Then I reined the bay around, made sure Roland was following on the zebra dun, and we rode out of the Slash Diamond headquarters.

"So much for Mrs. Dobbs," I said to Roland when we were on the trail back to our ranch.

"She mean, Momma," Roland replied.

I was surprised to hear him say that. "She's probably not mean, son. She's just upset and can't figure things right."

The reaction of the Dobbs woman to me bothered me all the way back to the Quarter Circle L. I was really and truly wanting to reach out and comfort the lady, but she completely pushed me away. Remembering the corrals at the Slash Diamond, I wondered how many of my calves had been hair-branded inside those walls made of stacked-up mesquite poles.

By the time I had done all the chores and made supper for Roland and me, I had put most of those bothers out of my mind. I decided that I'd take Roland up to the high country in the morning to check on any cattle what had drifted up there. Most of the herd was grazing the foothills, but there was always a few that stayed behind in their favorite spots. I wanted to get most of the cattle off the mountain by November, and working that country alone took a spell. I hoped Luis would come riding in soon.

By the time I got the mule packed with our camp gear the sun was peaking over the mountain. We started up the trail, taking it slow because I didn't want to have wore-out animals once we reached the high country. I wanted to get the camp set up so's we could start looking for cattle early the next morning. Since we was getting short of venison, I made sure I had plenty of ammunition for the Sharps. I was a pretty good shot with that old carbine, but not near as good as Custis. If I got the camp set in time, I figured to scout out a deer by the creek that run down into Grapevine Canyon.

I'd taken Roland hunting with me before. The first time he jumped and yelled just as I was about to fire the Sharps at a two-year-old buck. Of course, the buck was out of my sights in a second. I had to laugh when I looked down and saw that boy of mine grinning from ear to ear. It was almost like he didn't want me to shoot that buck. I explained to him that we needed to eat, and that was the only reason I'd ever kill a deer. After that he learned to keep still.

We made good time going up the mountain. The pine were all green, and there was lots of grass between the trees. Along the way, I spotted eight cows with calves and one bull with the bunch. By midafternoon we had reached the camp in the middle of a pine grove; here Custis had built a small lean-to shelter and a fire circle.

I unloaded the mule and unsaddled the horses. I put hobbles on them so they could graze. I strapped a bell around the zebra dun's neck so I could find them in the morning. Then I set about making our camp, first off making a fire to cook supper on. Roland and I carried a bucket over to the small mountain spring a hundred yards away, filled the bucket with water, and hauled it back to camp.

I commenced making some stew out of part of the jerky I'd packed in. In another pot I put some beans on

to heat. Of course, there was the old standby, the coffeepot. While supper was getting ready I spread out our
bedrolls under the lean-to. I figured we had plenty of
time to eat before dusk, so I'd try my luck finding a
deer watering from the creek about a half mile or so
from camp.

After supper we walked slowly and quietly over a nar-
row trail through the grass and trees. Around a pool where
I knew the deer liked to come in for water, there were some
large boulders that we could hide behind. The sun was setting over in the west, coloring the sky with gold. I had
Roland sit down next to my favorite boulder and motioned
him to keep still while we waited.

It wasn't long before I heard a twig snap by the pool. I
put my finger to my lips to tell Roland to be real quiet and
edged myself around the boulder to see what was coming
into the pool.

There were four deer: a doe with a fawn, a yearling doe,
and a yearling spike buck. I had already pulled the hammer
back on the Sharps, so I raised it up slowly and took aim on
the spike buck's heart. Just as I was about to squeeze the
trigger, I saw an arrow fly into the buck right where I was
aiming. The deer went down. The others bolted off into the
surrounding forest. I looked around to see where the arrow
had come from, and there behind me stood Hiding Fox,
grinning at me.

"What in the world?" I said in English, too surprised to
think what to say in Apache.

"I saved you a bullet," he said. "It is your deer."

Roland got up from his perch behind the boulder and ran
squealing over to Hiding Fox as soon as he saw him. Hiding Fox picked him up and gave him a hug.

"How did you know I was here hunting?" I asked.

"I followed your track from your camp. Blue Humming Bird is there with our son and daughter. I will carry the deer back to your camp and dress it there."

He went to the pool, picked up the deer, put it over his shoulder, and we started back to camp. Roland walked next to Hiding Fox all the way. I saw their hobbled horses grazing beyond the camp.

Blue Humming Bird's face was full of smile when she saw us coming. She left the cooking fire and walked out to meet us. Roland left Hiding Fox's side and ran to get his hug from Blue Humming Bird. Then she and I hugged each other.

I was glad to finally meet their son and daughter. The boy, Man Who Talks to Wolf, looked to be near fifteen years old and resembled his father in his piercing eyes. Yellow Flower was younger by a year or so, and I could see she would someday grow up to be as beautiful as Blue Humming Bird. Her bosoms were already pushing out her buckskin blouse.

Hiding Fox dressed out the deer while Roland and the other two young'uns watched. Blue Humming Bird scraped some coals a ways from the fire and put some strips of meat down on them to broil. I just sat there and watched.

As she turned the strips of meat to broil the other sides, Blue Humming Bird looked up at me and said, "Horse."

I knew Apaches liked horse meat better than beef, so it didn't surprise me.

"Horse from soldiers Hiding Fox and others steal from your ranch," she said.

I smiled to let her know that I understood.

"Soldier horses too slow. Better to eat than ride," she said.

111

Hiding Fox had finished dressing the deer, and brought the liver and heart over to the fire. Blue Humming Bird sliced them up and laid the slices on the coals next to the strips of horse meat. She put more wood on the fire for light. Then she took the cooked strips from the coals and laid them on a length of firewood, telling everyone to help themselves after handing the first strip to her husband.

I wasn't hungry, but I ate what they were sharing. When we were finished, Hiding Fox tossed more wood on the fire, and I could tell he had something on his mind.

"I come to tell you that my people are leaving for Mexico in two days," he said, solemn-like. "I come to invite you to leave with my people because you are our sister because your husband was my brother. My wife's brother is a scout for the soldiers. He came to our place to tell us that the horse soldiers are planning to search us out because I killed the murderer of my brother, Man of Good Heart."

I was suddenly sad to learn that my dear friends would not be nearby in the mountains. It was real hard for me to keep the tears back. I reckon Hiding Fox could see my eyes getting wet in the firelight.

"We will take care of you as our sister, White Summer Cloud," he said. "Man With Strength of Cougar is the same as my son. I will teach him the ways of hunting and tracking."

I didn't know what to say. I knew these people would do exactly what they said they would do. The temptation to go with them was strong, because, aside from Paula, Angie, and Luis, I had no friends around. But I had a cow herd to think about. I had to think what Custis would want me to do, even though he was gone. If I left the ranch to go with these people, I wouldn't know what would happen.

112

"I thank you," I said. "I have to stay behind to care for the cattle of your brother and see that his resting place isn't disturbed. I can't forget Man of Good Heart, because I still love him."

"We respect your wishes," Hiding Fox went on. "You are our sister, but you have different ideas about the land. You must claim the land as your possession. We look at the land as a place to live with and all that is with the land. When your people came and put us where we did not want to be, we came to these mountains to live with these mountains. Our brother, Geronimo, went to Mexico. Our people have strong feelings about our families. Think about the brother of Blue Humming Bird coming to warn us of the horse soldiers. That was more important than what the soldiers might do to him later."

Hiding Fox looked into the flickering flames of the dying fire. I knew he wasn't finished saying what he wanted to say. I could feel the strength of him as he sat there across from where I was.

"We are small in numbers," he began again. "We do not want to live where the white man tells us to live, because that is not our way. Others of us have gone to San Carlos and are not happy. We will leave for the mountains of Mexico in two days. We will disappear in the mountains, away from the horse soldiers."

"Will you ever come back to these mountains?" I asked. "Will I ever see you again?"

"Nothing is certain. I do not know what tomorrow will bring."

Hiding Fox stood up and walked away from the fire. Blue Humming Bird and I looked at each other. Tears began to roll down our cheeks.

We were all out of our bedrolls before the sun had even winked through the trees. I put the coffeepot on the rekindled fire, and when it was heated we shared two tin cups I had packed in. For breakfast we had the slices of liver and heart from the deer along with more strips of horse meat that Blue Humming Bird broiled. Nobody seemed up to talking. Hiding Fox went out and brought in their horses. He told me where ours were, so I went out and brought them in too. He told me there was something he wanted to show me before he left the mountain, so me and Roland followed along behind.

We were riding about due north along the top of the mountain through pine and juniper. About an hour out of camp Hunting Fox reined off the trail onto a narrower one that headed toward a canyon. It was rough going, and I commenced to wonder what was so important that he was wanting to show me. When we bottomed out in the canyon, we were riding next to a small stream lined with sycamore trees. Up ahead I saw a bunch of boulders where the canyon made a twist. Hiding Fox reined in his horse and waited for the rest of us to catch up.

He beckoned me to ride up to him. When I reached where he was, he pointed to a small sycamore what was growing bent in two places near the ground on the bank of the stream opposite the boulders.

"Look at that tree with the bent trunk," he said. "When this stream is dry you can dig here and you will find water. We call this a 'water tree.' There are several water trees in the canyons of the mountain. Now that you have seen this one you will be able to see others."

Hiding Fox went on about how his people always bent young saplings at points along streams where they could dig and find water during dry times. They bent the young trunks, tied them with rawhide, and in that way the tree would grow with the two bends as long as it lived. The tree we were looking at had a trunk about two inches wide. He explained that there were some water trees that were much larger.

We climbed back toward the main trail, and when we reached it Hiding Fox reined in his horse and dismounted. We all followed by dismounting too. He had a real serious look on his face, and I knew we were about to say our good-byes.

Hiding Fox held out both his hands. I took his hands at arm's length.

"If you need a place to go sometime, follow this trail until you reach the highest point on the mountain. There is a canyon going off in the direction of the rising sun. Follow the canyon until you see the first juniper. Just beyond there is a side canyon. Go up the side canyon until it opens into a grove of oak trees. That is our place, among the oak trees. You will see our wickiups, but they will be empty. Good-bye, White Summer Cloud, our sister."

"Good-bye, my true friend and brother, Hiding Fox. Have a safe journey."

He turned to Roland, squatted down, and gave him a hug. Then, without further words, Hiding Fox mounted his horse and waited for the rest of his family to finish their good-byes.

I said good-bye to the children and turned to Blue Humming Bird with tears streaming out of my eyes. We put our arms around each other and held on close. I felt our bosoms heave together from the sadness we both felt.

"Come back, my sister," I said through my tears.

She took my face in her hands and kissed my forehead. Then she turned to Roland, who seemed to understand, because he was sobbing. She looked back once after she mounted her sorrel mare. I stood there watching as they rode off along the trail. I felt empty. I felt sad. I felt afraid I would never see my dear friends again.

Chapter Eight

I rode back with Roland, caught up the mule, and broke camp. I was sad after seeing my friends leave. I decided not to check for more cattle, because we had ridden most of the highest country. Besides, I wanted to get back to the ranch with the mood I was in.

As we came down the hill in back of the corrals I saw someone come out of the barn, waving his arms in the air. I grabbed the Sharps, then saw the blue uniform like the ones worn by the Buffalo Soldiers. I let the Sharps slip back in its scabbard, and as we got nearer I recognized Matthew Cooper, the man with the knot on his head I had nursed.

"Missus Ames, it's Matthew Cooper," he yelled.

"What are you doing back here, Matthew?"

"It's not a nice story, Missus Ames. I run away from the Army."

"Well, you can tell me all about it when I get these horses unsaddled and put up. Why don't you go to the house and wait. I won't be long."

"I'll help with the horses, Missus Ames."

He lifted Roland down to the ground, unsaddled the zebra dun, and carried the saddle into the barn. Then he put grain in three morrals for the horses and the mule. I took the morrals and gave them to the bay and the dun as he commenced unpacking the mule.

I lugged the bedrolls while he carried the deer carcass. Roland wanted to help, so I let him struggle along with the cooking gear.

"How long have you been walking?" I asked.

"Three nights, Missus Ames. I hid out along the river during the days."

"You must be hungry."

"I'm so hungry I think I could eat a whole leg off that deer."

"Well, let me get you something to eat, and then you can tell me all about what happened."

I started the fire in the cookstove, put water on for coffee, and put the big, cast-iron skillet on to heat for frying up some venison. I had some biscuits that were a bit hard from age, but I gave him some to chew on while the meat was cooking. He told me that he hadn't eaten in two days, so I figured he needed something in his stomach before packing it with the rich venison. When I set the meal in front of him, Matthew didn't say a word until he had finished.

"Missus Ames, that was the best meal I ever lit into."

"I'd have heated some beans to go with the venison, but I don't have any cooked. Roland and me have been up on the mountain checking cattle. Now, Matthew, tell me what's going on if you're a mind to."

118

"Well, Missus Ames, I come here because you'all seemed different. I'm trusting y'all to speak nothing o' this to nobody."

"Whatever you say, Matthew."

"When we got back to Huachuca after losing all the horses, we could tell the lieutenant was real embarrassed. The next morning, Corporal Johnson, he's a good friend of mine, told me that the lieutenant was telling the captain thet losing the horses was caused by me falling asleep on sentry duty."

"Were you asleep?"

"Missus Ames, I was wide awake and walking 'round the corral. The only thing I 'member was a strong hand slapping across my mouth to where I couldn't yell or even breathe. Then things went blank until I woke up with you standing over me."

"Why don't you tell the captain what you just told me, Matthew?"

"The captain and the lieutenant are officers. I'm jus' a private Buffalo Soldier. The captain ain't gonna listen to me over the lieutenant. Jody Sanders told me the lieutenant was telling the captain that he wanted an investigation. The captain told the lieutenant to confine me to post. I got my backside out of there afore the lieutenant tells me anything. I figured it was better to leave afore I gets thrown in the stockade."

"An investigation doesn't mean you go to the stockade, Matthew."

"Missus Ames, you don't know the Army, 'specially when the officers is all white and the soldiers is all niggas. My mammy and pappy was slaves. I woulda been, too, if it hadn't been fo' the war. This here Army seems like what my pappy told me about slavery, exceptin' we get paid."

"What are you planning?

"I got no plans at all. When I heard about what the lieutenant was saying about me, I thought about all the other things I don't like about the Army. They're using us to fight Indians because they don't care if we gets killed. An' they think because we used to be slaves that we'll follow orders even if it means getting killed."

"The Army's bound to come looking for you. You can stay here as long as you want to, but what would happen if you got caught?"

"I knows I can't stay here, Missus Ames. I just headed fo' here 'cause I figured you to be good people the way you taken care of me. I don't know where to go, I just knows I gotta get away somewhere."

"Why don't you stay here and rest up. I'll go to town and get you a horse and saddle, because if you light out of here walking you probably won't get far enough away and they'll find you."

"They won't look fo' me. They's too busy looking fo' Apaches. I jus' gotta make sure I ain't where they's lookin' fo' Apaches. That Lieutenant Holmes is bound to come back here, because he's thinks you knows much more than what you told him. Are you really friends with Apaches?"

"Matthew, who my friends are is my business. Maybe you came here as some kind of spy for your Lieutenant Holmes."

"Missus Ames, I told you the truth. I sure ain't no spy for nobody. I didn't mean to pry. Lordy, I don't even know why the Army is so stubborn to kill all the Indians they can find. There's some Apache scouts that works for the Army. They seem like fine people. One of those scouts and me got to be friends."

We talked for quite a spell. Matthew told about joining

the Army because he thought it would be better than chopping cotton. He said he'd been up north fighting Indians, and didn't like killing people no matter who they were. I got well acquainted with Matthew that evening. I wished he could have stayed and helped work the cattle, but with the Army all over the hills looking for Hiding Fox and his band, I knew they'd find Matthew easy.

In the morning, he came down to the house from the barn. We had finished breakfast and was finishing our coffee when I had a good idea. I went into the sleeping room, opened the trunk where I kept all Custis's clothes, and took out some denim breeches, a couple of shirts, and a pair of high-top shoes. I put all the clothes on my bed and went back to the table.

"Matthew, you look about the size of my Custis. One thing you better do is get out of that army suit and look like a civilian. Go on in to the sleeping room and see if Custis's clothes will fit you proper."

He was gone for a bit, and came out looking like a black Custis.

"The clothes seem to fit real good, even the boots," he said, smiling.

"Then they're yours, and I'll dig out some more if you want. We'd better find a way to get rid of that army suit in case your lieutenant comes sniffing around here again."

I went over by the door where Custis's hat was still hanging on a peg. I took it and handed it to Matthew. "See if the hat fits."

He put it on, moving it around a bit, and said, "Fits like I bought it fo' myself, Missus Ames."

"Then get all that army stuff together and we'll put it in the stove."

The burning clothes smelled a bit, but most of the stink

121

went up the chimney with the smoke. I was right proud of myself for thinking about Custis's clothes fitting Matthew. Now he could ride wherever he was going without standing out. I even thought for a minute that he could stay here and work, but that idea flew out of my head when I thought back to what he'd said about the lieutenant coming back to question me again.

We hitched up the mules to the buckboard after I got dressed for town. I told Matthew to hide in the barn no matter who might come by.

"We'll be back tomorrow," I said.

I got Roland up on the seat next to me, and we started for Tombstone to buy Matthew a horse and saddle. I wondered why I was going so far out of my way to help this runaway soldier. I reckoned I liked him. Part of it was I didn't like Lieutenant Holmes. Custis wouldn't have liked him either.

I remembered back when I was working at Paula's. There was a couple of lieutenants what come in for joy, and the way they acted, you'd have thought they was doing us girls a big favor.

Dunbar's Corral, on Fremont and Third, was where I went to look at horses. Dunbar was sitting on the bench outside the small shack he used for an office. Actually, he called it his office, but it was just a place for him to get out of the weather. I stopped the mules and climbed down from the buckboard. Roland wanted to come too, so I lifted him down to the ground. He was growing bigger and bigger every day, and I knew it wouldn't be long before he'd be too much for me to be lifting.

There was fifteen head of horses in the corral. I looked them over through the gate for five or ten minutes. Dunbar had tipped his hat toward me when I had pulled up in the buckboard, but hadn't spoken a word. He sat looking out across the street as he puffed on his cigar.

"Would you mind if I went in and looked at your horses?" I asked.

"Not a bit," he replied, and pushed his large hulk off the bench. "Lemme get the gate for ya."

Dunbar waddled over and opened the corral gate. I took Roland by the hand, and we entered the corral. Dunbar closed the gate behind us. He stood leaning on it from the inside.

"What kind of horse are ya looking for, ma'am?"

"A good saddle horse what's broke and sound."

"That roan gelding's well broke and looks sound to me. He's 'long around eight, by his teeth."

I looked over at the roan standing along the far side. He was Roman-nosed a bit, but Matthew wasn't going to ride his nose. His feet needed trimming and he was barefoot, but he looked like a horse that would carry Matthew. He was taller than the zebra dun mare, and just a mite shorter than the bay gelding.

"How much are you wanting for the roan, Mr. Dunbar?"

"Thirty."

"I'd like to try him once."

"That's fine. Soon's I get him saddled, you can take him around town if you're a mind to."

Dunbar grabbed a halter from the gatepost, caught the roan easily, and led him out to the hitchrack. I was glad to see the horse seemed gentle enough. Dunbar went into his shack and brought out an old three-quarter rigged saddle with some saddle blankets. He didn't bother to brush the roan before tossing the saddle on his back.

"There you are, ma'am. Those stirrups might be a mite long for you."

I took Roland back to the buckboard and put him on the seat, telling him I'd be right back. I mounted the roan, and we started out down the road a ways. He walked out real nice. The stirrups were a bit long, but I wasn't going very far. I kicked the roan into a trot, and he responded real good. When we had gone to the end of the block, I reined him around to go back to the corral. Dunbar was back sitting on his bench.

"I'll tell you what, Mr. Dunbar. The roan's a twenty-dollar horse once he's shod."

"Ma'am, the roan's a forty-dollar horse with shoes on."

"His mane and tail would have to be made of gold to be worth that much."

I dismounted, handed the reins to Dunbar, and headed for the buckboard.

"Tell ya what, ma'am. I'll have the roan shod, and you can have him for twenty-five."

I reached into my pocket for a ten-dollar gold piece as I turned around to face him. "You sold the roan, Mr. Dunbar. Here's ten dollars. When can I come back for him?"

"Probably in the morning, ma'am. The man what shoes my horses is most likely full of beer by now."

"I'll be back for the roan in the morning Mr. Dunbar. And I'd like a receipt for the ten."

Dunbar pushed himself up from the bench again, draped the reins over the hitchrack, and went into the shack. He came back with the receipt and handed it to me.

"Probably be nine o'clock."

From Dunbar's we drove over to a saddle shop, where I knew they had a bunch of used stuff. I reckoned to get Matthew a McClelland, both because he was used to one, and a used McClelland wouldn't run too dear. I told the man I was looking for a used McClelland to use for a pack-saddle so in case he'd heard about Matthew he wouldn't get suspicious. I was sure enough edgy. But I was trying to be careful.

He showed me a McClelland that had seen a lot of miles. "It needs a good coat of oil," he said. "I'll take five dollars for it, as is."

I gave him five dollars and packed the old army saddle out to the buckboard. We drove to the livery, left the mules and buckboard, and walked to Paula's. She seemed worried about something. As we talked over coffee, there was a frown kept coming on her face.

"What are you worried about?" I asked her finally.

"I'm not really worried, Gen. I'm thinking about selling out and moving to Tucson."

"What's making you think that way?"

"It's the mines. Every one of them has problems with water. They've installed pumps, but the water is still a huge problem. The four-month strike by the miners didn't help business, and the Contention Mine didn't open when the strike was settled."

"Are you thinking that all the mines will close down?"

"No, Gen, it's just a feeling I have that one of these days the bottom's going to fall out of Tombstone, and I want to sell out before that happens."

"Is business still good?"

"Oh, heavens yes. I have no complaints. The girls are busy every night, especially weekends when the officers come into town from Fort Huachuca. That's another matter I need to talk to you about."

"What do you mean?"

"There was a blond lieutenant here last night. He came in for Angie, but he talked to me for quite a while about some Buffalo Soldier who's a deserter from the post. He

125

showed me a wanted poster and told me about the incident at your ranch when the Apaches stole his horses. His story was just like yours that you told me the day you brought his men into town. However, the lieutenant said the deserter fell asleep on sentry duty."

"I can tell you that the lieutenant is just trying to pass the blame on to Matthew Cooper to save his own hide. I nursed Matthew, and I know him to be honorable."

"You wouldn't possibly know where your Matthew is hiding, would you?"

"What else did the lieutenant have to say?" I asked, rather than tell Paula about Matthew staying at the ranch. I reckoned the less she knew about Matthew, the better. Then she wouldn't have to lie if Lieutenant Holmes showed up again.

"Angie told me a funny one after the lieutenant left. Before they went to Angie's room, he wanted to know if she slept with Buffalo Soldiers. Angie told him she didn't know, because it was always too dark in her room to tell."

"Good for Angie! Lieutenant Holmes is a pompous ass."

"He said he was going back to your mountains to hunt down the Apaches who killed Harry Dobbs."

"When did he say he was going?"

"He didn't say when. I agree with you that Holmes is a pompous ass, but he dropped a good amount of money with Angie. He spent the night with her. Angie got him for forty dollars."

"I can handle Holmes if he comes back to the ranch, but what I'm worried about is you selling out and going to Tucson."

"I'm just thinking about what might be best. I'm not going to sell out next week, but I also have to think about

Angie and the others. I'm also thinking about moving to Bisbee."

"At least Bisbee is closer than Tucson."

"Don't worry, Gen. Wherever I end up we will always be friends, and we'll get together."

We talked until midnight. Paula kept telling me I should be careful if I knew where Matthew was because hiding a deserter from the Army could get me into a bunch of trouble. I didn't come out and tell her that Matthew was at the ranch, but I knew that she knew.

We had a good breakfast in the morning. The roan was shod when I drove to Dunbar's corral, so I paid for him, tied him to the back of the buckboard, and headed for the ranch after buying some grain for the mules and saddle horses.

Matthew was nowhere in sight when we arrived. I took care of the mules and the roan, unloaded the grain into the barn, and looked around to try and pick up any sign where he might have gone. Since it was getting along toward evening, I got the fire going in the stove and put the beans on to heat. When I went outside again I noticed the dogs was missing. I looked up the trail to the mountains, and there he was with the dogs close behind, carrying the ax on his left shoulder, his rifle on his right.

"I hope you didn't think I'd run off," he said when he came close to the corral.

"If you'd have run off, the dogs would've stayed here," I answered.

"I been cutting stove wood. It looked to me like you could use some."

"Thanks, Matthew. I was reckoning the other day that I'd better get some in pretty soon."

"I cut a bunch of oak and some juniper. I'll take the sled up behind the mules tomorrow and bring the logs in. Probably be three, four loads. I'll get it all bucked up and split oncet I git it all down here."

"Come over to the corral. I bought you a roan horse that ought to get you where you're going."

We went over to the corral where I had put the roan gelding. Matthew looked him over, then turned to me.

"Missus Ames, I don't know how in the world to thank you for yo' kindness to me. Ain't nobody ever done for me what you been doing."

"Matthew, you're my friend. You came here trusting me, and that's good enough thanks. I got an old McClelland saddle for you, too. It's in the barn with the other tack."

After we finished supper I told Matthew about Paula telling me that Lieutenant Holmes was fixing to come back to hunt Hiding Fox. He didn't seem to worry about the lieutenant, telling me that it would take a week for the troop to get ready.

"I'll git the logs down tomorrow," Matthew said. "I be quick about doing it so's I can git them all bucked and split afore I leave."

I could see that he had made up his mind and nothing I could say was going to change him. He took Roland with him in the morning after he hitched the mules to the sled with a double-tree and chain. Roland looked happy to be with Matthew. I was glad to see that both had become good friends.

The dogs had gone with Matthew and Roland, so I didn't notice the buggy coming in until I heard a woman's voice asking if there was anybody home. I opened the door to find Clara Dobbs standing there with a slight smile on her face.

"Mrs. Ames, I had to come over to tell you that I am so

sorry for what I said to you. You are absolutely right that we have widowhood in common. I have thought about the entire matter, and hope that we can be friends."

"Come in, Mrs. Dobbs. The coffee's hot."

She sat down at the table while I poured us both a cup of hot, fresh coffee.

"I'm glad to see you, Mrs. Dobbs."

"Please call me Clara."

"If you call me Genevieve," I offered. "I must admit, Clara, that I was some upset when I left your place the other day. Now I feel much better."

"Well, I know Harry killed your husband, and there's nothing I can do about that. I was angry with Harry when all that happened. He had such a peculiar way about him, temper and all. But what those Apaches did to him is unforgivable."

I didn't say anything about the Apaches. I had my own views on what happened to Harry Dobbs. I commenced to be worried that Matthew might come back before Clara Dobbs decided to leave. I went to the cooking room and brought back some turnovers I had made. Clara said they were delicious, and ate two.

"We can be good neighbors, Clara," I said after we were finished with the turnovers. "Luis should be back any day now, so he'll be ready to help with roundup."

"Another thing I must tell you, Genevieve. I have sold the ranch and cattle to Tom Smalley. He came to the ranch the other day and made me an offer I couldn't refuse. Besides, running that ranch alone, depending on cowboys to do all the cow work, would be too much for me. I don't know how you manage your place and raise that boy of yours at the same time."

"It seems like a lot at times, but I manage. Luis is a great help, and he's dependable. I grew up on a farm in Missoura. Cow ranching is different here in Arizona, but cows are cows, and out here on the Quarter Circle L there's no farmland to work."

"All the same, it's tough work for a woman. You must be very strong."

"I'm probably stubborn, too."

We palavered a while longer. I actually got to liking Clara Dobbs. In a way I was sorry to hear that Tom Smalley had bought her out. We might have become close friends, in spite of her being afraid of running her ranch alone. After we'd gone through three cups of coffee, Clara stood up and told me she had to get back home.

"Tom will tally the cattle during the roundup," she said, climbing back into her buggy.

Just then Matthew came in, driving the mules pulling the sled loaded with oak and juniper logs. Roland and the dogs trotted behind. When the dogs spotted Clara's buggy, they come running and barking to the house. I shushed them up, because I didn't want Clara's buggy horse to get spooked.

"Who's that?" she asked.

"He come by the other day headed for Tucson. He's coming from Texas looking for cow work."

"You had better make sure of him. You never can tell about that kind telling the truth. I saw a wanted poster in town. It seems one of the Huachuca Buffalo Soldiers deserted and headed this way."

"He doesn't act or talk like a soldier. He's been cowboying in Texas for five years. If Luis wasn't due back shortly, I'd hire him on."

"Well, Genevieve, I would be very careful if I were you."

"I'm always careful, Clara."

I waited until Clara had driven her buggy out of the

barnyard before I hurried over to where Matthew was unloading the logs from the sled.

"That was Clara Dobbs, Matthew. She saw a wanted poster for you in town. I think she suspects you're the deserter. I reckon you'd better be heading out away from here."

"What about the wood, Missus Ames? I needs to git it bucked and split."

"I appreciate what you're doing, Matthew, but I'd rather buck and split the wood myself than to see you get caught by that snobby Lieutenant Holmes."

"He's probably still waiting orders at Huachuca."

"He could be on his way here this very minute. Matthew, I believe you're just about as stubborn as I am. Put those mules up and come to the house for supper now. I'll take care of the wood in the morning."

The stew I had added jerky to simmered on the stove, filling the house with a smell that made my stomach growl with hunger. I packed a good amount of jerky in a flour sack so Matthew would have plenty to eat until he got away to where nobody would be looking for the deserter on the wanted poster. He and Roland came in after a while. I filled plates with stew and beans.

"I've been thinking that you'd be better off heading south across the border than trying to make it over into Texas," I said as we sat drinking coffee after supper. "I have an idea. You've heard me mention Luis, the vaquero from Arispe who comes here for roundups. Luis is a fine man in all respects. I think you should head for Arispe, find Luis, and I'm sure he'll help you."

"I don't speak much Spanish, Missus Ames."

"Luis speaks enough English. He's worked up here for many years."

"Supposin' I git down there and can't find Luis?"

"When you reach Arispe, ask for Luis Huerta. He has a small ranch near the town. You'll find him easy. Tell him that I sent you, and he'll help you get something to do."

"I know about where Arispe is. I reckon I'd be best off riding straight to Mexico, and go west."

As we sat talking about his trip, I got to feeling close to Matthew Cooper. Here was such a gentle, loving man what ought to be able to go and do as he pleased except that he decided to run away from the Army. I got to thinking how I'd almost like to give him part of myself before he left. But if I did that he might not leave in time to get away from Lieutenant Holmes.

"There's just enough moonlight so you can find your way past Tombstone before sunrise."

"Thank you, Missus Ames. I'll make it all up to y'all someday."

He saddled the roan and led him back to the house. I gave him the sack of jerky, some coffee, and beans, along with an old pot he could cook with. He had tied two canteens full of water onto the old McClelland. We walked over to Custis's grave, Matthew leading the roan.

"Custis Ames, I never knowed you," Matthew said, pulling his hat off. "I'm wearing your clothes, and I hope I don't disappoint you."

Tears come to my eyes. I put my arms around him and kissed him strong. "Take care of yourself, Matthew. If you need anything, ask Luis."

I could hear the roan's hooves hitting the trail toward town after the darkness put them out of my view. I stood there wondering if I would ever see Matthew Cooper again, an' what would happen if I did.

132

Chapter Nine

I woke in the morning feeling lonely. While I was waiting for the coffee to heat, I commenced thinking about how the few friends I had all seemed to be going out of my life. First, of course, it was Custis what was taken from me. Hiding Fox and his family were gone from the mountains. Now Matthew was on his way to Mexico. Paula was thinking about selling out and going to Tucson. I didn't know but what Hannah and Angie might leave. That left me with only Roland. He was becoming better company every day, because he was talking up a storm.

We rode up to the high country looking for cattle to drive down. Riding through the pines with the fall wind whistling through the needles and that nice clean smell took away the loneliness. Along about midday we come across five cows, three calves, and a two-year-old bull that

133

didn't like the idea of being drove away from the mountain. But we finally got the bunch headed down toward headquarters. Once they was started, they knew the way and didn't give us any trouble. Custis always said that it's a lot easier driving cattle to water than away from it.

The cows and calves were doing good. One of the calves we'd missed didn't wear a brand. I had shut the gate to the big corral, so when they got to it, we kept them going lower to Turkey Tank. When Luis got back we could brand the one calf with any others what might show up. I didn't worry about hair-brands anymore with Harry Dobbs in his grave.

After making sure all those we'd driven off the mountain drank water at the represo, we headed back to headquarters. Hopefully, they would locate there instead of going back to the high country.

The soldiers in the barnyard weren't visible until we rode over the hill north of headquarters. The dogs took off running from us to see who the visitors was. They was all sitting under the trees. I took a quick glance around to see if they had caught Matthew. I counted ten Buffalo Soldiers and two Apache scouts. Lieutenant Holmes was standing near the house. We rode up and stopped in front of him. He had commenced to take his glove off his right hand.

"What brings you back to the Quarter Circle L, Lieutenant Holmes? Didn't you lose enough horses last time?"

Hearing chuckles from the men sitting under the trees, I noticed Holmes's face turn color with his embarrassment and anger. When he saw I wasn't going to dismount and shake his hand, he wriggled his fingers back into the glove.

"Mrs. Ames, I am here to find out what you know about the whereabouts of the Apaches who killed Harry Dobbs, and who, most likely, stole our mounts. I am also here to find out where Cooper, the deserter, might be, since he was seen working here the day before yesterday."

"Well now, Lieutenant, it seems you have quite an assignment, especially when I already told you I have no idea about the Apaches. As for your deserter feller, someone must have seen Clyde Washburn hauling wood for me. He was passing through from Texas on his way to Tucson, looking for cow work."

"Momma, what about—"

"Roland, get on to the corral and water your mare."

I'd plumb forgot about Roland listening to what I was telling the lieutenant.

"You'll have to excuse us, Lieutenant Holmes. We've rode these horses all day, gathering cattle. They deserve to be put up proper."

"We can wait, Mrs. Ames."

I followed Roland up to the barn. We unsaddled the bay and the zebra dun. I brushed them off better than usual, just to make the lieutenant stew awhile. One of the Buffalo Soldiers with corporal stripes on his sleeves was sitting under the tree nearest the barn. When I had put the horses in the corral, I asked him to help me stack some grain sacks. When we were inside the barn I asked him if he was Corporal Johnson.

"Yes, ma'am. I is Corporal Johnson."

"I just wanted to tell you that your friend Matthew is all right."

"Where dat Matthew go, Missus Ames?"

"Matthew is in good hands. That's all I'm telling you for your own good."

"Thank you, Missus Ames."

I latched the barn door behind us when we were back outside. The Apache scouts were sitting near the house

under the apricot tree. I walked up to them and started talking Apache to them. I saw the lieutenant out of the corner
of my eye looking at us with a puzzled look on his face.

"You are well known among my people, White Summer
Cloud," one of the scouts said in Apache. "I am Lone
Hawk Flying, brother of Blue Humming Bird."

"Why do you work for the officer?"

"Money and whiskey."

"That seems a wrong reason."

"It is a way to live without being hunted down all the
time."

"Hiding Fox and his family are well."

"I know they are well, because I warned them myself."

"I am told that."

"I am pleased to see White Summer Cloud and Man
With Strength of Cougar."

"We are also pleased to know the brother of Blue Humming Bird, our dear sister forever."

Holmes had ambled over to where we was palavering. I
could tell by the look on his face that he was annoyed that
I was talking Apache with his scouts.

"You two, mount up and start up the mountain ahead of
the troop. I need to know what to expect."

I told Roland to get to the house and wait for me.

The two scouts looked at Holmes with looks that said
they didn't like being interrupted in a palaver.

"We call him 'Man With Yellow Lip That Holds Nose to
Sky,' " Lone Hawk said as he turned to mount his horse.

"Mrs. Ames, what do you find to talk about with my
scouts?" Holmes asked.

"Just passing the time of day, Lieutenant."

"You seem to speak Apache very well."

"I expect enough to get by with."

"Why don't you cooperate with the United States Army? By the way, I have a voucher from our quartermaster for repayment of the food and transportation you furnished us the last time we were here."

He took an envelope from his pocket and handed it to me. I thanked him and put it in my pocket without looking at how much the voucher was for.

"As a citizen of the United States of America, you must cooperate with us by answering our questions."

"Now, Mr. Holmes, get one thing straight. Don't you go to threatening me with your Army stuff. The Apaches were here long before the United States become the United States. I happen to be friends with some Apaches. I consider them just as much citizens of the United States as I am."

"If you would just tell me where these friends of yours are living, it would make things much easier."

"Easier! You have no idea what it means to work for a living to survive in these parts. You spend all your time either riding around the mountains looking for Apaches who you can't find, or down in the parlors with the whores in Tombstone. You are on my property, Lieutenant Holmes. I am telling you to get on that horse and leave."

Holmes grabbed me by the shoulders and started shaking me, saying, "Why don't you listen to reason?"

Something snapped inside of me when he started with my shoulders. I reckon the memory of that bastard Gillian clouded my mind against everything else. Without giving another thought to anything, I kneed the lieutenant between his legs with all my strength. He dropped his hands from my shoulders and, moaning real loud, grabbed his privates as he sunk to the ground. All I heard was his saber jingling as it hit the dirt.

I whipped around, stomped my way to the house, and went in, slamming the door behind me. Roland was standing wide-eyed at the window.

"What did you do to the lieutenant, Momma?"

"I did what should have been done a long time ago."

"Why did he fall on the ground, Momma?"

"Because he shouldn't have shook me by my shoulders."

I sat down at the table, still shaking from what had happened. I was glad to hear Corporal Johnson order the men to mount and then "Forward, ho." I imagined that Holmes was bent over in his saddle. I hoped I'd never see the man again. Roland come over, and I put my arm around him.

For another week, we rode the high country. All told, we drove eighty head down to Turkey Tank. The two-year-olds and threes gave us a bit of trouble, because they was wilder than the cows. Roland stayed with the cows, following them on that gentle zebra dun mare. The steers was my droving job. It was important to get those steers out of the mountains so everything over yearling could get sold. I hoped Luis would come riding in any day, because there was only about two weeks before roundup. We needed to drive everything out of the mountains before then.

Roland was a big help. That little boy seemed to have a built-in knack for working cattle. I still kept him strapped into his saddle. At the end of the week, we had just rode in and put the horses up when the dogs went a-running out of the barnyard at a lone rider on a jog-trotting horse. We stopped and waited by the barn door. It was Tom Smalley.

"Afternoon, Mrs. Ames. That boy of yours sure has grown."

"Yeah, he's becoming quite a hand, too. Clara Dobbs tells me you bought the Slash Diamond."

138

"I wanted to get back into the cattle business. We'll tally the Slash Diamond cows during the roundup."

"We can start as soon as Luis gets here from Arispe. You'll find he's a good hand to have on roundup."

"Fine. I will try to be a good neighbor. Hopefully, you'll forgive my brashness when we last met here. I have regretted saying the things I said."

"Mr. Smalley, I don't hold nothing against you."

"Thank you, Mrs. Ames. We might start by dropping the 'Mister,' and call me Tom."

"Genevieve sounds more neighborly than Mrs. Ames. Why don't you come in for coffee?"

"I'd better get back. I'll join you for coffee next time. Let me know when your man arrives. I'm staying at the Slash Diamond. Clara has moved to the Grand Hotel until we finish our business. Then she plans to live in Tucson."

"I'll have Luis ride over when he gets here."

I watched Tom Smalley ride away. He seemed a whole lot different than when he come over with that note on the ranch. I wondered where he came from before he bought the Quarter Circle L.

A week later, I was happy to see Luis ride in. He was leading the roan horse I'd given Matthew. Roland was glad to see him too, and gave Luis a big hug.

"I see that Matthew found you, Luis."

"He sends his *saludes* to you, señora."

"Has he found a place to stay?"

"He is with my family, taking care of the farm. We like him very much. My wife and daughters are glad to have a man to do the farm work while I am here."

"That makes me happy. Matthew is a good man."

Luis unsaddled the sorrel and handed me two sacks he

139

unpacked from the McClelland on the roan. One sack was beans, the other held a variety of squashes. While we were having coffee in the house, Luis told me that Matthew had said he was glad there was no cotton to chop. It sounded like Matthew had found a home.

Early the next morning, Luis rode the high country with Roland and I rode over to the Slash Diamond to tell Tom Smalley that we were ready to start roundup anytime he was. He had talked to Luther Breeland about roundup, so the plan was to start in three days.

Tom invited me in for coffee. I come near to telling him I had to get back to the ranch, but he seemed to want to make amends. I put the roan horse in the corral and joined Tom in his cooking room.

"You'll be riding with us, won't you, Genevieve?" he asked.

"I'll be sending Luis. I don't hanker to be around Luther Breeland."

"I understand there's quite a rift between you because you have Apache friends."

"It's more than that, Tom. Breeland was with Dobbs when he shot my Custis."

"I believe I heard about that. I never cared much for either Breeland or Dobbs. I always suspected that they had fast horses and long ropes. Every time I told them that I thought I was missing some cattle, they were too quick to blame my losses on the Indians."

"I'd just as soon change the subject. I've been curious about you. You don't sound like someone what's been out in this country too long."

"I came out here from New York, Genevieve. I was a real black sheep in my family. My grandfather started an importing business that, shall we say, prospered. My father took over the firm when Grandpapa died. I have an older brother I never got along with. He became a member of the firm while I was still in college."

"What made you come out to this wild country?"

"When I graduated from Princeton, I went to work for my father in the business. But my brother insisted on being my boss. My father was very disappointed when I told him I was leaving. He was aware that my brother and I had always been at odds with each other, so he tried to make it up to me by offering to back me in whatever I wished to do."

"So you decided to buy a cow ranch?"

"Not at first. I found a job on a ranch in Texas, where I learned something about cattle. I already knew horses from summers spent riding in upstate New York."

"When did you buy the Quarter Circle L?"

"Three years before I sold out to your husband and you. Father died, and left the business to my brother and me. I quit my job in Texas and went back to New York. I informed my brother that not under any circumstance would I work under him in the business. We finally agreed that he would buy out my interest in the firm. That's when I married Katherine, brought her out to Arizona, and bought the Quarter Circle L."

"Did your wife like living way out away from any city?"

"It was, at first, difficult for her. She was getting used to the life when she took sick. That's when I decided to sell the ranch. I wanted to be with her in Tucson while the doctor treated her. As you probably heard, she didn't last long. Three doctors failed to diagnose or cure her sickness."

"That's too bad. I reckon you must be lonely without her."

"Sometimes it's worse than others. Since I've been here

at the Slash Diamond I manage to keep busy. Husbanding a herd of cows keeps plenty on my mind."

"I know what you mean, Tom. I was terrible lonely after Custis was killed, even with Roland to take care of. I still miss my Custis very much."

There come a knock on the door while we were talking. I hoped it wasn't Luther Breeland come to call. Tom yelled out "Come in," and in walks a cowboy black as the ace of spades. He looked sort of familiar.

"Jonas," Tom said. "This lady is Mrs. Ames, our neighbor at the Quarter Circle L."

"Howdy, Missus Ames. I'm Jonas Tucker. I was with Lieutenant Holmes at your place when the Apaches stole our horses."

"I remember you, Jonas. You were helping carry Matthew."

"That I was, Missus Ames. You done took good care of Matthew. Didja know Matthew deserted from the Army?"

"I saw the wanted poster in Tombstone."

"Right after we got back to the post my enlistment was up, so I skedaddled. I'd had a bellyful of that Lieutenant Holmes. Mr. Smalley was good enough to hire me on."

"I'm glad, Jonas. I'm glad you're my neighbor."

"Thank you, Missus Ames."

Jonas turned toward Tom and told him that he'd put all the working horses in the big corral. "There's three that needs shoein'," he said. "I might as well get to it."

"Good idea, Jonas. I'll be out there as soon as Mrs. Ames and I are finished talking."

Jonas tipped his hat to me and smiled. Tom and I palavered a bit more, and then I told him I needed to get back home.

"Genevieve, I wish you would reconsider, and ride with

us on roundup. I'll make sure Breeland doesn't cause any trouble."

"I believe you would, Tom, but I think it's best I meet up with you at the Willcox corrals when the buyers show up."

I felt real good on the ride back. Tom Smalley was a whole lot different than the first time I'd met him. I commenced to like him. He was a handsome devil with a kind of rugged-looking face and his hair sprinkled with gray. All of a sudden, I realized I was smiling and humming a song.

Chapter Ten

Roland didn't understand why he couldn't ride with Luis on roundup, but when I told him he could come with me to ride the mountain country before the roundup, he seemed content. I wanted to make sure we had found all the older steers up there. I also figured to look at the feed coming up.

As we rode the high country, I was happy to see the grasses growing well between the trees. The mountain streams flowed gently with nice clear water, and I could see that after the roundup I would let the mother cows drift up to the high country. They would take advantage of the green feed to produce more milk for their calves. In four days' riding we didn't spot any steers that I wanted to sell, so we went back to headquarters.

After the roundup, Luis and four other cowboys drove the Quarter Circle L mother cows, calves, and yearlings back to Turkey Tank. He rode in and gave me the tally he'd

Genevieve of Tombstone

made. There would be three hundred twenty-four three-year-olds and three hundred forty-eight twos on the trail to Willcox. Hopefully, they would bring as good a price as the year before, when I got close to thirty dollars a head.

We went out to Turkey Tank the next day and started some of the cows and calves drifting up to the high country.

Paula arrived, driving a one-horse buggy, just as we had finished putting the horses up. As I walked down from the corral I wondered what might be the occasion for her visit.

We gave each other hugs. Paula bent down and gave Roland a big squeeze and told him how big he was getting. Roland fed the hens while Paula and I went in to sit and palaver.

"Gen," she said, looking away from me. "I sold the place, and I'm moving to Tucson."

"I'm sorry to hear that, Paula. You're about the only real friend I got in Tombstone."

"I feel the same about you, but Tucson is not the other end of the world."

"It seems like that to me. Even Tombstone seems to be getting further and further away for me. If you aren't in Tombstone, my trips for supplies will be no pleasure at all."

"As I said before, with the mines having such problems with the water flooding the shafts, and some of them already shut down, I thought it best to sell out while I could get a good price."

"What about Angie and the rest of the girls?"

"They've all agreed to stay on with the new owner. She's had a bunch of parlor houses in California and Nevada. I'm just glad I found a good buyer for the place."

"I'll sure miss seeing you, Paula. It seems like I've known you all my life. If it wasn't for meeting you on that stage in Downing, I don't know what I would have done."

145

"I still remember what you told me about finding the right man. Maybe Tucson's the place to find one."

"You won't have any trouble finding a good man, Paula. You're the most beautiful woman I ever knew."

"I hope you're right."

We sat around the table after I rustled up some supper. I poured out a couple of glasses full of mescal, and I toasted Paula's new adventure to Tucson. I have to admit I cried a bit when she told me she was leaving in a couple days.

I shed a lot more tears the next morning. Paula left after breakfast. I stood out in the barnyard watching the buggy go down the road until it was plumb out of sight. I'd no sooner got the cooking room cleaned up than Tom Smalley came riding in to tell me the cattle drive to Willcox was going to start the next day. I invited him in for coffee after sending Roland out with a bucket of grain to wrangle in the mules.

"I would really like to have you accompany us on the drive, Genevieve. I asked Luther Breeland what he thought about you helping on the drive, and he said that it would be all right with him."

"Tom, you don't seem to realize that I don't like living ten miles from Luther Breeland, and riding a cattle drive with him would be too much just having to see the varmint. It's bad enough having to be in Willcox to meet my buyer with Breeland in the same town."

"If you won't ride on the drive, will you join me for dinner in Willcox when we finish dealing with the buyers?"

"That sounds like something I can really look forward to," I replied, changing the tone of my voice. Immediately I wondered if I had showed too much enthusiasm. Then I decided I didn't care. I reckon it was in my eyes, because a big grin come onto Tom Smalley's handsome face.

The next thing I knew, Tom's arms were around my waist, pulling me close to him. My hands went around his neck, and we were kissing each other. My whole body felt like it was shaking from the tingling all this was causing in me. Before we went to the sleeping room I glanced out the door toward the corrals. The mules or Roland weren't anywhere in sight. I shut the door and bolted it just in case they might have been behind the barn.

Tom was sweet, gentle, and got me to the point of frenzy by the way he made love. I didn't think about Custis until we were lying in bed afterward. For the first time since I could remember, I hadn't thought about cows, horses, Roland, or anything else. I reckon Tom felt good too, because he told me I was a magnificent woman. As he was leaving, I almost told him I'd join the trail drive.

I went outside and kissed him before he climbed back in his saddle. I watched him ride out of the barnyard. When he got to the gate, he turned around and waved. Again I almost ran out after him to tell him I'd be with him on the drive. Then I saw Roland bringing the mules in from the horse pasture.

Roland and I kept on drifting cows from Turkey Tank and four other represos for three more days. Then it was time to hitch the mules to the buckboard and load our gear for the trip to Willcox. I reckoned we'd get there at least a half day ahead of the drovers. That would give me time to buy a bunch of supplies that I needed.

We stopped in Tombstone for half a day to get the mules shod. While the mules were at the blacksmith's, I went over to see Angie and the girls, and also met Rosey Kincaid, the new owner. She seemed like a nice sort, but lots different than Paula. Angie and the others didn't mind working under somebody new. I reckon as long as they

147

made the same kind of money, they didn't much care who was in charge. It was sure different to me without Paula there, and I didn't go to the parlor for coffee.

The drovers kept the trail drive close to the Dragoons, but with the team of mules and the buckboard, I stuck to the well-traveled road along the San Pedro River. We made good time, and we made camp the first night out on Curtis Flat, just above the river. The next morning we headed out early. In order to reach the pass between the Dragoons and the Little Dragoon Mountains by evening, it was a long day's haul. It was almost dark before we reached a good campsite near a water hole. Roland slipped into his bedroll as soon as he'd eaten some beans I warmed up. After hobbling the mules for the night, I was glad to stretch out under the stars.

My thoughts about Tom Smalley kept me awake for a spell. I reckon I was more anxious to see him than to get the cattle dealing over with. Doggoned if that Tom hadn't got my mind spinning. When I finally fell asleep, I was still thinking about him.

The next morning, it was all downhill to Willcox. The drovers' dust was off in the distance. The mules kept a good pace, and we pulled into Willcox before dark. After putting the mules up in the livery stable and getting Roland and me a hotel room, we had good hot baths to get the trail dust out. Then we moseyed over to the Cattleman's Café, where we filled our bellies with beefsteak and apple pie.

While we were getting ourselves around supper, Frank Soldner, the buyer I'd been dealing with for a couple of years, come over and joined us.

"When do you reckon your steers will get here, Mrs. Ames?"

"If I saw the right bunch back on the trail, they should be in by noon tomorrow."

"How many you gonna be selling?"

"Three hundred twenty-four three-year-olds and three hundred forty-eight twos."

"Are they about the same as last year?"

"Same daddys and mommas. I reckon they're in about the same flesh, maybe a tad lighter."

"There's a few Arizona cowmen who are buying Durham or Hereford bulls to upgrade these Texas cattle. You might consider that for your cows, Mrs. Ames."

"Why would I want to do that?"

"Your calves will bring better prices."

"That's just fine for some what's got waterholes close together. My cows might be leggy, but they'll range further. I saw some of those Durham crosses what Colonel Hooker had here last year, and those Durham bulls sure enough shorten their calves' legs."

"Colonel Hooker's developed a lot of new water holes. Perhaps that might be something you could do."

"Well, Frank, you might have a good point, but I don't see as how I'm ready. Those Durham and Hereford bulls are pricey, and making more represos ain't exactly cheap. Besides, I've got a good bunch of bulls what I've selected over the years since my husband was killed."

"I just thought I'd mention what some fellers are doing with their cattle. The time's coming soon when you won't be selling threes and twos. Yearlings and weaner calves will be what the grass boys up north will be looking for."

"Tomorrow, you'll be buying all the threes and twos I have."

"What about yearlings?"

149

"I've got three hundred and fifty-four yearlings back at the ranch."

"I've got a Montana buyer who's looking for yearlings if you'd want to sell them."

"Let's wait and see what happens when the herd gets in tomorrow."

"I'll see you out at the corrals around noon, Mrs. Ames."

"All right, Frank. Like I said, if I saw the dust right they'll be here by noon, maybe before."

"I've got six Durham bulls for sale out in the corrals. You might have a look at them in the morning."

"I'll be out as soon as I get my supplies bought, Frank."

We turned in early. It felt good to sleep on a mattress instead of the ground. But I couldn't sleep for thinking about Tom. It might have had something to do with sleeping in a bed. Wondering what I could do with Roland the next night, and thinking about what Frank Soldner had said about selling calves and yearlings, also kept me awake. If that's what was happening to the cattle market, I'd be in good shape by getting rid of all those agey devil steers. And the way the grass was getting grazed off, I could save all I had for the mother cows.

It was nice to have breakfast made by somebody else for a change. Roland had another piece of apple pie besides eggs and sausage. He was growing fast, and had the appetite to go with it.

I got the shopping done early and drove out to the corrals to look at Frank Soldner's Durham bulls. They were pretty animals, all reddish brown with real short horns. But they were short-legged critters. How they could get far enough up on one of my leggy Texas cows to get the job done might be interesting. Frank walked over to see if he could sell his bulls to me, but as we were palavering I looked up to the west and saw the point rider in the distance. Pretty soon I recognized him as Jonas Tucker.

"Here they come, Frank," I said. "Are the gates ready?"

"I expect so, but I'll make sure."

Several people seemed to appear out of nowhere once the herd coming in was spotted. Jonas got the leaders through the gate, then rode around to make sure none of them bolted away from the main herd. The rest of us stood well away from where the cattle were coming in so as not to spook them. Give a steer the slightest reason to spook and he will. Otherwise they'll follow one another once the leaders are heading in the right direction.

Once the herd was safely in the holding trap, the drovers commenced separating them by brand. They started cutting out Breeland's Mexican steers first. He had something in the neighborhood of fifteen hundred head, so his herd went into the biggest corral. Once the cowboys had half of Breeland's steers separated, they commenced with Tom's and mine, calling out the brands so the fellers working the gates knew where to put them.

It was well into the afternoon before all the steers were separated. It was a tired and hungry bunch of cowboys what unsaddled their horses and went to the Cattleman's Café. Luis looked tired from the drive and all the work cutting the cattle, but he grinned as he told me that all the Quarter Circle L steers made the drive without any problem.

Finally, there was Tom. He told me that the trail drive had gone well with the exception of nine head of Breeland's steers breaking back and brushing up in a thick bunch of catclaw along an arroyo. With that bit of news told, he went to the Cattleman's with the others.

"Don't forget to leave room for that dinner you promised me," I said.

"Dear Genevieve," he replied. "I have been thinking about that dinner since before the drive began."

I walked back to the corrals where Frank Soldner was looking at my steers. He had climbed halfway up the corral fence to get a good look at them. I joined him on the fence. They had all filled up with water and looked as good as when they started the drive.

"They look about the same as last year's, I'd say."

"Pretty much," Frank muttered. "I can give you twenty-two dollars a head."

"Now, Frank, Sierra Bonita steers brought thirty straight across."

"There were a bunch of Durham crosses in those steers. Like I was telling you last night, those cattle bring better prices."

"That might be, but not that much better. I was thinking twenty-five. They're in good shape and healthy."

"Mrs. Ames, my man would quit giving me orders if I was to give you twenty-five dollars a head for those steers."

I knew I could get more than twenty-two dollars for my steers, and I reckoned Soldner would probably go the difference. I also knew that there were several other buyers in town. They had moseyed out to the corrals while the separating was going on. I had spotted Clyde Johnson, and he might have a better order than Soldner.

"I'll be at the Cattleman's, Frank. I need to get something to eat for me and my boy."

Soldner stayed up on the fence looking at my steers. I took Roland across the railroad tracks to the café. We sat down at the only empty table. Tom was across the room sitting with Luther Breeland and another man I didn't recognize. The room was noisy with all the talking going on. We ate biscuits and beans. As we were getting up to leave, Tom came over.

"Where are you going, Genevieve?"

"I reckon to get back out to the corrals and see if I can sell my cattle."

"Before you let them go to Frank Soldner, Luther and I have been talking to Jed Hawkins. He's over at our table. You might see what he'll offer."

"Thanks, Tom. Soldner offered me twenty-two dollars a head, and I'm not letting my steers go at that price."

"Hawkins hasn't had a good look yet, but he's talking twenty for Luther's Mexican steers. Yours and mine should bring more than that."

"Tell him that my cattle are still for sale, but he'd better get a move on and look at them."

"He should be out there soon. I think Luther's ready to take his offer of twenty. By the way, I've missed you."

"Yes, me too."

Roland tagged along after me back to the corrals. Frank Soldner was up on the corral fence looking over Tom's steers. I didn't go over there, because I didn't want to seem too anxious to sell. Roland sat with me on an old bench that was next to the corrals. We had a good time just talking together. Luis came back and joined us.

He told me about Breeland's steers breaking out and brushing up, and how Breeland wanted to stop the drive to get his steers back with the herd. The drovers had the cattle strung out and moving easy and wouldn't stop, so Luther rode back into the brush to get his steers. He rode back to the herd two hours later, all scratched up with no steers.

In a while, Frank Soldner ambled over to where we were sitting, rolled a cigarette, lit it, and commenced talking with the cigarette dangling in his mouth.

"Mrs. Ames, how soon could you get your yearlings here?"

"It all depends on how far up in the high country they've drifted."

"Do you reckon on three weeks or a month?"

"I expect I could get them gathered in a week to ten days if I can borrow a cowboy or two. I reckon three weeks."

"Have you seen my Durham bulls?"

"I looked at your bulls. To tell you the truth, I never saw such short-legged cattle since I come to Arizona."

"I'll tell you what I'll do. I'll give you twenty-three dollars a head, straight across, for your steers. I'll give you a deposit on your yearlings at twenty-one, delivered here in three weeks, and I'll let you have my Durham bulls for a hundred apiece."

He took the cigarette out of his mouth and stomped it out in the dirt.

"I don't want the bulls, Frank. You can probably sell those short-legged devils to Tom Smalley—he's been talking Durhams. As far as my steers and yearlings is concerned, figure the steers at twenty-three fifty and the yearlings at twenty-two, and you got yourself a deal."

"Mrs. Ames, I've run into cowmen that are not near so tough to deal with. I reckon I'll take your prices. Otherwise, I can see us arguing all night. Why don't we go over to the bank and settle up?"

"Sounds good to me, Frank."

We walked back across the railroad tracks and down Main Street to the bank. When it was all over I had $15,792 for the steers in the corral, and a thousand-dollar deposit on the yearlings. For the first time since I buried Custis, I felt like I didn't have to worry about having enough money to keep the ranch and cattle going. It was a good, comfortable feeling.

Frank went back to the corrals. He said he was going to try and buy Tom's cattle. I didn't say nothing about Tom talking with that Jed Hawkins feller. I'd sold mine, and felt good about it.

I saw Tom heading out to the corrals. I caught up with him and asked about borrowing Jonas to gather the yearlings. Tom didn't hesitate a second, agreeing to let Jonas go back with Luis in the morning. He did seem surprised to hear I'd sold my yearlings.

"Keep Jonas as long as you need him, Genevieve. I'll try to get over and give you a hand as well."

I found Luis, told him that the steers were sold, and paid him what he had coming in wages. I told him about us having to gather the yearlings and driving them to town. I also mentioned that Jonas would be helping. He assured me that we could get the job done in three weeks. It was another good feeling to know I could always count on Luis Huerta.

Luis said he'd start back to the ranch in the morning and get started gathering the yearlings. He didn't much care about drinking with the others. Suddenly the idea popped into my head to have him take Roland for supper. Luis said he'd be happy to take Roland for Mexican food at La Casita. Thank goodness for Luis. I wanted to be alone with Tom.

I got back to the café just as Tom and Luther Breeland walked out with the cattle buyer, Jed Hawkins. Tom walked over to me and Roland.

"I'll see you for dinner," he said. "I have to go to the corrals and see if I can get the steers sold to Jed Hawkins.

Luther ended up taking twenty dollars for his Mexican steers."

"Frank Soldner has some Durham bulls for sale. For short-legged devils they don't look too bad."

"Thanks for the information, Genevieve. I'll see you at the hotel at seven. Then we can have dinner."

"I'll be there."

I was getting excited about having supper with Tom. It was funny to hear him calling supper, dinner. I wondered if he'd ever lose his eastern talk.

I took Roland to the general store and bought him a pair of brand-new boots and new britches. I saw a dress that looked like it should suit me, so I bought it too. When we got back to our room, I got the bath ready. I wanted to be clean and as pretty as possible for supper with Tom.

I stood in front of the mirror and was glad I had bought the new dress. It was made of bright green cotton, trimmed around the collar and sleeves with black lace. I hadn't been dolled up like that since I worked at Paula's. Roland said I looked beautiful. He had his new outfit on, and we stood together looking at ourselves in the mirror and grinning. We went down to the lobby of the hotel, where Luis was waiting for Roland.

"Have a nice time," Luis said with a twinkle in his eye. Nothing happened without Luis noticing.

I sat down in an overstuffed chair to wait for Tom. I could see the old clock on the wall behind the desk. I had ten minutes to wait. I hoped he wouldn't be late. I thought he'd be coming in the front door of the hotel, but at exactly seven o'clock Tom came down the stairway to the lobby. He was all cleaned up, shaved, and had on a pair of fancy-looking trousers. I wondered if he had packed the trousers in his saddlebags.

"Well," he said. "You certainly look beautiful, Genevieve. Your hair is like the feathers on a raven."

"Thanks, Tom." I could feel my cheeks heating up. "You're mighty handsome yourself."

At that moment I could have taken that man up to my room and done without supper. He took my hand as we walked to the Cattleman's Café. When we walked through the door, every man in the room seemed to be staring at us. The noise of the talking almost stopped as conversations paused. I looked up at Tom and saw him smiling. He was leading me to a small room off the main part. It was where cattlemen and buyers often went when they were dealing.

I noticed the table had a tablecloth and candles in the middle. Tom pulled my chair out to seat me proper. I really felt like a lady. He sat down opposite me, leaned his arms on the table, and smiled.

"It's wonderful to be with you, Genevieve."

"I must say I feel the same way."

Ginger, the barmaid, brought us a bottle of wine with two glasses. Tom poured the red wine into the glasses, then held his up for a toast.

"Here's to us," he said, clicking his glass to mine.

"And here's to the sale of our steers," I said.

"By the way, how did you do with Frank Soldner?"

"I got twenty-three fifty for the steers straight across, and twenty-two for the yearlings."

"I guess I should hire you to sell my steers from now on. Hawkins paid me twenty-two dollars a head for my steers. Luther told me mine was the highest price he'd heard of after Hawkins made his offer."

"I thought Luther was real savvy when it come to cow trading."

"I did too, but I guess I was fooled."

"He also told me that he's bringing in two thousand Mexican steers as soon as he can."

"That's crowding our country, don't you reckon?"

"I guess you're right. Maybe we should hire some cowboys to keep Luther's Mexican steers off our water holes."

We talked cattle. We talked about ourselves. The supper was delicious steaks cut from a tenderloin. It was a wonderful time for me, and I could tell Tom enjoyed himself too. He had some brandy brought in after we'd finished the meal. I couldn't help thinking back to the time Custis proposed to me when we had that brandy at the Crystal Palace. It seemed like a long time ago.

With supper finished, there was no question where we wanted to be. I checked my room to see if Roland was all right, and was glad to see him asleep. We walked down the hall to Tom's room. He took the glass chimney off the coal-oil lamp and lit the wick. With the chimney back on, he adjusted the wick so that there was just a glimmer of light coming from the flame. When he took me into his arms, I felt warm and comfortable with my head on his chest.

We didn't say much. I reckon the sighs said it all. I commenced tingling as he helped me with taking off my new green dress. We didn't hurry. Our separate passions melted into each other.

First morning light was creeping through the window when I opened my eyes and untangled myself. I was slipping out of bed when I felt Tom's arms circle around me and pull me back. I wanted to get back to Roland before he woke up, but it didn't take much of Tom's caressing to make me stay with him.

Roland was still asleep when I tiptoed into the room. He didn't wake up until I had changed back into my regular clothes.

"Did you have fun with Luis last night?"

"Yes, Momma, we ate Mexican food. It was good."

"It's time to get up and have breakfast, so go get yourself dressed."

We met Tom at the café. Tom said he'd seen Luis and Jonas heading out to the southwest with his Durham bulls. He had also learned that the cattle train would be ready for loading by afternoon. It was customary for the sellers to help load the cattle onto the train. That meant another night at the hotel. We smiled at each other.

"I'd like to ride back in the buckboard with you and Roland," he suggested.

"We'd enjoy your company very much," I replied.

"I'm still wondering why you sold your yearlings."

"Like I said, I think it's best to save my grass for the mother cows. It might not be a good rainy season this winter. After all, we've had two good summers in a row. I'm also tryin' to take advantage of the good prices."

"You almost have me convinced to sell my yearlings."

"Go talk to Frank Soldner. I'll bet he'd buy."

We finished breakfast and walked over to the corrals. Frank Soldner was standing by the holding trap, smoking a cigarette and talking with Jed Hawkins. Tom ambled over there with Roland following him. I sat down on the bench, waiting to hear if Tom could make a deal with Soldner on his yearlings.

I commenced thinking about Paula in Tucson, wondering how she was going to like living there, and what she might figure to do for a living. I hoped she'd find a man to love. Tucson seemed a long way off for me to go visit her. Besides, the ranch kept me busy every day.

The thought of Luther Breeland bringing in two thousand Mexican steers gave me some worries. Here I was trying to take care of my grass, and that many cattle were sure enough going to crowd the range. It seemed too bad that the Apaches had all left for Mexico. They could have thinned out Breeland's steers in a short while. There was always the rustlers. I decided that I'd best hire an extra hand to keep Breeland's cattle away from my water. That would keep his steers off my grass too. I was wishing Luis would stay instead of going back to Arispe.

Tom and Roland came back to where I was sitting on the bench.

"Did you get your yearlings sold?" I asked.

"No, Soldner said he didn't have any more orders for yearlings, and Jed couldn't use them either. I'll just grow them out to two-year-olds."

"You'll do all right as long as the market holds."

"That's always a gamble, but I'd hate to be gambling on two thousand head of Mexican steers like Luther Breeland plans to do."

"I was just thinking about that, Tom. Luis will be going back to Arispe, so I reckon I'd better look around for someone to ride my water holes."

"I would venture to say that if we both don't keep Luther's cattle off our country, there won't be enough grass or water for our own stock."

"I'm wondering if there could be someone around here what needed work."

"I expect the best place to start looking is at the Cattleman's Café. Let's walk over there and see who we can find. I'll hire an extra hand myself."

There were a bunch of cowboys in the Stockman's waiting for the train to pull in so they could pick up a few dollars helping with the loading. We sat down at a table and ordered coffee. Tom asked the waitress if she knew of any

Get Four Books Totally F R E E* — A Value between $16 and $20

Tear here and mail your FREE* book card today!

PLEASE RUSH
MY FOUR FREE*
BOOKS TO ME
RIGHT AWAY!

LeisureWestern Book Club
P.O. Box 6613
Edison, NJ 08818-6613

cowboys looking for work. She said she'd pass the word around. It wasn't ten minutes before a young feller stepped over to our table. He was tall, brown-haired, and had the look of a cowboy, even though I could tell he was young.

"Howdy," he said. "Are you folks looking for a hand?"

"We might be," Tom replied. "Sit down."

"I'm Will Sorrels. I've been working in that San Pedro country, but I'm looking to change."

"Where are you from originally, Will?" Tom asked.

"I was born on a ranch out of Clovis, New Mexico."

"How old are you?"

"I'm seventeen last month."

"How come you're clear out here in Arizona?" I asked.

"My pa and ma was killed in a wagon wreck. The team spooked, ran away over a cliff. There was no work around home, so I drifted out here."

"I'm Genevieve Ames, Will. I'm looking for someone to ride water holes. I run cows and calves."

"I'd sure like to hire on. I left that San Pedro country because there's a bunch of feuding families there, and I sure didn't want to get caught in their cross fire. I'm not scared of work."

"Do you have your own gear?"

"Yes, ma'am. I've got my own saddle horse, too."

"I'll hire you, Will, if you can skedaddle to the Quarter Circle L today. You just follow the tracks made by the cattle drive, and if you ride hard enough today, you'll catch up with Luis Huerta and Jonas Tucker. They'll be driving some Durham bulls, so you'll be able to catch up easy. They're heading there to gather my yearlings. Luis will tell you what to do. He knows the country and the cattle."

"Thank you, ma'am. I'll go saddle up right away."

"Better get some grub to get you there."

161

"My saddlebags are plumb full."

"Good, I'll be out there in a few days."

I took a liking to Will Sorrels right off. He might have been young to be out drifting around the country, but I could tell he would work out just fine. Tom agreed with me. He hired another man who heard about us looking for hands. His man was past forty, been a cowboy all his life in Texas and Arizona. He'd been hanging around Willcox for a month.

The train pulled in at two in the afternoon. Everyone left the café to help with the loading. Every time we started on an empty car it took some prodding to get the lead steer to walk up the loading chute. But once we had him going the rest would follow easily. There was a couple of wild ones here and there, but we managed to get them in with some gentler cattle so we wouldn't have to fight them singly.

Supper was late, but we had the train loaded with everything that was headed out. Roland went to bed right after supper. I stayed in the room with him until he was asleep.

Tom was reading some book by the light of the coal-oil lamp when I opened his door and went in the room. We didn't waste any time getting our clothes off. I can't speak for him, but I had been thinking about sliding into bed with Tom all afternoon.

We were on the road back shortly after sunrise. With the three of us sitting on the seat of the buckboard and Tom's horse tied on behind, it felt to me like we were a family. It scared me a bit to be thinking that way. I sure had no notions about hitching up with anyone. But, I have to admit, I had a smile on my face all day.

By the time we made camp the sun was dipping its golden way behind the purple mountains to the west. I watered the mules down at the river while Tom and Roland gathered firewood. We hobbled the mules and Tom's horse, leaving them in a big stand of sacaton grass by the river. The new green shoots from the bases of the big clumps would fill their bellies overnight.

The three of us sat around the fire after supper. We didn't talk about much of anything. It was nice and peaceful just to watch the flames licking up from the mesquite logs. Even after Roland snuggled down in his bedroll, Tom and I sat there by the fire for a while. Tom unrolled his bed on the far side of the buckboard just as the near full moon poked over the Dragoons and lit up the valley. We stood naked in the moonlight, looking at each other.

"You are so beautiful and feminine, Genevieve, yet you can run a cow ranch, deal with cattle buyers, and drive a team of mules as well as any man. You are absolutely remarkable."

I couldn't answer, because my lips had gone to his.

Chapter Eleven

Tom left us at his ranch road. He promised he'd ride over to help gather the yearlings. Roland was full of questions as we drove on to the ranch.

"Is Mr. Smalley like my daddy?"

"He's not your daddy, dear. But he's a nice man."

"No, I don't mean that he's my daddy. My daddy's buried in the barnyard. I mean, is he like my daddy was when he was alive?"

"Everybody's different. Mr. Smalley is different than your daddy, but he's a nice man like your daddy was."

"Do you love Mr. Smalley, Momma?"

"I guess I love him in a way, Roland. But not like I love your daddy."

"I just wondered."

I put my arm around Roland and gave him a hug. I could

feel the tears welling up in my eyes, thinking about Custis and how Roland never really knew him.

I noticed the three bedrolls in the barn when we pulled in and unhitched the mules, took their harnesses off, and hung them on the wooden pegs. Roland gave the mules their grain, and we went to the house. I started the fire in the stove, put the coffeepot on, and started soaking jerky. There was not enough time to make up a pot of stew. I was glad to see that someone had gathered eggs. I decided to make a supper of scrambled eggs and venison jerky.

I heard the three of them ride in just as the coffee commenced to boil. I went outside to learn how the gather was going. They finished unsaddling their horses and put the horses in the corral away from the mules. Luis looked tired. I couldn't blame him after all the riding he'd been doing. Will and Jonas took the grain out to the horses.

"How's the roundup?" I asked Luis.

"*Bueno,* señora. We got most of the high country covered. Pushed maybe thirty head down to Turkey Tank. Maybe two more days up on the mountain."

"How's the new man?"

"Good boy, Will. He *sabe* cattle good."

"That's good to hear. There's coffee ready."

"*Bueno,* I tell them."

I went back to tend the supper. The men came in shortly, and I was glad that there was hot, fresh coffee ready for them. I soon had the supper ready.

I was real happy watching those three getting along so well together. Will fit right in with the older two, and I could see they had respect for him in spite of his age. After listening to their conversation, I was confident that we'd get the yearlings to Willcox in plenty of time.

The three men saddled up early and breakfast was ready for them before sunrise. When they finished they were gone to the high country. A big stew and pot of beans had to be made. I had picked the rocks out of about ten pounds of beans the night before. They had soaked overnight.

Some fresh venison would have added more flavor to the potatoes and carrots I'd bought in Willcox, but that would have to be for another stew. Hunting yearlings was more important than hunting deer. With plenty of jerky, and with a handful of red chili mixed in, I'd have a tasty enough meal for my cowboys.

Tom rode in around midday. It was glad to see him, and I gave him a hug and kiss when he dismounted.

"I guess I'm too late to ride the mountain country," he said.

"You're never too late to be here with me. There's more riding tomorrow, and I've got three of the best cowboys in the country to do it."

"Where's Roland?"

"He's up by the barn. Get your horse put up and we can sit."

"There's more I would rather do than sit," he said, and laughed.

"We can take care of all that tonight after Roland's asleep."

Tom put his horse up in the corral and found Roland talking to the chickens. We sat down at the table with a bottle of mescal. The stew and beans commenced to smell good as they simmered on the stove. I could tell there was something on Tom's mind.

"Is there anything bothering you, Tom?"

"Not exactly bothering. I can't help wondering about you, Genevieve."

"I don't know what there is to wonder about. I'm me, Genevieve Ames, just a woman trying her best to run a cow ranch and raise a son out here in Arizona."

"I don't mean all that. I'm well aware what you're doing, and, I might add, doing very well. What I'm trying to say is I know you once worked in a parlor house in Tombstone. You must have known a lot of men in that profession, yet you seem to enjoy what you and I do more than any woman I have ever known."

"Oh, Tom, I reckon I have to explain whoring to you. Whoring is a business. A whore trades her body for money to live on. She doesn't necessarily enjoy what she's doing for that money, but it's a very good way to earn a decent living."

"But you're so passionate. I have never known a more passionate woman."

"I'm passionate with you. You're passionate with me. I may have been a whore, but I'm still a woman."

"Were you passionate with your husband?"

"Now, Tom, I'm not about to talk about Custis with you. Custis was Custis. You are you. I have never, and never will, ask you about your wife."

"You're right, Genevieve. Nothing would be accomplished by that. I'm not bothered or wondering anymore."

"That's good. I don't want you to be wondering about anything."

I got up to tend the stew and beans. I also mixed up the batter for the sourdough biscuits everyone liked. Tom wandered into the cooking room, and after I got the batter mixed he took me into his arms.

167

"You are a wonderful woman just the way you are," he said, and kissed me.

I could feel his passion, so I pushed away gently. It was good that I did, because Roland came in the door and told me he was hungry. I took the big stirring spoon to see if the beans had boiled to tender. They tasted good, but needed more time boiling to be just right. I scooped out a bowl for Roland.

"You'll have to wait until supper for biscuits," I said.

I always liked letting the sourdough batter set awhile before putting the biscuits in the oven.

Roland gobbled up the beans and went outside again. Tom poured us another mescal.

"How soon do you think your yearlings will be rounded up?"

"At the rate the men are working, I'd say another three days, maybe four."

"Are you going to ride with them tomorrow?"

"I'm planning on it. I stayed home today to get the food cooked. I'll see how they did today, and maybe go out tomorrow for some venison."

"I can help with the roundup while you do your hunting."

"That sounds like a good idea. That way I can feed all you fellers some fresh steaks and sweeten up the stew some."

The men rode in about two hours before sunset. Luis told me they had one more day in the high country. There were a few what broke back as they were heading them off the mountain. Luis was trying to let the mother cows stay where they were, cutting out the yearlings as they found them.

I told him Tom would be riding with them in the morning, and I would take Roland out to get us some fresh venison. Will overheard our conversation and told me he'd seen a small herd of deer on his way back. He offered to go back to try and get one, but I told him that supper was ready even though I appreciated his offer.

The deer that Will had seen the afternoon before were just leaving Sullivan Tank when we saw them. We approached downwind from them. I slowly dismounted, handed the reins to Roland, and stalked the deer as they commenced to nibble at the weeds a hundred yards up the arroyo from the represo. I knelt down and sighted the Sharps on a two-year-old buck. It was an easy shot. The rest scampered away up the arroyo when they heard the Sharps fire.

After cleaning out the guts, I lifted the deer onto the back of Roland's saddle and tied it down with the saddle strings. The zebra dun had done this many times before, and never spooked. We rode back to headquarters before midmorning.

I spent the rest of the morning slicing up the venison into steaks, roasts, and thin strips to put in the jerky drying box. Instead of hanging the strips out in the open to dry, I used a big screened-in box with strings inside to hang the strips of meat on. This arrangement kept the flies away while the air was drying the meat.

The mesquite-broiled steaks made for a happy roundup crew that evening. I had enough venison to last until we got the yearlings to Willcox. Luis told me that all they lacked gathering was the hill country. That meant only another day before we could commence the trail drive.

Two days later, Will, Jonas, and Luis camped near Turkey Tank. They took turns night herding to keep the yearlings from drifting off. Luis had given me the tally. He had counted three hundred fifty-one head ready for the drive. Two had been so wild that the men left them in the high country. Luis reckoned we didn't need them in the herd to spook the rest into a stampede. He said he'd take Will and bring them in once the drive was done.

It was the beginning of the first week in December. The men started the drive early in the morning. They had the herd moving out well in a short time. They let the steers set their own pace during the middle of the day, and when they come to a water hole, the crew let the animals take their time before starting them out again.

The mules hitched to the buckboard served as chuck wagon, since we didn't have Breeland's to use. The country was too rough in places to get the wagon through following the herd. The *bajada* of the Dragoons was cut into a few deep canyons. So I drove over the road by the river and around midafternoon I turned up a road that went clear to the foot of the mountain. By the time the herd arrived, supper was ready for the crew.

We were in Breeland's country, and I noticed the grass was a lot more grazed off than on Tom's or my country. I wondered about Breeland bringing in two thousand Mexican steers with such scant feed to get them through until the rains arrived. I was glad to have Will, because Breeland's Mexican steers were bound to push their way into my country scavenging for feed and water.

Tom had told me about some big outfit bringing twenty thousand Texas steers into the Sulphur Springs Valley east of us. Some of those would probably range up into my mountain country. I felt like everyone was squeezing at me. But with the money I had from selling the steers and yearlings I could always hire another hand to help out.

The yearlings got delivered without mishap. I was relieved when Luis closed the gate to the corrals. Frank

Soldner was there to count them, and wrote me the draft. Everything seemed to be going as planned. Tom rode with Roland and me on the buckboard. We had one night in the hotel and one camped by the river. I was getting used to enjoying my times with Tom.

Two days after we got back to the ranch, Luis left for Arispe. He rode out early, but as I was hauling buckets of water to the house, I saw him coming back. I put the buckets in the cooking room and went back out to see why he had returned so quickly.

"Señora, I came back to tell you I met El Señor Breeland's trail herd of steers. He's driving them through the lower country, but you might want to keep watch. There are *muchos novillos*, many steers. There's enough to dry up the represos."

"Gracias, Luis. I'll ride down there to make sure he doesn't try and water them at Tecolote Tank."

"I'll see you in the fall. I'll give your *saludes* to Matthew."

"Gracias."

I went to the corral to get saddled. Roland was happy when I told him that we had riding to do. Just as we were mounted and ready, Will came riding in.

"There's a big bunch of steers down below heading north. I thought you ought to know."

"Luis came back to tell me. Roland and me were just about to ride down there to make sure they keep moving. They're Breeland's Mexican steers. Why don't you ride with us. That way you can see them, and know they don't belong on our range."

We rode down the ranch road and soon saw the dust Breeland's steers were making as they headed north. After a couple of miles we rode across the *bajada* in a northwest direction to catch up with them. By the dust it looked like Breeland was driving them slowly. It wasn't long before we had them in sight. I stopped on a long ridge where we could get a good look at the cattle. I counted ten drovers. By the way they were working those steers it was obvious they were letting them graze as much as they could along the way. They were chomping out a swath a quarter mile wide. I could feel myself getting angry at Luther Breeland. Wherever those steers went they left the country bare as a man's clean-shaven face. Then I realized they were heading for Tecolote Tank. It was about half full, but two thousand steers could suck it down to mud in an hour.

"Will, we've got to get to Tecolote Tank before those steers do, or we won't have any water left in it once they're through."

We took out at a fast pace. I was glad I'd tied Roland in or he might have bounced out of the saddle. The way I reckoned, we'd beat the leaders by half a mile. I figured to close the gate in the water lot. Custis had built fences around the largest tanks to close off the water when he wanted to trap cattle what needed branding. As we rode hard, I was glad Tecolote Tank was one of those.

Just as we came in sight of it, I saw Luis on his horse, standing by the closed gate to the water lot. I was real happy to see him, because another man on horseback might make a big difference if we ran into trouble. Luis saw us coming, dismounted, and opened the gate for us to ride through. When we were inside he quickly closed it, and got back on his horse.

He pulled his Remington carbine out of its boot.

"Señora, those steers are going to be thirsty. When they smell the water, they might decide to break through the fence."

"We'll find out shortly," I said as I pulled the Sharps out. "Here they come!"

The lead steers had smelled the water and had broken into a trot. They stopped at the fence and began walking around, trying to find a way through to the water. Two Mexican vaqueros soon arrived. Luis hailed them in Spanish, telling them to keep the steers moving away from the tank. The two men managed to start the leaders around to the west. Then one of them rode back around the water lot to keep the steers moving northward.

We watched the fence to make sure none of the steers were trying to break through to get to the water. Luther Breeland rode up at a lope. He sure looked funny with that missing ear.

"What the hell is going on here. Open that gate! My steers need water!"

"Mr. Breeland," I said, raising my voice. "This is my water. If you want to water your two thousand steers, drive the devils to the river."

"Mrs. Ames, the river's too far out of the way. Open that goddamn gate, and let my steers have a drink."

"The gate stays shut," I said firmly. "Any of your steers that take a notion to try and break down my fence will end up buzzard bait."

"You heard Mrs. Ames. Get those steers moving north," Will said.

I was surprised to hear him back me up with such strength in his voice.

"You young pup," Breeland said, his eyes fiery with anger. "You watch how you talk to me. I'm old enough to be your father."

"Mister, you're not man enough to be my father."

Breeland dropped his right arm to the pocket in his

chaps. I pulled down on him with the Sharps, pulling the hammer back.

"Leave your revolver in your pocket," I said. "Besides, the man's unarmed, just like someone else I remember you tangling with."

Breeland lifted his arm and put his hand on the saddle horn.

"You best be getting your steers moving out before they start messing up my fence."

Breeland reined his horse around and commenced driving his steers away from the fence. He yelled at the rest of the drovers to head the cattle toward the river. We patrolled the fence, making sure none of the steers tried sticking their heads through. It wasn't long before the herd had been pushed away from the water lot and were following the lead steers toward the river. We stayed where we were until they were far gone.

I was proud of Will, and told him so. I was also grateful to Luis for doing what he did. We said good-bye to Luis again.

That evening at supper, I told Will the story about Custis being killed, and about Hiding Fox's revenge. "That's how come Luther Breeland looks so funny with only one ear."

"He comes across real mean, Mrs. Ames. But he don't scare me none."

"Now that you've seen his two thousand Mexican steers, you have an idea about the problems they're going to cause when they run out of feed on Breeland's range."

"All we can do is keep driving them back."

"I have an idea that might help," I said. "If we build water lot fences around the rest of the represos and the springs in the high country, we'll have better control. Whoever controls the water, controls the range."

"Just tell me when to start, Mrs. Ames. I know how to build fence."

"I'm sure you do, Will, but you'll need to be riding while the fences are getting built. I'm planning to hire a couple of fence builders from Tombstone."

"When do you figure to start?"

"Tomorrow, I'll go to town. We've got a while. Breeland's got some feed left, and I'm sure there's still water in his tanks or he wouldn't have brought all those steers in. But by June it will be hot and dry. Those steers are going to suck up a lot of water. And you never know when the rains will come."

I was pleasantly surprised to find that Will had the mules in and hitched to the buckboard before breakfast. I got an early start with Roland up on the seat with me. I needed to find a couple of fence builders and buy some wire and another shovel. I told Will that I might be gone overnight so he could fix some supper himself if I didn't show up by sundown.

Tombstone had been all worried about the water coming in to the shafts. Now some of the mines had closed down, some had installed huge pumps. There were a few miners out of work, but none of them seemed to want to build fence for thirty dollars a month and keep. I went over to the part of town where most of the Mexican people lived to see if I could find someone wanting work. There was a couple of cantinas there. I left Roland on the seat of the buckboard while I went in to ask around. First I told the bartender I was looking for men to build fence. The bartender moved down along the bar, telling his customers about my request.

A stocky, smiling fellow came over to where I was standing. He asked where the work was, how much I was paying, and how long would the work last. My answers seemed to please him, because he said he had a cousin who was looking for work also. I asked him to bring his cousin to the buckboard and we could get things settled.

I thanked the bartender and went outside to wait in the buckboard with Roland. About fifteen minutes went by before Antonio, the stocky, smiling man, and his cousin Abelardo came ambling up to the buckboard. We talked awhile, and I decided the two men would work out all right. They agreed to thirty a month and keep. I told them I would pick them up in the morning.

By the time I got the wire and shovel bought it was getting on in the afternoon. I went over to the Grand Hotel and paid for a room for the night. Then I went to Paula's old place to see Angie. Rosey Kincaid, the new madam, was pleasant enough to me, but I could tell she wasn't happy with me visiting her parlor house. I talked to Angie for a spell. Angie didn't seem as jovial as she generally was. Of course, she was glad to see Roland. She told me that several of the girls had quit and gone elsewhere because Rosey was charging them too much for keep.

With the mules at the livery stable, we went to supper. It was still light afterward, so I took Roland on a stroll through town. There didn't seem to be many people in the Crystal Palace when we passed by, so I went in to see Hannah.

We talked for a while. Since the place was near empty, Hannah come over and sat down with us. She seemed tired of Tombstone, and talked about moving up to Colorado. She hadn't heard a word from Paula in Tucson, and didn't know what she was doing. I went away from the Palace feeling like I didn't care much about Tombstone anymore.

I knew things are bound to change, but the friends I had left there seemed to have gotten into a deep rut. Roland and I started walking back to the hotel when I saw Tom coming out of the Oriental Saloon.

"Well, Genevieve, what brings you to town?"

"Just errands," I replied.

"Whatever it is, I'm sure glad to see you."

"It's good to see you too, Tom."

"Where are you staying?"

"We have a room at the Grand."

"So do I, number forty-seven."

"We're in thirty-two. We should be close by."

"Why don't we have a drink together."

"I think I'd like that. What brings you to town, Tom?"

"Errands, and I'm looking for a couple of horses. I would also like to find another cowboy to help ride water holes. Did you know that Luther brought in his two thousand Mexican steers?"

"I saw them. We arrived at Tecolote Tank in time to close the gate on the devils. Breeland rode up, and we almost had trouble."

"What kind of trouble?"

"He was getting real angry that we wouldn't let him water his steers. My new man, Will, had some words with Breeland. If I hadn't pulled down on him with my Sharps, Breeland might have gotten his revolver out of his chaps pocket."

"You never cease to amaze me, Genevieve."

"I reckon I amazed Luther Breeland, too."

We went to the Crystal Palace for our drinks. It was nice to be with Tom, and I was looking forward to going to his room in the Grand. I didn't want to tell him about my plan

177

to fence the water holes. He might get upset, since a couple of springs I had in mind to fence were close to what he thought of as his range.

Hannah was surprised to see me again, especially with Tom. She brought our drinks to the table. I ordered a sarsaparilla for Roland. We palavered for an hour or so, until Roland started getting restless. I could also see that Tom would just as soon go back to the hotel.

Roland finally went to sleep so I could go to Tom. I was ready for him before I got to his room.

He had a bottle of brandy on the dresser. After we had joined our passion, he got out of bed and poured two small glasses full from the bottle. The brandy tasted good. It wasn't as fiery as mescal, and seemed just right for the time. We didn't talk much, but finally Tom put his glass down on the nightstand.

"Why not move over to the Slash Diamond, Genevieve? That would make life a lot easier for both of us."

"Dear Tom," I answered. "I have a cow ranch to run and a boy to raise. Besides, the Quarter Circle L is home."

"You could be at home at my place."

"Not worrying about my ranch and my cows."

"You certainly have a stubborn streak in you."

"I reckon you can call it what you want to. I have a responsibility I aim to live up to somehow."

He didn't go on about me moving to his ranch. I didn't feel like telling him that I still loved my Custis. I was enjoying being with Tom, but I had no thoughts about getting hitched up with him. We finished our brandy and went back to each other's arms.

The three of us had an early breakfast together. I wanted to get back to the ranch after one more errand I'd thought of. Tom said he would spend the day looking for another cowboy and try to buy a couple of horses he had seen.

There was a store on Allen Street where they sold guns and ammunition. I went there to look at carbines. After the episode with Luther Breeland, I had got to thinking about Will being out there in the mountains or in the hills without any protection. I found a Remington that would make a good saddle carbine, so I bought it. I also bought some ammunition for it. I picked up Antonio and his cousin Abelardo. The four of us reached home in the early afternoon.

Will was in the corral shoeing the bay when I pulled up the mules in the barnyard. He had been riding over some rocky ground near one of the mountain streams, and the horse had thrown a shoe. I told my two fence builders to unload their gear but to leave the wire in the buckboard. I had in mind to fence two represos first. I could haul everything they needed in the buckboard easier than packing it in.

When Will finished with the bay, he came to the house. I gave him the Remington.

"This is just in case you might need to protect yourself, Will," I said. "I wouldn't want to see you get dry-gulched."

"Thanks for your concern, Mrs. Ames. That Breeland feller had me a tad worried the other day."

"We can haul the wire, tools, and our fence builders out to Skeleton Tank tomorrow morning. I'll get some grub together for them, and you can get the boys started on the water lot fence."

I commenced getting supper ready. The night in Tom's room was nice. I hoped he wouldn't keep talking about me moving to his place. I reckoned that if I didn't have the ranch and Roland, I would consider going there. But I was too attached to the Quarter Circle L.

John Duncklee

We packed up the buckboard in the morning and were at Skeleton Tank by midday. Will and I agreed where the fence should be built, and Will showed the new men. Antonio and Abelardo were setting up their camp when we pulled out for home. I felt good about getting started with that project.

After supper, Roland said he was tired. Will stayed around for an hour or so, telling me about how his young life had already been full of disappointments. He seemed to feel better about his life after me telling him about some of the things what had happened to me.

The next morning Roland said he didn't feel good. I felt his forehead, and it seemed a little warm. I put him back to bed. After I had cleaned up the cooking room, I went in to see how he was. He had gone back to sleep. I had planned to take Roland out to check on Turkey Tank, because I wanted to see how the cows and calves were drifting up to the mountain country. With the little feller not feeling good, I couldn't leave.

I looked in on him every so often, and felt his forehead. Along about midday I ladled some broth from the stew pot and heated it up enough to make it taste good. I took it in his room and sat down on the bed next to him. I woke him gently.

"Here's some soup for you, Roland."

"I don't feel good, Momma."

"I know, dear. But if you have some soup you'll feel better."

I lifted him up so he was sitting. Then I took a spoonful of the broth, blew on it to make sure it wasn't too hot, and held it up to his lips. He sipped a little.

"Momma, I got a sore throat."

180

"Take a little more soup, and it'll make your throat feel better."

I got him to sip more of the broth. I could see it was hurting him to swallow. I reckoned he was coming down with some sort of children's thing. He'd had sore throats before. He finished half the bowl of broth and wanted to lie down again. Very soon, he went back to sleep.

Every half hour or so, I looked in on him. The fever seemed to stay about the same. I didn't know anything more I could do except try and get him to drink soup and water. Will rode in from the high country at dusk. I went out to the corral.

"How's Roland?" he asked

"He's a sick boy. He's still got a fever, but I got him to drink some broth from the stew."

"The cows and calves are drifting good."

"Any sign of Breeland's steers?"

"I didn't see any. I did find a Slash Diamond cow with her calf. I drove her back into Smalley's country."

"If Roland's better tomorrow, I might ride out to Skeleton Tank."

"I rode by there on the way in. They've got a bunch of posts cut. I'd say they have a couple more days cutting posts before they're ready to start setting them."

Will took care of the gray horse he'd been riding while I went back to the house. Roland was still sleeping, so I went into the cooking room to get supper out for Will and me. After we ate, I woke Roland again and managed to get some more soup down him. He seemed a mite better, but when I felt his forehead I knew the fever was still inside him.

In the morning Roland was still complaining about his sore throat. I got him to gargle with warm salt water. That seemed to help, because after that he drank some more broth. I sat on his bed talking to him for a while. I tried to get him up to walk around. He stood up for a little bit, then wanted to lie down again. He still had the fever.

This went on for three more days. I was getting tired from the little sleep I was getting. Roland hadn't been able to eat anything except the broth. The gargling helped for a little bit, but he wasn't getting better. Then one morning he wouldn't drink any broth, and he commenced talking strange.

Will came in for breakfast and told me he was figuring to ride out to Skeleton to check on the fence builders.

"I think you better ride to Tombstone and get the doctor out here as soon as he can get here. Roland's talking strange, and the fever seems hotter than it has been. Which horse is up?"

"I kept the roan up for today."

"Good. He'll make it trotting all the way. Best you start right away, Will. I'm real worried about the boy."

Will didn't waste any time getting the roan saddled and off to Tombstone. I heard him leaving as I was getting the cooking room cleaned up. It seemed like a long day waiting for the doctor to arrive. I stayed by Roland's bed most of the time, putting cool, damp flour sacks on his forehead to try and keep the fever down. I tried to get him up to gargle and drink some broth, but he didn't want to sit up or do anything except lie down on the bed and curl up like a puppy.

At near sunset the dogs commenced barking as they ran out to the gate into the barnyard. I went to the door and saw the doctor in his buggy coming in, the horse moving at a trot. I called off the dogs. The doctor grabbed his black satchel, stepped off the buggy, and started toward me.

182

"I'm sure glad you're here, Doc," I said. "Roland's not better. In fact, he seems like he's worse."

"Let's have a look at the boy," he said without stopping on his way to the house.

I led him into Roland's room. He put the satchel on the bed and opened it. First he felt Roland's forehead and around his neck. Then he took out the instrument that he put in his ears with the tubes going to the thing in his hand. He moved it all around on Roland's chest as he sort of hummed to himself. He took the ends out of his ears, let them stay around his neck, and put the listening end in a pocket in his vest. He took a stick out of the satchel.

"Mrs. Ames, if you will sit him up, I'll have a look at his throat."

I put my arms around Roland and got him sitting against the pillows leaned on the headboard. The doctor took the lamp from the nightstand, turned up the wick, and handed it to me.

"I'll need the lamp held so I can see into his throat."

He gently opened Roland's mouth with his left hand, and with his right hand poked the stick in over his tongue. I held the lamp so the light shined into Roland's mouth. Roland coughed. The doctor was humming to himself again. When he took the stick out of Roland's mouth, he put it on the nightstand. I put the lamp down and eased Roland back to lying down. The doctor put his listening thing back in the satchel and closed it.

"Let's go into the other room, Mrs. Ames."

I followed him out of Roland's room. He sat at the table while I went into the cooking room to get us both some coffee. I sat down opposite the doctor. He took a sip of coffee and leaned back in the chair.

"Mrs. Ames, you have a very sick boy there. He has diphtheria. The symptoms are plain."

"What can we do?"

"You've been doing all you can do, Mrs. Ames. Just keep up the same treatment. Diphtheria is strange. As the disease runs its course, your boy will either get well eventually or he may end up with paralysis—or he won't get well. There is really nothing you or I can do except keep trying to have him take liquids, keep the cool, damp towel on his forehead, and, if he has trouble breathing, keep him in a sitting position."

"Is Roland going to die, Doc?"

"He might, Mrs. Ames. Then again, he may be able to fight off the disease. I have had several cases in town this past month."

"Did they die?"

"Some."

"Will you spend the night, Doc?"

"Thank you, no. I have patients in town who need tending to. My horse is used to traveling after dark. I really must get back. If I thought there was something I could do to help your boy, I would certainly stay. Just continue what you've been doing."

"Thank you, Doc."

"You're welcome, Mrs. Ames. I wish there was something more I could do."

He stepped back in the buggy, took the reins, and turned around in the barnyard. He waved as the horse began a slow trot, pulling the buggy and the doctor back to Tombstone.

Will came riding in after an hour. Both he and the roan were tired. I told him to come to the house for supper once he had the roan taken care of. I told him what the doctor

184

had said. I saw the worry lines on his forehead. He looked in on Roland before he sat down to eat.

"The boy's a tough one. Don't you worry about the cattle, Mrs. Ames. I'll take care of them. You just tend Roland."

"I'm sure glad you're here, Will. And by the way, you can drop the 'Mrs. Ames'. Just make it Genevieve."

"I'll pack some grub to the Mexicans building fence in the morning."

I managed a few naps during the night. My little boy seemed to rest a mite easier. He sipped a little of the broth, and I kept the towel on his forehead. Once, when I went to look at him, I couldn't help thinking about how the doctor sounded almost hopeless. As I looked down at his face flushed with the fever, I had to go back to my chair and cry.

The next time I looked in on him I said, "Roland, son, you're going to get better. Keep fighting, my dear."

I reckon it was about two weeks since Roland had took sick. I had lost all thought of days. I was weary, so very weary. It was around sunrise. I had fallen asleep in my chair in the sitting room. I woke up with a start. Will was standing in front of me, telling me to wake up.

"Roland's groaning, Genevieve. I think you best look in on him."

I got up from the chair and went into his room. He was lying on his back with his head moving slowly back and forth. I could tell he was having a lot of trouble breathing. I propped him up against the pillows. That seemed to help some. His face was real flushed with fever, and his little chest was red too.

I told Will to dampen the flour sack and bring it to me. He was back in a minute, and I put it on Roland's forehead like I had been doing.

185

"Will, get the stove going and heat up that broth what's in the pan," I said. "It don't have to be hot, just enough to take the chill off. Then put some in that cup what's on the table."

The poor little feller was struggling hard to get his breath. I put my arms around his back to keep him sitting up. I was holding him that way when all of a sudden his head quit moving and he wasn't struggling anymore. I put my ear down over his heart. No thumping. No sound at all.

I looked up. Will was standing at the foot of the bed with the cup of broth in his hand.

"He's gone, Will. My boy's dead! Oh, God, my Roland's dead."

Will stood there like a statue with tears streaming down his cheeks. I looked back at Roland. I brought him close to me. Suddenly, I commenced to wail. I felt Will's hand on my back, patting me gently.

I don't remember how long I was there wailing with Roland's lifeless body in my arms. I do remember putting him back down on the bed and heading for the cooking room. Will was standing by the table, still crying. I took him into my arms, and we kept patting each other on our backs.

"I'm so sorry, Genevieve. I'm so sorry," Will kept repeating.

We stood there for quite a spell. Finally, I went to the cupboard and took the bottle of mescal and two glasses to the table.

"Better sit down, Will."

I poured out two hefty belts into the glasses. I lifted mine up.

186

"Here's to my son's journey. Wherever it takes him, I hope he meets up with his father."

We both drained our glasses, looked into each other's eyes, and commenced crying again. I don't remember when I finally stopped.

Chapter Twelve

My mind stopped. Half stumbling into Roland's bedroom, I stood over my son, just looking at him. First Custis, then Roland. I stopped crying and went to sobbing.

Will came in after a while and asked if there was anything he could do. I still couldn't think. I felt completely numb. Will put his hand on my shoulder.

"Genevieve, if there's anything you need, I'll be out at the corral."

"Thank you, Will. I reckon I'll think of something once my mind commences to work again."

Sometime during the afternoon I was in the cooking room. Thanks to Will, the coffee was hot. He had kept the fire in the stove going. I poured out a cup and sat down in my chair. When I finished the coffee, I got up and went outside. As I stood over Custis's grave, I wondered if Roland had met up with him somewhere.

Will was sitting on the bench by the barn, whittling on a piece of wood, when I sat down next to him.

"I reckon Roland's going to need a casket. I don't want to take him to town. I'll dig his grave next to Custis."

"I can make the casket and dig the grave, Genevieve."

"I'll dig the grave, same's I did for Custis. There ought to be something around you can make a casket out of."

"I think I saw some boards stacked in the barn."

"I just happened to think that the fence builders have the shovels and the bar. If you ride out there and bring me the bar and the new shovel, I can get busy as soon as you return."

"I'll be going as soon as I get the roan saddled."

Will hadn't been gone an hour when Tom came riding into the barnyard. I came out of the house as he dismounted and tied his horse to the hitchrack.

"Hello, sweetheart," he said, and then he must have noticed my eyes. "What's the matter, Genevieve?"

"Roland died this morning."

"My God, how did that happen?"

"Diphtheria."

He came over and put his arms around me. "I've been in Tucson since we were together in Tombstone. I had a lot business to take care of. This is a terrible shock."

The tears began again. Tom's arms around me was comforting. I was really glad to see him. I had wondered why he hadn't been around to see me. It wasn't in a way that I wanted him. It was just that I wondered why he hadn't been by when I was so worried about Roland. But once he was here, it was all right, especially since he was comforting me by taking me in his arms.

I quit crying and took Tom by the hand to lead him into the house, then to Roland, who looked so peaceful.

"I am so sorry, my dear," he murmured as he looked at my dead son. "I wish I had known."

"It just happened, Tom. You had to do what you had to do. God knows I did what I could for my baby. Doc Means told me I was doing all that I could do."

"Genevieve, is there anything I can do?"

"I don't guess there's anything, Tom. My baby's dead, and I've just got to put him next to his daddy. Just hold me like you're doing. I'm not real right now, so just try to understand."

Will came riding in with the new shovel and the crowbar. I took the bar and shovel and went to Custis's grave. I started to dig Roland's grave next to his father's. Tom tried to stop me, but I told him it was what I had to do. I was already tired, but I commenced to dig with the bar and shovel.

I saw Tom, looking at me with a funny look on his face.

"I have to do this, Tom."

"I understand," he murmured.

"Will is making Roland a casket. Maybe you can help him."

I needed to be alone while I was digging the grave. Tom went up to the barn as I continued to loosen the upper layers of dirt with the bar, clearing it away with the shovel into a pile at the side of the grave.

I quit for the night when I was three feet down. Tom rode home, but promised he'd be back in the morning. Will worked on the casket until darkness set in, then went to the cooking room to heat up some beans for supper.

I went to sleep after crying some more, and slept clear through the night until the morning sun coming through the window woke me up. Earlier, Will had come down from the barn to make fresh coffee. I didn't hear him come in the house. I reckon I was finally catching up on sleep.

He made some breakfast for us, and I went back to digging Roland's grave when we finished eating. Tom rode in, gave me a hug, and went to the barn to help Will.

I reckon the best way to describe how I felt while I was digging is empty, plumb empty. Nothing seemed right. Little Roland dying so young didn't strike me as the right order of things in life. Custis being killed just when he was getting his cow ranch going wasn't the right order of things either. I thought about Tom and what I had with him, but I really didn't know what I had with Tom. I hadn't known Will Sorrels very long, but he seemed like a son to me. I did feel good about Will.

All my other friends had disappeared from my life. Hiding Fox and Blue Humming Bird had taken their family to Mexico. Matthew had gone to Mexico. Luis would be back for roundups, but he belonged in Mexico. Paula had sold out and gone to Tucson. Angie and Hannah were talking about leaving Tombstone. I really felt plumb empty.

I finished the grave by midday. Will and Tom had made the casket and carried it down for me to see. It wasn't as fancy as one from a funeral parlor, but it was nicer in my eyes because Will and Tom had made it.

"I reckon we should get this all over with," I said.

I went into the house and dressed Roland in his new boots and britches, combed his hair, and kissed his cold forehead. Tears streamed out of my eyes to where I could barely see to put him in the casket. Then I placed the carved wooden doll Blue Humming Bird had given him at his side. When he was all situated, I bent down and kissed him again. We carried it outside. Will nailed the lid down, and we lowered my son into his grave.

I tossed the first shovelful of dirt onto the wooden box. The small rocks made a hollow rattle as they struck the lid. I broke down again and commenced to wail. I handed Will the shovel. Tom put his arms around me and let me cry.

When Will had all the dirt replaced, the three of us went to the house, and sat down at the table. I had stopped crying. I reckon I felt it was over. I got up from the table and got the bottle of mescal with three glasses down from the cupboard. I uncorked the bottle and poured the glasses full.

We didn't say much. Each of us sipped at our mescal, having our own thoughts. I kept thinking how life seemed so unfair. I knew I was feeling sorry for myself, not just for Custis and Roland.

Will announced that he was going to do some riding and left. I knew he was thinking about the fence builders. Tom stayed for a while. He talked about buying more Durham bulls and what they would do for his cow herd. I didn't say anything, but I was glad that he was with me. He finally got up to leave.

"If it would help you, I'll spend the night, Genevieve."

"Thanks, Tom, but you needn't. I'll be just fine. It'll take a long time, and I might just as well get used to it."

I didn't sleep well that night. I kept waking up from bad dreams.

Two days later, we moved the fence builders from Skeleton Tank to Coyote Tank. They had done a good job at Skeleton. The water lot fence looked like it was stout enough to hold a mad bull from getting in or out.

The first week in June, Will and I rode the mountain country, looking for any of Breeland's steers what might have drifted over, but there was none. June heat smothered the low country. July came with no sign of summer thunderstorms. The sky was clear blue, and the land was hot.

The fence builders finished the last water lot fence around Piedra Spring during the third week of July. I thanked them for their good work, paid them, and took them back to Tombstone. We had begun finding a few of Breeland's Mexican steers ranging into our country. Some of Tom's cattle wandered over, too. Keeping those strays off my grass became near a full-time job for both of us.

There was still no rain to speak of. One storm come in over the mountains and dropped a lot of rain, but the foothills and *bajada* was dry as powder. I reckon Breeland had run out of feed, because his steers were showing up in my country more and more. I felt sorry for those poor devils. They were just acting natural, ranging out to find enough to eat. Survival. Yet I had to do the best I could for my mother cows. Breeland had gotten too greedy, and those Mexican steers were suffering on account of it.

Tom rode over about once a week to spend the night with me. It took a while before I wanted to try and go back to enjoying what we had before. He was real patient with me. Those times with Tom came to help me get past the low feelings that ate at me most of the time.

He was worried about the rain that didn't come. He had come over during the first week in August. It still hadn't rained. Tom had heard that steers were being contracted for three dollars a head. I was real glad that I didn't have any steers to sell. Tom also decided to fence his water holes, and asked me where to find Antonio and Abelardo. He was having more trouble with Breeland's steers ranging on his country than I was.

A week later, I was just finished putting my horse up. Will was seeing to the grain. I had started walking to the

John Duncklee

house to commence making supper when I saw a horse plodding up the road. I stopped and waited to see who it might be. As it got closer I noticed the horse was carrying double.

Gasping, I recognized Blue Humming Bird with Yellow Flower riding behind her. They both looked bedraggled and almost ready to fall off the tired, Indian pony. I went over and helped them get down. Blue Humming Bird had a deep, sad, hollow look in her eyes. Yellow Flower had a similar look to her, but not as severe. We didn't speak. I took them both in my arms for a long moment, then called to Will to ask him to come and put the pony in the corral. He started down from the barn as I took Blue Humming Bird by her hand and led her to the house. Yellow Flower trailed behind.

I led mother and daughter to the table and put some stove wood on the coals. I still had a half pot of coffee left over, so I moved it over to the hot spot.

"We are very tired, but we must talk," Blue Humming Bird murmured. "We are very sad. We have come to the only place we can come to."

"I am glad you are here," I said. "You are always welcome here, for as long as you wish."

"Yellow Flower and I are alone. The one who was my husband and the one who was my son are both dead. They were killed in a battle with the Mexican Army. Life for the Apache is no longer good in the Sierra Madre. He who is called Geronimo by the Mexicans, he who is our leader there, talks surrender to the American Army. That means for us to live on the reservation like caged animals. The one who was my husband spoke to me about the reservation many times. He said it would be like living dead.

"Did Geronimo surrender to the American Army?"

194

"Not yet, but he will. That is why we came here. We will not surrender to the Americans. We left our camp in the Sierra Madre by ourselves. We had to steal away in the middle of the night. Geronimo had forbidden anyone to leave. The Apache guards of our camp were drunk on tiswin. We were lucky."

"Come with me, friend. I have had sadness also."

I led her out to Roland's grave. "Roland was very sick. There was no medicine to cure him. He is dead beneath this mound, next to his father."

Tears filled her eyes. She took me in her arms. I began to cry too. We stood there for a while. She bent down and put both her hands on the mound of the grave. Then she straightened up, and we went back in the house. The coffee was hot. I poured it into three cups before sliding the bean pot over to heat.

I watched Blue Humming Bird as she sipped the coffee. She had the look of an old woman because of the sadness written on her face. Aside from being dirty, Yellow Flower still bloomed with youth. But I could tell that she was very tired from the ordeal.

Will came in with a quarter of venison from the barn. He put it in the cooking room and came back with a cup of coffee. I told him that Blue Humming Bird and Yellow Flower were the Apache friends I had spoken about. I also told him that Hiding Fox and their son had been killed. I then turned to my Apache friends and told them that Will was my cowboy. I also told them that Will was their friend.

I got up from the table, broiled some venison steaks, and we ate a big supper. Blue Humming Bird and Yellow Flower went to bed right after we finished eating. Will sat for a while before going to the barn.

"Yellow Flower is a beautiful girl," he remarked.

"You'll find her more beautiful once she has a bath and combs out her hair. They've been on the trail a long time. There's a lot of rough country between here and the Sierra Madre."

"You speak their language really good."

"I wish I knew more. Now that they're here, I will."

"Please teach me Apache so I can talk to Yellow Flower."

"Maybe you should teach her English, too." I laughed for the first time in weeks.

The following morning, Will rode out early to check water lots, chase Breeland's steers back where they belonged, and make sure all our mother cows had water. It was a lot of riding, and I generally helped. But with Blue Humming Bird and Yellow Flower at the ranch, I stayed behind to fix them a bath and talk some more.

Blue Humming Bird told me a lot about what she and her family had gone through after they left here. She told how they were almost always on the move. When the band was hungry, the warriors raided Mexican ranchos for horses and cattle. Sometimes they found rifles and ammunition, which they took with the livestock. After the raids, when the Mexican Army went searching for them, they came across the border and raided ranches in Arizona and New Mexico. When the United States Cavalry came after them, they fled back to their hideouts in the Sierra Madres.

Here and there warriors were killed, so some of the women were given rifles and sometimes went on raids. Young boys were made into warriors before they were ten years old.

They went hungry a lot of the time. The band became unhappy with Geronimo, and there was talk about having another leader. After her husband and son were killed, she decided to come back and live in these mountains. I told her that she could live here with me for the rest of her life. She cried when I said that.

Neither Blue Humming Bird nor Yellow Flower had ever had a bath in a tub, so that gave them something to laugh about. Once she had told me all about their life in Mexico, she seemed better. Somehow, I felt better too. I reckon we were both good for each other to be able to palaver about things.

They looked much better after their baths. The water was pretty dirty after they got out of the tub. Yellow Flower was beautiful. She had bloomed into womanhood with full, firm bosoms, copper-brown skin, and long blue-black hair that glistened in the sunlight. I wondered what Will would have done if he had been at the house instead of riding.

After a couple of days' rest and good meals, they both lost the hollow looks in their eyes. We were able to laugh when I told them about what I did to Lieutenant Holmes.

I told her about Tom. She didn't say anything, so I didn't know if she approved or disapproved. I also told her the story of Matthew, and him going to Arispe. She remembered some warriors coming back from scouting Arispe and talking about a black man they saw working in a field.

Will didn't say much at supper, because we women were palavering in Apache. I noticed he had a tough time keeping his eyes off Yellow Flower.

"When are you going to teach me how to talk Apache?" he asked as he was leaving for the barn.

I told him how to say good night. He managed pretty well for his first time. Blue Humming Bird and Yellow Flower told him to sleep well and smiled at him. I told Will what they had said. He smiled back at them and slightly waved his hand.

Two days later, Tom came riding in about suppertime.

He was surprised to see my Apache friends. He thought they would be in Mexico. I told him what had happened to Hiding Fox and his son, and how Blue Humming Bird had escaped from the band to come here.

"Suppose someone finds them living here, Genevieve?"

"I aim to keep them safe, Tom. I reckon that as soon as Geronimo surrenders, people won't be so plumb scared of Apaches. I'll fight for Blue Humming Bird. She helped me in birthing Roland. She's like being my sister."

"Geronimo surrendered once before, and look what happened. It is my belief that we cannot trust those savages."

I was glad my Apache friends had gone to bed. Otherwise they would have seen my anger.

"Tom Smalley, you've been listening to the likes of Luther Breeland and Lieutenant Holmes. The Apaches are no more savages than we are. Would you like to live on a reservation? Would you like to be split away from your family and loved ones? Would you fight back if someone came into the Slash Diamond and claimed it was theirs? Savages. The Apaches don't try making other people believe the way they do."

"I knew you could get your dander up, but I didn't know you were so set on being friends with Indians."

"Tom, I'll be friendly towards anyone if they're friendly to me. And I don't look at their hide or listen to what they believe before I make up my mind about being friends with them."

"You may be taking on too much by harboring these two women."

"Just promise me you won't go around blabbing that they're here with me."

"I can promise you that, Genevieve. What you do with your Indian friends is strictly your business."

"Good, I'm glad to hear you say that. Now, what do you say about us getting into bed together?"

"I would say that I would be happy to say yes."

September of 1886 didn't bring us any rain, but when I went to Tombstone for supplies I learned that Geronimo had surrendered. It didn't surprise me, since Blue Humming Bird had told me about what was happening. She and Yellow Flower recovered from their hard times, and both began helping with the riding. I gave Yellow Flower the zebra dun. The mare was getting some age on her, but she was always in good condition. I felt good seeing her on the mare what Roland used to ride.

Checking the water lot fences, driving Breeland's and Tom's steers away, and making sure all our cows got watered was more work than I ever expected. Will rode in one afternoon and reported that the gate on the Skeleton Tank water lot had been left open and fifty of Breeland's steers were inside. Skeleton Tank was the farthest north of our water holes, and with that many of Breeland's stock there we had a good idea who had left the gate open.

Will wanted to camp there to catch whoever rode in and opened the gate. His idea didn't seem good to me, because if it was Breeland himself what showed up, there would be more trouble than the water was worth. The water level in the tank was getting low anyway.

Yellow Flower and her mother rode the high country with me for a couple of days while Will kept his eyes on Turkey and Skeleton Tanks. Blue Humming Bird asked me about the canyon where she used to live. After checking the springs, we rode over there. When we reached the clearing in the canyon, both Indians gasped at seeing what the cavalry had done. The blackened remnants of their former home brought tears to their eyes. Their sadness made me angrier at the thoughtless Lieutenant Holmes.

The next day, we found the fence around Coyote Spring cut. We had arrived there too late to find out whose cattle had been there. They had already drifted away to graze. We made a couple of circles and saw several of Breeland's Mexican steers and one of Tom's cows with a calf.

The next morning, Will patched the fence. I had temporarily restrung the strands of wire, but he took enough wire to put the fence back in shape. While I made the ride to Turkey and Skeleton Tanks, my Indian gals rode with Will to help drive the strays away from our range.

While at Turkey Tank, I met Tom riding toward my place. He was happy to see me.

"I was riding over to tell you that Luther has decided to round up his steers early. He's just about out of water, and his feed is gone."

"When does he figure to start?"

"He told me he wanted to get started tomorrow. That doesn't give much notice to his neighbors."

"What about your steers, Tom?"

"I'm thinking that I might as well sell all my big steers now, too. I still have water, but the feed is short."

"I'm glad I don't have any steers to sell this fall."

"You turned out to be way ahead of the rest of us. With steers going for three dollars a head, Luther will lose a lot of money on his Mexican steers. I understand he paid sixteen for them."

"I reckon I can't feel sorry for the man."

"Are you planning to help with the roundup?"

"Tom, you know I don't hanker to be around Luther Breeland. Luis hasn't come in from Arispe. I'm afraid to send Will, after the way Breeland came close to drawing his revolver on him. We'll work our mountain country by ourselves. As far as joining in the drive to Willcox, count us out."

The four of us rode through the mountains, gathering Breeland's and Tom's steers, driving them down to the foothills, leaving the Quarter Circle L cows and calves where they were. There weren't many of the strays, because we had worked hard keeping them away from our range.

Tom came to the house a couple of weeks later. There was an unhappy look to his face when he rode into the barnyard.

"Well, Genevieve, the drought has taken its toll."

"How do you mean?" I asked.

"I managed to get three dollars a head for my steers. A year ago, the market was high in the twenty-dollar range."

"What did Breeland get for his Mexican steers?"

"Luther's broke. The best he could get was two and a quarter. To make matters worse, he lost a hundred and eighty-four head."

"That doesn't surprise me. Look at how those steers ate all his grass and part of yours."

"He couldn't pay his loan. The bank is going to take his ranch unless he can sell."

"A ranch without feed or water isn't a ranch, Tom."

"I know that, Genevieve. It will rain someday, though."

"You're not thinking about buying Breeland out, are you?"

"With what I got for my steers, I'm not in a good position to buy anyone out. I came by to tell you I'll be in Tucson on business for a while."

"How long will you be there?"

"It's difficult to say. It all depends on how my business goes."

"I'll miss you, Tom. Can you spend tonight here?"

"I wouldn't miss it."

Chapter Thirteen

Breeland being forced to sell his ranch made me wonder if I should try to buy him out. I could probably deal with his bankers and get a better price. I wouldn't think of talking to Breeland. I had a bunch of money from my steers, and if I could find some heifers during the low market, I'd have a big ranch. I got to thinking about how bad Breeland's country was after those two thousand Mexican steers finished chomping it down. I'd have to hire more cowboys, especially with the two outfits separated by the Slash Diamond.

I was managing to get by with just the Quarter Circle L, and there was no telling when the drought would break. I decided to stay with what I had and not take any chances just to be able to run more cows. There was no sense in getting greedy. Whoever was to buy that ranch was bound to be a better neighbor than Luther Breeland.

One day Will and I rode into town together and bought

four two-year-old colts. There was a team of young mules for sale, so I bought them too. We led the colts and mules back to the ranch. As soon as we arrived I hitched the mules to the buckboard, and they worked fine. Whoever had broke them knew what he was doing. A week later, someone bought the old mules what had come with the ranch. They brought almost as much as I'd paid for the new young team.

Tom was gone for almost a month. I was making venison jerky from a deer Will had brought in when he drove into the barnyard in his buggy. There was a man in a funny hat with him, who Tom introduced as his brother Hiram. They looked like brothers, except Tom was more handsome.

"I've been showing Hiram around the country," Tom said. "These wide-open spaces are far different than New York. I'm pleased to tell you that we have purchased the Breeland place."

"I thought you were broke from those low steer prices," I said.

"That's where Hiram came in. He is now my partner."

"What are you going to do with a ranch that has no feed and precious little water?"

"We'll wait for the rain to return before restocking. We came over here today to talk to you about raising Durham crossbreeds."

"We've talked about that before, Tom. I haven't changed my mind about those short-legged devils."

I didn't invite them in, because Blue Humming Bird was there helping me with the jerky. Will and Yellow Flower were riding the high-country springs.

"We've been talking with Colonel Hooker. What he says makes good sense. Using Durham bulls on Texas cows

204

improves the quality of the calves. He received thirty dollars a head last year."

"He sure didn't get thirty for this year's steers," I answered.

"Prices are bound to go up when it rains. But that's beside the point I am trying to make with you, Genevieve. You keep the crossbred heifers, breed them back to Durham bulls, keep doing that, and within four crosses your calves look like straight Durhams."

"I reckon that's just fine and dandy if you like Durhams."

"It's a matter of keeping up with the times, Genevieve."

I could see Tom was getting frustrated with me.

"With our cattle sharing much of the same range, your Texas bulls are bound to breed our cows. If you would use Durham bulls, everything would work out better."

"Better for you and your brother, Tom. But not for me."

"I know that replacing your bulls with Durhams would be a substantial expense, so we're prepared to make you an offer."

"I don't want to sell the ranch."

"No, no, no, that's not what we have in mind. If you sell your Texas bulls, we will furnish enough Durhams for both our herds. That way you will not be out a nickel."

"Tom, I like my Texas bulls. I like my Texas cows. I don't want your short-legged Durhams messing with my cows any more than you want my Texas bulls breeding your cows."

"You really can be stubborn, Genevieve Ames."

"I may be stubborn, but I just had an idea. Since we're good neighbors, we can swap calves."

"What are you talking about?"

"The calves from your cows that come from my bulls we brand with the Quarter Circle L. The calves from my cows that have your short-legged calves we brand with the Slash Diamond."

"Suppose there are more of my cows bred by your bulls, or the other way around?"

"If there's more Durhams on my cows than Texas calves on your cows, you buy the extras. If there's more Texas calves on your cows than Durhams on mine, I buy the extras. I'll probably end up buying, because my leggy bulls will outrun your shorties."

I had to laugh at my own joke, but Tom didn't seem to enjoy it.

"That sounds like an equitable solution, Tom," Hiram said.

"It would be a lot simpler if Genevieve would get rid of her rangy, leggy, Texas bulls."

"I reckon you're about as stubborn as I am, Tom Smalley," I said.

Tom went on about how they planned to buy straight-bred Durham heifers with the idea of raising their own bulls as well as to sell. It sounded like their plan was going to cost a bundle of money. It sounded odd that Hiram had become partners with Tom after him telling me how they didn't get along. I recalled Tom saying not getting along with his brother was the main reason he came west in the first place.

I was glad they left before Will and Yellow Flower rode in. Hiram might be scared of Apaches for all I knew, and I sure didn't hanker for any trouble for my friends.

A few days later, Luis came in from Arispe. He knew that we wouldn't be rounding up since I'd sold everything except the calves. He was just showing up, as usual, in case

I needed him. He looked tired, not the same Luis I was used to. I asked him if he was feeling poorly, but he said he had no complaints. With Luis to ride the cow herd, it was a good opportunity to have Will break the four colts I had bought. My saddle horses were getting old, so I reckoned I should start some young colts to replace them.

I enjoyed watching Will with the colts. He had a gentle but firm way with them. It was almost like he was fooling them into enjoying being trained. Yellow Flower was at the corral most of the days, watching Will.

Yellow Flower was teaching Will Apache, and he was teaching her English. It was nice to see two young people getting along so well. I had a notion they were getting to be more than just friends. It was good to see Yellow Flower laugh and smile after watching her carry the pain she felt when she first got back from Mexico.

When the colts were far enough along in their training for Will to begin riding them, Yellow Flower was right there in the corral helping. She held their heads while Will got into the saddle. Only one of the colts, a brown with a white blazed face, tried to buck. Will handled him firmly, keeping a tight rein on him so he couldn't get his head down to buck. After ten days of schooling, the colts were ready for riding out on the range.

Will saddled the blaze-faced brown. Yellow Flower chose the chestnut sorrel. Blue Humming Bird and I watched them ride away toward Turkey Tank. We went back to the house to make biscuits for supper. I was finding it nice to have company. We worked well together, and in spite of our miseries, we was able to laugh together.

A big winter storm rolled in during the last week of November. It was a gentle rain that lasted four days and nights. It seemed to arrive, hunker down for a visit, and then move on. The ground was soaked. None of the arroyos ran, because after a summer with no rain, the ground was thirsty. Luis reported that the mountain country had a little snow that melted by midday.

He drove seventeen cows down to headquarters. Twelve had calves by their sides. Luis said he thought the cows would do better where it wasn't as cold. I could tell they were getting some age. They all had lots of age rings on their horns, and their eyes were getting slanted. The cows nursing calves looked thinner than the rest. That was to be expected, but I agreed they ought to do better off the cold mountain. Three of the cows looked barren. Luis put them in the corral. The rest he drove to Turkey Tank. The following morning, he and I drove the three barren old Nellies to the butcher in Tombstone. The price I got made me think it would have been better to make jerky out of them ourselves. At least they wouldn't be freeloading feed and water without giving anything back.

Another winter storm came through, dumping rain for three days and nights. Toward the last day of the storm, the arroyos commenced to have some runoff water in them. It wasn't enough to fill any of the represos, but Turkey and Skeleton Tanks caught about a foot each.

I hadn't seen Tom in quite a spell. I commenced to wonder if he was out buying Durham bulls after the two storms. I was hankering for some loving and wished he'd ride in for a night or two. Maybe it was me having Blue Humming Bird and Yellow Flower in the house that bothered him. Maybe he was angry with me for not going along with his Durham bull deal. I sure didn't know. But when Luis and Will brought one of Breeland's wild, stray steers into the corral, I decided to ride over to Tom's to see what he wanted to do with the critter. Will and Luis both had to rope the steer in order to lead him in.

I told Will I might be gone overnight, and saddled the roan to ride to the Slash Diamond. The cold morning air made the roan frisky, and he walked out like he was headed home instead of out for a day's work. Blue Humming Bird had made me a buckskin shirt that felt good under my jacket. A breeze had picked up when I was halfway to Tom's, so by the time I tied the roan to the hitchrack in front of his house, I was a mite cold.

The ranch dogs had run out to meet me, but when they knew I was no stranger, they ambled off to their favorite places around the old adobe house. Knocking on the door, I wondered if Tom was home. It was quite a spell before he opened the big door. I had turned to go back to the roan.

"Well, Genevieve, what brings you to the Slash Diamond?" he asked nervously.

I commenced to wonder what was going on with Tom. He generally greeted me with more affection.

"We've got one of Breeland's strays in the corral. He's a wild one. It took both Will and Luis to lead him off the mountain. Since you bought the Breeland outfit, I figure you bought the brand too, so he's your steer."

"Who's here, Tom?" a female voice asked from inside the house.

Tom turned his head to answer, "It's our neighbor, Mrs. Ames. She has one of our steers in her corral."

Hearing that female voice sure enough surprised me. I wanted to get out of there quickly.

"I reckon I best be leaving," I said.

"Please come in and meet Sara."

Tom took me by the arm, and I followed him into the

large living room where he and I had spent some nice times in front of the huge fireplace. The woman was quite beautiful in a strange sort of way. Her angular face went with the rest of her slim figure. Her clothes looked out of place on a ranch.

"Sara, dear, I'd like you to meet our good neighbor, Mrs. Ames . . . er . . . ah, Genevieve. Genevieve, this is my wife, Sara."

Completely stunned, I was speechless. All the desire for Tom that I had ridden over with vanished like the moon getting covered by a cloud. I wanted to run out of the house as fast as I could.

"It's so nice to meet you, Genevieve. I hope we can become better acquainted very soon."

"Pleased to meet you, Mrs. Smalley," I answered after clearing my throat.

"Do call me Sara. After all, we are going to be neighbors."

"What about your steer, Tom?"

"If he's as wild as you say, why don't you butcher him?"

"All right, but we'll bring you a quarter and the hide. I don't want a Breeland steer hide hanging on my corral fence."

"I'll send Jonas over tomorrow, if that's fine with you."

"That sounds good. We'll have the critter quartered by noon."

I turned to leave. Tom followed me to the door. Once outside, he closed the door behind him.

"Genevieve, I am truly sorry you had to find out about Sara this way. I tried to tell you when Hiram and I were at your place, but I couldn't bring myself to."

"I hope you both are very happy," I muttered, and walked out to the roan.

After I quit being angry, I started crying. It seemed a

longer ride back than usual. I realized that I had gotten too attached to Tom. Although I hadn't hankered to hook up with him, I felt he had betrayed me. There had always been a hollow space between us that I could never figure out. By the time I rode into my barnyard I felt better about things. I was even feeling good that I didn't go for his Durham bull scheme just because we were intimate. Men! I put the roan up, went over to the graves, and told Custis he was the only man I could trust.

I told Blue Humming Bird about Tom. She didn't quite understand the situation. She told me that Apache women who are unfaithful get their noses cut off. I thought about how Tom Smalley would look without his nose.

The Breeland steer was wild, but he was in good shape. Luis had ridden back to the springs, so the rest of us went to work getting the critter ready for quartering. When we had all the entrails out, each of the four of us took a leg and commenced skinning. Jonas arrived just before we had the backbone sawed. I was so disgusted with Tom that I gave Jonas a forequarter, instead of a tenderer hindquarter, to take home with the hide.

I put the liver and heart in a bucket of salted water and hung up the three quarters to age. For supper that evening we enjoyed broiled liver and beef heart. I was glad that the days were cool and the nights cold. That way the meat would stay fresh for a while, and I wouldn't have to make so much jerky.

That beef hadn't been hanging four days when Paula, with a man next to her in a buggy, drove into the barnyard. I trotted down from the barn and got to the buggy just as she stepped down. I was so happy to see her that I must have squealed like a sow. The man stood by patiently while Paula and me hugged each other.

"Genevieve, I want you to meet Nathan Russell. And, my dear one, I am now Mrs. Nathan Russell. You were right."

We squealed again. I shook Nathan's hand and hugged Paula again.

"I was right about what?"

"About going to Tucson. I did, and now I'm happily married to Nathan. We were married two weeks ago, and we're on our honeymoon."

"You're not going to spend your honeymoon in Tombstone, are you?"

"Part of it. Nathan knows all about my Tombstone days. He thinks it's great to be married to a former madam. We're going on to Bisbee in a few days. Listen, Gen, I heard about Roland, and I am so very sorry."

She took me into her arms, and we both cried.

"He was such a wonderful little boy," Paula said.

"I think about him most of the time."

"I have something to tell you, Gen. Nathan is a lawyer in Tucson. He gets around town and hears things. We were at a party a while back. Your Tom Smalley was there. Angie wrote to me about you and Smalley. He was drinking and, according to Nathan, talking rather freely. He was telling a small group of men that he had a ranch next to you, and he mentioned your name."

"What for?"

"I'm getting to that. He told these men that you were stubborn. He wanted to buy you out, but you wouldn't consider it. Then he said he tried to get you to move in with him and you turned him down. Then he said you were harboring Apache savages."

"He promised me he wouldn't tell anyone about Blue Humming Bird and Yellow Flower."

212

"Gen, he's not a man to be trusted. He was after your ranch, and using you to get it."

"Don't be worrying, Paula. I was over to his place the other day, and he introduced me to his wife. I didn't know he was married."

"I was going to tell you about him getting married to a socialite from Boston."

"Here we are palavering, and your Nathan hasn't got a word in."

"He does enough talking in court."

Paula stepped over next to her husband and put her arm around his waist. I was real glad to see my dear friend with such a happy look to her. After insisting that they put their buggy horse up and stay the night, we had us a feast of a bottle of mescal Paula'd brought and steaks Will boned out of a tenderloin from the beef. That steer might have been owned by a sorry neighbor, but those steaks were tasty and tender.

I could see that Nathan and Paula enjoyed themselves with Blue Humming Bird, Yellow Flower, Will, and Luis. We managed to drain not only Paula's bottle of mescal, but also the half-full one I had in the cupboard. I hated to see their buggy go down the road the next morning.

Luis headed back to Arispe just before the next winter storm. The day he left, I rode around the lower country to check on the represos. It was good to see that all the tanks had caught runoff.

By the middle of February we had been fortunate to have four more storms. The cows were scurrying around the foothill country, grazing the spring weeds that were popping out of the ground. New calves were bouncing by their sides, and the weaned calves were slicked off and growing. We worked the water holes, branding the new

213

calves as they were born. Will and Yellow Flower worked
well together. I kept wondering why Luis hadn't showed
up. I had plenty of help with Will and Yellow Flower, but it
would have been nice to have Luis there to ride with.

Tom Smalley sent Jonas over one day to tell me he was
starting spring roundup in a week. Will went over to work
the gather. I stayed home and rode with Yellow Flower.
Blue Humming Bird was content to stay home to have our
suppers ready. I could see that Yellow Flower missed not
having Will around during the two weeks of roundup. She
sure enough lit up like a high-burning lamp when he got
back.

Will brought news of Tom Smalley's Durhams. He had
bought fifty Durham bulls and seventy-five two-year-old
straight Durham heifers. He had put the heifers and six
bulls on what had been Breeland's country to keep them
away from my leggy Texas devils.

"He'd better keep Jonas with those sweethearts of his," I
told Will. "Once our bulls get wind of all those two-year-
old heifers, they'll go visiting real quick."

By the time the spring weeds commenced drying up, we
had branded four hundred thirty-seven new calves. It was
time to commence drifting the cows up to the high country.
The grasses had greened up and the springs were flowing
real good. We took the cattle up in bunches as we found
them coming in to water. I felt like I had things on the
ranch under control. All I needed was to have some good
summer rains to grow feed on the foothills and mountain
country.

Then came May 3, 1887. The whole earth commenced
to shake. After it was over, I marked the calendar. It was
the only earthquake I'd ever been in, and I was one scared
Genevieve. It didn't last long, but I'll never forget how it

felt. I was inside the house, fixing to go to the corral. The dishes, pots and pans, and windows all commenced to shake like they was going to start flying any minute.

When the shaking quit, I went outside to have a look around. There was dust clouds in the air toward Tombstone. I wondered if the town had been swallowed up or something. A while later the shaking commenced again, but not as strong. It took me quite a while before the scare left. The next time I went to town, I found out that I had been in an earthquake.

Chapter Fourteen

I knew it would be just a matter of time for Will and Yellow Flower to realize they was in love. We had finished supper one evening around the middle of May. Will and Yellow Flower, together as usual, had gone up to the corral to turn out the mules. At least that's the excuse Will had. Of course, I knew it didn't take two people to turn out the mules.

After a bit, they come back in the house. Blue Humming Bird and I was sitting at the table. Will and Yellow Flower was standing in front of us. Will looked uneasy, standing on one foot and then the other.

"Yellow Flower and me want to get married," he announced.

"That's wonderful," I replied.

Blue Humming Bird told them they were good together.

"But with our people scattered, I don't know how we can have the ceremony."

"We don't need a ceremony, my mother," Yellow Flower said. "We are married in our minds and hearts. That is all that matters to us."

"That is true, daughter. That is true. But it is sad and not right to not have the wedding ceremony."

I commenced to think they could be married by a judge, but the territory law didn't allow for whites and Indians to get married. Suddenly, I had an idea.

"I'll take you to Mexico," I suggested. "Arizona Territory won't allow whites and Indians to marry. But if you're married somewhere else, there's nothing the law can do about it."

"Are you sure, Genevieve?" Will asked.

"I'm no lawyer, I'm just supposing."

"What if we go to Mexico to get married, and they won't let us come back?"

"There's plenty of border. We'll just ride out of town. If the cattle smugglers can drive herds across to here, we can sure enough get back."

Blue Humming Bird decided it was best for her to stay at the ranch while I took the young couple to Naco. Before the trip, we caught up all the ranch work. Actually, ranch work is never caught up. There's always something to do, but we did all we could before leaving early one morning before the sun was close to rising over the mountains. I wanted to get as many miles behind us as we could before the midday heat set in to slow us down.

Yellow Flower dressed up in plain ranch clothes. At a distance, nobody could tell her for an Indian. I reckoned that once we found a judge in Mexico, I could grease his palm so's he wouldn't mind performing the ceremony.

We'd passed Tombstone by ten miles or so by the time the sun rose. Keeping the horses at a good trot, we covered a lot of country. The plan I had was to make the thirty miles to the border by nightfall. We would camp close to the village on the American side of the border. I'd leave camp and ride across the border to figure out the situation. If I could find some judge willing to do what we wanted him to do, I'd ride back and get Will and Yellow Flower.

The village came into sight before sunset. I was happy we could make camp before darkness set in so we would know exactly where we was. The border was less than a half mile from where we had camped, so it wasn't but a few minutes before I rode across the line. There was one main street on the Mexican side. I rode down slowly, looking for some sign of an official. There was several cantinas, so I picked one to go in and ask where there might be a judge. Cantina Paloma looked the least busy, so I dismounted and tied the blaze-faced brown to the hitchrack.

Two Mexican men stood at the bar. The bartender, a short, bald man with a large mustache, ambled over to where I stood near the door. I asked him where I could find a judge. He was very helpful when I told him I needed the judge to perform a marriage. He took me outside and pointed to a small adobe house a block away. I thanked him and got back on the brown horse.

Shortly after I knocked on the door, the judge opened it and asked what it was I wanted. I told him. He said he was tired, and to come by in the morning. Reaching inside my pocket, I pulled out a ten-dollar gold piece.

"Would this make a difference?" I asked. "I can have the couple here in half an hour."

The judge's eyes sparkled when he saw the gold piece.

"I will have everything ready for the ceremony, señora."

Wasting no time, I hurried back across the border and to camp. Will and Yellow Flower followed me across the line to the judge's house. We dismounted and tied the horses to the hitchrack. As he had promised, the judge had all his papers out on his desk.

I understood most of what the judge said. He had a little trouble pronouncing Will's and Yellow Flower's names. When he was finished, he told Will and Yellow Flower to sign the license. Will wrote his name, but Yellow Flower didn't know what to do. Will put the pen in her hand and guided her fingers as he formed the English letters of her name.

It seemed to satisfy the judge, but I expect the ten-dollar gold piece made everything legal. Will put the papers in his pocket and thanked the judge. We started back across the border into Arizona Territory, but an American customs officer stopped us at the line. He asked us where we were coming from. I told him we had just been in the village across the border. Then he wanted to know where we was all born. I told him Missoura.

"New Mexico," Will said.

Yellow Flower, not knowing what was going on, didn't speak.

"Where were you born, young lady?" the man asked.

"She was born in Arizona Territory," Will said, answering for Yellow Flower.

"Are you a Mex?" the customs man asked.

"She is my wife," Will said sternly.

"All right, you folks may pass."

Sighing with relief, we spurred the horses and trotted them back to camp. When the horses was hobbled, Will piled some wood on the fire. I gave the two newlyweds hugs. I felt real happy that I had gotten us through without any scary stuff happening. Yellow Flower, being Apache, could have caused problems. I was glad that we got everything done at night.

I made sure my bedroll was at the opposite side of the fire from them. After the day's hard ride, I fell asleep as soon as I squirmed into my blankets.

First morning light woke me up. Out of bed and putting wood on the fire, I looked over and saw Will and Yellow Flower still sleeping with their arms around each other. Seeing two young people so happy brought tears to my eyes. I couldn't help remembering how happy Custis and me had been.

I had some pleasant memories of Tom and me, but after listening to Paula the pleasant memories had seemed to fade away. I wondered if there would ever be another man in my life, or would I have to be satisfied with the memories of Custis.

They didn't wake up when I got the fire going, so I went out to look for the horses. I could see that as close to town as we was, there wasn't much feed for them around camp. I tracked them to about a quarter mile, where an arroyo with a bunch of mesquite growing along its banks hid them. They were nibbling away at the new leaves when I saw them. I was glad they hadn't gone into Mexico. I'd heard that once a good horse crossed over the border it was rare, if not impossible, to get it back.

Will and Yellow Flower were up and out of bed when I came in with the horses. Yellow Flower had bacon and coffee going on the fire. Will had all the bedrolls tied, ready to put behind the cantles on our saddles.

The ride back to the ranch was pleasant. We didn't hurry

the horses, and it was a good time to look around. We rode through a grassland what had been mowed down by too many cattle. The dry heat of May had already browned what was left of the grass down to its roots. I was glad I had the high country where the snow, even when it wasn't much, kept the feed in better shape than down on the *bajada*.

I wondered how Tom Smalley's Durhams would do. I'd heard he had bought his short-legged darlings back near Kansas City. Being from Missoura, I knew those cattle would be used to a whole different kind of feed than they would get on the Slash Diamond.

The cowmen, what put twenty thousand steers over in the Sulphur Springs country, must have taken a real whipping, even had they gotten three dollars a head. We hadn't seen many up in the mountains. Will had drove one bunch of twenty-four head off down the east slope just before the Sulfur Springs cowboys rounded up for shipping.

A time or two, I looked back and saw Will and Yellow Flower riding side by side, holding hands. I smiled, and they smiled back at me. I thought about them staying in the barn, and decided I'd better get some lumber from Tombstone and have Will build an addition so they could have more room. I reckoned that between us, we could add another room onto the barn in no time once we got everything we needed.

The day after we got back to the ranch, I took the buckboard into Tombstone and bought a load of lumber for the barn addition. The young mules worked well with the heavy load. We began framing the floor and walls the next day. I had to go back for the boards and battens for the outside. Three weeks later, Mr. and Mrs. Sorrels had a nice place to live.

Blue Humming Bird accepted their marriage in spite of

there having been no Apache ceremony. It was one happy family. They took their meals at the house as usual, and Yellow Flower rode with Will, taking care of the cattle. June was hotter than I could remember, but the big white thunderheads started flying in before San Juan's Day, June 24.

The first storm to hit the ranch began in the morning, with the thunderheads lower than the days before. They commenced getting blacker and blacker. I had ridden out to Turkey Tank. By the time I was headed back, the lightning and thunder started exploding. For some fool reason I had forgotten to tie my slicker behind the cantle, so I was soaked to the skin by the time I rode into the barnyard. Will and Yellow Flower had seen the storm coming and had beat it to the barn.

Hurrying to the house, I got out of my wet clothes. Blue Humming Bird had the fire going in the stove, and the coffee hot. She came into my sleeping room while I was getting the wet clothes off.

"This is for you, White Summer Cloud," she said.

She handed me a skirt and blouse made of buckskin. The beadwork and feathers were beautiful.

"Oh, thank you, my dear friend."

I hugged her close, then put on my new clothes. I had seen her working on the skirt and blouse. I had assumed it was for herself or Yellow Flower.

"I started making it for my daughter. She has her husband to make her happy. You need the new clothes to make you happy."

"What do you want to make you happy?" I asked her.

"I watch my daughter happy. I was happy about everything when my family was together in the mountains."

I didn't know what to do to make Blue Humming Bird happy. I reckon she felt the same hollowness I did. I was doing my best to live my life the way the cards were dealt. I understood how the changes in her life, without her own people around, made her hollow feeling worse than mine. I hoped that Will and Yellow Flower would make a baby soon. That might give my dear friend a spark to her life.

Two days later, I was riding to check the cattle around the represos again. Most had drifted up to the high country, but there were always a few what stayed below unless we drove them to the mountains. I wanted to let the grass on the foothills grow during the summer so the herd would have plenty of winter feed. I could see a tinge of green appearing after just one storm.

There were only a dozen cows and calves at Turkey Tank, but I gathered them and drove them to Skeleton Tank, several miles closer to the base of the mountains. It was midmorning. By the time I got the cows and calves to Skeleton Tank, the billowing clouds were getting black. The country around Skeleton Tank didn't get the full brunt of the first storm, so I was happy to see this second storm forming overhead. I hadn't forgotten my slicker this time, so I untied it and put it on.

The cattle I was driving got to the water hole long before I did. When I rode over the hill next to Skeleton Tank I saw a sight that made me laugh out loud. There was one of my cows with a young calf, and one of Tom Smalley's Durham bulls. The cow was bulling and just hotter than a pistol. The short-legged Durham was chasing after her, smelling her hindquarters. Out of the brush along the arroyo above the represo, one of my leggy bulls trotted up with his head high and swinging back and forth, checking the situation.

Reining in my horse, I watched to see what would happen. My bull had the smell of that cow in heat in his nostrils. He kept trotting toward her, paying no attention to that Durham. Just as the Durham tried to mount the cow, my bull lifted him up with one long horn and the Durham fell off to one side. My bull commenced to court his cow. He gave her a good nosing on her rear, then curled his upper lip up over his nose. The Durham had recovered from the attack. He stood there watching, but he was too close to suit my bull. That leggy devil turned toward the Durham like he was batting a fly, and butted "Short Legs" out of his way. With snot running out his nose, the Durham shook his head but he didn't make any further advances toward the cow.

My bull was ready. As he rose on his hind legs, his thing come out of its sheath, all pink and looking like a long carrot. He poked around his target a couple of times before he found it. He thrust it inside the cow and commenced to hump. It didn't take but a few seconds. The cow curved her back up, my bull slid off behind, and I knew there was another calf started. The Durham thought he was going to get another chance at the cow, but as he warily approached her, she turned around quickly and butted him away.

I wished Tom Smalley could have seen what I had. Somehow, all I could think of was the calves from my bulls and his cows I would have to buy. I cut the Durham bull away from the rest of the cattle, and just as the first rain commenced pelting down from the storm, I started driving Short Legs toward the Slash Diamond.

The storm continued to deliver its rain. I was glad to have my slicker on. When I got close to the Slash Diamond headquarters, I reined my horse away from the bull and headed back toward Turkey Tank over the foothills. The small arroyos had started to run little streams. The farther I rode, the more water was coming down the arroyos. I was just about to cross one of the bigger arroyos when I heard the roar of rushing water. I reined up and turned around. After hustling back about twenty yards, I reined up again and turned around again.

A wall of muddy water, four feet high, full of sticks and dead tree trunks, came gushing down over the sandy bed of the arroyo. I sat there on my horse feeling sure enough glad that I hadn't been in the middle of that arroyo with all that water and stuff coming down. This runoff was what filled represos. I wondered if mine had caught any. Suddenly, the rain stopped like someone had turned off a faucet.

I reckon I sat there for over an hour before the flow of water went down to where I dared try to cross. Sometimes the sandy bottoms of these arroyos would get so full of water that a horse would sink down and drown. I finally urged my horse into the stream. He took it slow until he was sure. I gave him his head once we started. The bottom seemed good enough to cross, so we forded to the other side.

There were a couple more to cross before we reached Turkey Tank. They had run too. I rode in from above the represo, and the wonderful sight of a full tank met my eyes. The frogs had already commenced to croak, beginning their mating season. I felt like screaming with joy. The spillway was still trickling water. I headed for the barn.

The grasses greening up and growing good on the foothills gave me good feelings. By the end of August the grasses had seed heads, lots of leaves, and all my tanks were full. The mountain country was lush too. The springs were all running good. The grasses had grown, and the cattle were all in good shape. I wanted to give the grass on the mountain time to grow more before summer quit and fall commenced, so I decided to move the cattle down to the foothills.

Will, Yellow Flower, Blue Humming Bird, and me camped on the mountain while we gradually got the cattle drifting down to the hills. We were up there a week. I reckoned we had found most of them, so I left Will and Yellow Flower to find any we missed. Blue Humming Bird rode back with me to the house. I think it had been good for her to go up to the mountains again, even though none of her people were there anymore.

I packed half a venison on the packhorse, leaving the other half for Will and Yellow Flower. When we reached home, I got some beans going and broiled some steaks. We was just sitting down to eat when the dogs commenced to bark. I went to the door, and there was Matthew and a young Mexican girl holding a baby in a buckboard Matthew was driving into the barnyard. I didn't even close the door, and ran out to meet them.

"Matthew, what a surprise! It's good to see you!"

He reined in the team of horses, stepped down off the buckboard, and gave me a hug.

"It's good to see you too, Missus Ames. I brought my wife, Oralia, and our baby girl, Domatila."

"Well, you old rascal. I'm pleased to meet you," I said, looking at Oralia.

She was smiling with a twinkle in her eyes. Matthew had found a very pretty wife.

"Oralia is Luis's daughter. I guess I fell in love as soon as I got down to Arispe."

"It doesn't look like you wasted much time," I said, and laughed with Matthew. "Tell me, how is Luis? I missed him last spring."

"That's why I came up here, Missus Ames. Luis asked me to tell you that he's sorry he missed the roundup and the drive. He knows how much you count on his help. He said he's getting too old for the long ride from Arispe. He isn't feeling good in his stomach, either. He wanted me to come here to tell you he won't be able to help out anymore."

"Is it serious?"

"I don't know, Missus Ames. We all hope his stomach will get better. And I want you to know that I'm real sorry about little Roland."

"Thank you, Matthew. It's been real tough on me, but I seem to be getting to where I can live with the sadness."

"You're a strong woman, Missus Ames."

"Well, get yourselves unloaded, put your team in the corral, and I'll broil up some more venison."

Matthew unhitched his team, took them to the barn, and removed their harnesses. Oralia came with me to the house, carrying little Domatila. I introduced her to Blue Humming Bird, and when Matthew arrived I introduced him too. I broiled the steaks, and we all sat down to eat.

"Luis said he'll send his son, Marcos, to help with roundup if you want him to," Matthew said. "Your horse is still at the farm. Marcos can ride him back."

"Tell Luis that I think we have enough help. Also, tell him I'm giving the horse to him as a gift. I've got four young colts what are working good. Will and Yellow Flower do most of the riding. They're camped right now in the high country. Blue Humming Bird and me just got down from the mountains, where we were drifting the cattle down to the foothill range."

"He'll be glad to know that everything's all right with you."

227

"How long can you stay here?"

"I got to get going back tomorrow, Missus Ames. I've got crops to get in."

"It sounds to me like you've found a home, Matthew. I'm happy to see that."

"You is right, there. I've never been happier in my life. I learned Spanish real good, too."

I told him about kneeing Lieutenant Holmes, and Jonas working for Tom Smalley. Matthew asked if I could get Jonas over here to visit with him. He was still worried about the wanted poster for him deserting the Army. I told him I'd be happy to ride over and tell Jonas about him being here visiting. But Matthew decided he'd best get back to the farm.

Matthew and his family stayed in Will's and Yellow Flower's place in the barn. They were up and ready to leave early in the morning, but I made them stay for breakfast. Sadly, I watched them heading down the road. I stood there wondering about Luis, wondering if I'd ever see him again. Then I got to wondering if I'd ever see Matthew again.

Chapter Fifteen

A couple weeks after Matthew left, Jonas come riding in to tell us the Slash Diamond would be starting roundup in five days. Tom wanted to know if that would be all right with me. I told Jonas that we'd be ready. He was happy to hear that Matthew was doing well and had a family.

With all the cattle located on the lower country, it was just a matter of gathering at the water holes, cutting out Tom's steers and my yearlings. There were a few late calves to brand, and then we drove the mother cows back to where they belonged. Tom was still keeping steers until they were two and three years old. I had changed to selling yearlings to save feed. I got less money for the younger steers, but I reckoned the mother cows needed good feed to be able to raise good calves. Another reason I liked my idea was that a lot of those older steers got pretty rank and wild ranging up in the mountain country. Sometimes that could mean a bunch of work to rope, hobble, and drag the rascals down to the corrals.

Frank Soldner had been happy to buy my yearlings before, and told me he would, most likely, have orders from Montana and Colorado for them. I had run into Frank in Tombstone a month before roundup, and he said he had orders for the kind of yearlings I had.

As it turned out, when we had driven all the sale cattle to Willcox, Frank paid me a dollar a head less for my steers than Clyde Johnson paid Tom for his big steers. The market had improved since the year before, when I didn't have any for sale.

I got along fine with Tom during the roundup and drive to Willcox. Just because we had once been close didn't mean we couldn't work cattle together. His new wife, Sara, met him in Willcox in their buggy, and after a night in the hotel, they drove home together. Jonas put Tom's horse in with their remuda. Then Jonas and the two other Slash Diamond cowboys left after the steers were loaded. Will and I rode back by ourselves.

The first of Tom's crossbred calves commenced dropping the following spring. I didn't see much difference, except they were closer to the ground and smaller than the calves I was used to looking at.

One evening in the middle of February, we were all sitting at the table after supper, palavering. Will seemed a mite nervous, and wasn't too talkative. Finally he spoke up.

"Yellow Flower is going to have a baby," he blurted out.

"That's wonderful news," I said, and got up from the table to give her a hug.

Then Yellow Flower told Blue Humming Bird the news in Apache. Her mother smiled and told Yellow Flower she was very happy.

"I don't think she should ride until after the baby's born," Will said. "But she wants to keep helping."

"It won't hurt her to keep riding," I said. "When I was carrying Roland, I rode clear up to my sixth month. You're just a nervous first-time father, Will."

The news of Yellow Flower being with child made me happy. It also seemed to perk up Blue Humming Bird and give her something to share with her daughter. She commenced making things, including the same kind of necklace she had given me when I had first met her and told her I was with child.

That winter we had some good soaking rains. By the time the days commenced to get warmer around the first of March, there was lots of green feed on the foothills. The calf crop looked good and healthy. The mother cows were in good flesh in spite of suckling their calves. We rode every day, branding the new calves as we found them.

I noticed there were still cows without calves, so I decided to gather as many of those what we could and sell the dry ones to the butcher in Tombstone. I also noticed there hadn't been a grass fire in quite a while. When Custis and me first moved to the ranch we saw a couple of fires every year. I reckoned with the shortage of feed a lot of the time, there wasn't anything to burn.

I was also seeing how little mesquite and catclaw was beginning to creep out from the banks of the arroyos. I rode up into the high country a time or two after storms to see how much snow had fallen. The springs were all running, and it looked like there would be good feed for the summer.

Yellow Flower commenced to show. She and Blue Humming Bird spent some times alone. Will got over his nervousness at the prospects of being a father, and we had some good palavers. I was glad to hear him talk about how much he loved his wife, and how he was happy that Blue Humming Bird would be the midwife at the birthing. It was a happy time for all of us. Of course, I had my moments thinking about Roland, and wondering about how big he would be if he was still with me. But I managed to get past most of the deepest hurt. I reckon that Yellow Flower and Will looking to be parents did a bunch to help me get my mind off what had happened to me.

By the time the June heat set in, Yellow Flower decided she was too big to ride. We had drifted the cattle up to the high country, so there wasn't much to do except keep our eyes out for any problems they might be having and watch for cougars. There was always the cougars taking calves, but as long as we kept the big cats thinned out some, we didn't lose too many.

Will did most of the riding, but I was out there a good part of the time, too. Blue Humming Bird and Yellow Flower always had supper ready for us when we got back to the corral. I took the buckboard to Tombstone on occasion to get supplies. The silver boom was pretty much a thing of the past. Several of the mines had closed. Some of the parlor houses was still going, but they wasn't doing the business they did before the mines commenced closing. Angie had left for Bisbee, and Hannah Turner moved to Colorado. Tombstone was still alive, but it sure wasn't the same as when I arrived with Paula.

I tried to keep up with happenings around the country. But, going to town only when we needed supplies, there was a bunch of happenings I never heard about. After the earthquake, there was a lot of artesian wells come in over around the little village of Saint David, near Benson. There was Mormons what farmed over there. I also heard tell of Colonel Hooker having a well drilled, and a windmill with a twenty-thousand-gallon storage tank installed. He was charging twenty-five cents a head to anyone watering cattle there.

That story commenced me to thinking about getting a well sunk. I had no notions of charging Tom to water his stock. I figured to have the well drilled at my headquarters so that when another drought hit, I'd have a more reliable water supply. I was glad I'd put away my money instead of buying short-legged Durham bulls.

On one trip to town I saw a well-drilling rig parked a little way outside of town. The owner was fiddling around with the machinery, so I stopped to ask about what it cost to drill me a well. We palavered awhile, me asking questions, him trying to answer.

"Now, lady, there's no guarantee that I'll hit water. You still have to pay me for drilling a dry hole."

"How about you coming out to the ranch and telling me what you think the chances of hitting water are?"

"You'll have to drive me out in that buckboard. All I have is this rig, and I don't hanker to drive it nowheres without a job to do."

The well man's name was Kenny Waddell. He was a nice sort, and a big-muscled man. After I got the supplies, I swung around to where he was waiting and took him to the ranch.

I told him where I wanted the well drilled. He asked me about the hand-dug well there at headquarters. I told him as much as I knew. He liked the idea of one well already there what had water, and advised me to have the new well drilled close by.

We decided that he had a good chance at hitting water. He said he couldn't promise how much water it would produce, but he pointed out that with a windmill running a pump it would probably keep a five-thousand-gallon storage tank full even with a lot of cattle drinking the water.

Although he didn't know how far he'd have to drill to get a good well, he did say he'd have to go deeper at headquarters than if he drilled lower down the *bajada*.

I wanted the well at headquarters. I thought the idea of not having to winch buckets of water up from the hand-dug well would be a lot better. Especially if I had a bunch of livestock around what needed watering. I told Kenny to bring in his rig and commence drilling.

It was close to dark by the time I got him back to his rig. I decided to spend the night in the Grand Hotel instead of driving the mules back at night. I put the mules up at the livery stable and figured to have some Chinese food at the Oriental Café. When I walked through the door I saw Tom and his wife, Sara, sitting at a table. I come close to turning around and leaving, but Tom stood up and asked me to join them. I thought that was kind of strange. I felt kind of trapped, but I went over to their table and sat down.

"It's nice to see you, Genevieve," Sara said. "We're neighbors, but rarely do we see one another."

"Cow ranching doesn't allow time for much socializing," I replied.

"The word is that you are going to drill a well, Genevieve," Tom said.

"The word sure enough travels fast," I said. "I just made the deal with Kenny Waddell today."

"I know," Tom continued. "I talked to him just before we came here for dinner. I asked him to come over to my place when he's finished with your well."

"Where do you reckon to drill?" I asked.

"I won't know until Kenny and I look at various potential well sites. He told me you were drilling at your head-quarters."

"That's what I decided. If he gets a good well there, I may have him try another somehere else."

"That will cost you a pretty penny."

"A ranch without water ain't a ranch," I replied.

"There is so much to know about ranching," Sara interrupted. "For a woman, you seem to know so much, Genevieve."

"A woman alone has to learn as much as she can. It ain't no different than a man."

"I'm glad I have Tom to make all the decisions. I wouldn't know where to begin."

I was beginning to think that Sara must be bored sitting around her house with nothing much to do. I wondered if she did any housework, because her hands looked like they had never worked a day in her life.

"By the way, Genevieve," Tom said. "We're planning to build a fence between the Slash Diamond and Luther's old Rocking T. I want to keep the straight-bred Durhams separate from the crossbreds."

"Is your brother Hiram still your partner?"

"Actually, no. Sara, er . . . ah, *we* decided to buy Hiram out."

It was then suddenly clear to me why Tom had married Sara, the socialite from Boston.

"I wanted to ask you what you think about building a fence between the Quarter Circle L and the Slash Diamond, Genevieve?"

"I've never given that much thought. You're talking about more money than I got to spend. The wells will put me out a bundle."

"If we shared the cost, it wouldn't be hard on either of us."

"I don't reckon I need a fence bad enough to spend a bunch of money on one."

"I would like to have a fence to keep your bulls away from my cows, since I'm trying to increase the quality of my herd."

"Tom, it's you what's trying to increase your herd quality, so why don't you put up the fence. I'm not afraid of your short-legged bulls getting to my cows. For one thing they're too short, and for another, they ain't fast enough. I watched one of your Durhams with a head start one day. The poor little feller was no match for one of my long-horned devils. I drove your bull home so he could have some fun with one of his own kind."

"Put some thought to the fence, Genevieve. You would be able to control your represos better."

We had finished supper. Tom paid for mine. I thanked him, and left to go to bed. Tom and Sara stayed for a glass of wine.

I was in bed, thinking about what Tom had said about controlling my water holes by having a fence to keep his cattle out of my country. The idea made sense, but I didn't want to spend that kind of money at the time. What I had saved up, I wanted for what some people called "a rainy day." Out here I was saving for a dry day.

I was almost asleep when I heard them walking down the hall. I recognized their voices.

"That Genevieve Ames is as stubborn a woman as I have ever known," Tom said.

"Tom, dear, you must give her credit for managing her ranch by herself."

"If she had any sense at all, she would get rid of those Texas bulls and buy some Durhams."

They must have gone into their room, because I didn't hear anything more. I commenced thinking about the time Tom and me spent a wonderful night in the Grand Hotel. I couldn't help wonder how passionate Sara Smalley was. It was clear to me, from the slip of his tongue, that Tom had most likely been attracted to her money more than anything else. I felt kind of sorry for her.

On the way back to the ranch the next morning, I kept thinking about the fence between the two ranches. I decided to wait and see what Tom would do with his wife's money. Maybe I'd get a fence without spending any of mine.

The day after I got home, Kenny Waddell came in with his well-drilling rig. It took him the rest of the day and half the next to get it set up over the place he figured was best to sink the hole. I had never been around such a noisy machine as that drilling rig. When he got the motor started and the bit running up and down, pounding and pounding, it was hard to talk to anyone out in the barnyard. Yellow Flower stayed in the house with her mother. I rode with Will to check the cattle.

We rode out together for a while. I asked him what he thought about a fence line dividing us from the Slash Diamond.

"It's Tom Smalley needing the fence. Let him pay for it," Will said.

"That's what I've been thinking," I agreed.

"He must have plenty of money to be buying Breeland's Rocking T, all those high-powered Durhams, and then go to building a fence between the two outfits."

"All of a sudden he gets married to a Boston socialite, and the next thing he's spending money what ain't made yet," I commented.

We went separate ways in our circles. I rode down the *bajada* to a spot I thought might be a good location for a well. It was about four miles down the slope from Turkey Tank. As I rode around I spotted a few cows and calves, but I figured with a well or water hole, more cattle would range there. When Kenny shut down his rig for the day, I asked him what he thought.

"For one thing, Mrs. Ames, you should file for a homestead. You can do that at the land office. That will make the spot where the well is, your land. I wouldn't drill a well on public land. Someone else could file on it and the well would be theirs."

"You sound like a lawyer, Kenny," I said.

"When it comes to drilling wells, I know what's best when it comes to filing a homestead."

"How about me showing you the place I got in mind to put a well. You can tell me if it's a good place to drill. If it looks good to you, I'll go to town to the land office and file."

"I can do that, but before you file, you'll have to get a survey so you file for the right location."

"I hadn't thought about that."

"Lots of people don't if they've never done it. If you drill a well that's not on the homestead you filed on, you might as well have not filed."

I hitched up the mules the next morning and drove Kenny down to where I wanted the well. He looked around some, then told me it looked like a good spot to drill. We piled a bunch of rocks into a cairn to mark the place for the surveyor. I took him back to start the well rig, then drove to town to hire a surveyor. This well-drilling was more complicated than I had reckoned on.

There was a couple of surveyors in Tombstone. I had to

wait around for one to come back from a job. The other had gone to Tucson for a week. It was late afternoon when the man showed up. Dave Hinton was a tall feller, with sandy hair and reddish mustache. He wore a pair of high-topped laced boots and a scruffy-looking hat like Custis had. I told him what I wanted and where I wanted him to survey.

"I can go out there with you in the morning, Mrs. Ames. You can show me where the homestead is, and I'll do the survey along with another I'm working on nearby."

"I'll meet you here in the morning. What time?"

"I get going early. Make it six o'clock."

"You said you were surveying nearby. Can you tell me where that might be?"

"Actually, I'm working on the boundary between your ranch and Mr. Smalley's Slash Diamond. He's planning to put in a fence. I just started the job. I located the section corner I needed today."

That surprised me some. I thought back to having supper with Tom and Sara a few days before. That rascal had already made up his mind to build the fence before he tried to talk me into paying for half of it. I was sure glad I didn't go along with him on that deal. Tom's fence didn't bother me a dingle as long as it didn't cost me.

I got a room at the Grand for the night, and got to thinking I was spending as much time in town as I was at the ranch. I met Dave and a young feller named Lawrence, who was Dave's rodman. I learned that the rodman held up a pole with numbers on it while Dave looked through his spyglass.

I took them out to where Kenny and I had built the cairn. "Where would you like the homestead surveyed, Mrs. Ames?" Dave asked.

"I reckon if you put this cairn right in the middle, that would be fine."

"We'll stake the section when we get it surveyed. I can see that it shouldn't take long, maybe three days."

"Should I come to town again in three days?"

"That should be all right. I'll have the map and the legal description for you in my office."

I drove back to the ranch. Kenny was standing next to the cable what lifted the big round bit up and down. I couldn't tell how far he'd got down, but the bit was out of sight. He left the rig running while he come over to tell me he'd hit some rock that would take some pounding to break. He said the hole was thirty-four feet deep. I told him what Dave Hinton had said about picking up the papers in three days.

"We'll have plenty of time," he said. "This baby might be tough going for a while."

I was glad I was paying Kenny to drill by the foot instead of by the hour or day. As it turned out, Kenny was there for two weeks before he hit water at two hundred twenty-eight feet. He was happy, but not near as happy as I was. It could have been a dry hole. He drilled down forty more feet before pulling the bit out for the last time.

"You've got a real strong well here, Mrs. Ames. There's sixty feet of water standing in her. I hit a good aquifer."

"What are you talking about?"

"An aquifer is like an underground stream. You have a good one down in that hole."

"I'll have to take your word for it."

Kenny smiled. "I'll start the other hole in a couple of days, once I'm set up. Once I get that one down, we'll know what size windmills and tanks to order. I sure want to thank you for the good meals you folks have cooked for me here."

"You're welcome, Kenny. It's been a pleasure. And thank you for the well."

I hadn't done much riding since Kenny and his well rig commenced drilling the well. I was either in town getting papers worked out, or watching what was going on. Will had seen Dave Hinton and his rodman surveying the boundary. He had palavered with Dave some, and told me that he figured Dave to be an honest sort. I was glad to hear that, because that's what I reckoned. After hearing that water-cooled engine popping along, and the drill rig thunking away for two weeks, the silence in the barnyard was welcome. I felt like I had my home back.

The summer rains had been coming in pretty regular. So far, the July storms were real spotty in the valley, but the mountain country looked like it was getting some good rain. That evening, after Kenny left with his rig for the low country, I went to bed early, right after supper.

I don't know what time Will come down to the house and woke up Blue Humming Bird and me to tell us Yellow Flower was having her baby. We got into our clothes as quick as we could and went up to the barn. Blue Humming Bird went to Yellow Flower immediately and began doing what she knew she had to do. I took Will outside to calm him down.

"She midwifed me with Roland," I assured him. "She knows more about birthing than both of us. Just let her do what she has to do, and everything will be fine."

"I know you're right, Genevieve. I just don't want anything to happen to my wife or the baby."

"Come with me to the house, and I'll heat up the coffee. There's nothing for you to do until the baby's born."

Will sipped at his coffee nervously, but I was glad he had listened to me instead of staying there to get in the

241

way. I commenced palavering with him about the wells and Tom's fence to keep his mind off Yellow Flower. After a while, I suggested that we should go up to the barn to see if Blue Humming Bird needed anything we could get for her. He jumped up like a cat chasing a mouse.

Yellow Flower was having big labor when we got there. I kept Will at the door, holding his arm. A few minutes later, we heard Blue Humming Bird say to Yellow Flower, "You have birthed a man-child, my daughter."

Will and me eased our way in through the door. Blue Humming Bird was chanting something, probably the same as she did for Roland. I patted Will on his back and left him to be with his wife, son, and mother-in-law.

They named the little boy Thunder Cloud, after the big white thunderheads of the rainy season. The baby brought a happy glow to Blue Humming Bird. Will was so excited, he couldn't leave Yellow Flower's side for two days except to eat. He brought her meals to the barn, and it was probably fifty times that he told me what a good-looking boy he had fathered.

I took the cradle board that Blue Humming Bird had given me for Roland and gave it to Yellow Flower. I couldn't help the tears. Yellow Flower's eyes filled, too.

"Come, Grandmother Genevieve. I would like you to hold your grandson."

That made me cry more, but I held little Thunder Cloud in my arms. He was a good looking boy. Yellow Flower had put a lot of Apache into him, but I thought I could see Will's eyes and nose.

The rainy season ended in September. Kenny Waddell finished the lower well, another strong one. By the middle of November he had installed pumps and windmills on both wells. He also put two ten-thousand-gallon storage tanks next to each windmill. Will made a water trough out of lumber for the lower well. He used the old trough in the corral for the other. Kenny showed him how to put the pipes in from the storage tanks to the troughs.

I was happy that both were good wells, and I paid Kenny the rest of the money I owed him. He had shown Will everything there was to know about the pumps and windmills while Will helped him install them. I was kind of sorry to see Kenny leave. He said he was heading out to the Sulphur Springs Valley to drill five wells for a rancher over there.

I sold the yearlings to Frank Soldner again. They brought a good price. After spending a big chunk of money for the wells and their equipment, I felt good to have my savings rejuvenated.

Tom had hired Antonio and Abelardo to build his fence. As usual, they were doing a good job. I rode over to ask them if they would fence the section well site when they were finished with Tom's. Also, I asked them to build a corral by the well. I figured if we had corrals around enough water holes, we could do all our branding with less chousing of the cattle.

Chapter Sixteen

After the boundary fence was finished, Tom rode over. He told me he wanted to round up all the cattle on both sides to get them where they belonged. I didn't agree with an extra roundup to disrupt the mother cows, so I suggested we could get the job done as we branded in the spring. He wanted to get all his stock on his side of the fence, and all of mine off his range. I reckon I gave him further reason to call me stubborn, but I didn't believe in working cattle any more than you absolutely have to. It disturbs their daily routines just as much as moving humans around disturbs humans.

Tom was peeved that I wouldn't do what he wanted. I told him that I would send Will over for his roundup, and that we would drive all his stock into his range as we found them. Will wasn't happy about having to go away for a few days. He liked spending evenings playing with his son.

Tom's roundup lasted two weeks. All told they gathered thirty-two of my cows and five bulls, and drove them through the gates into my range. After we had finished branding I counted forty-seven of Tom's cows as we drove them through the gates. Not one of them had a Durham-cross calf at her side.

Just after we finished branding, I noticed Blue Humming Bird losing her happy look and not saying much, even at meals when Yellow Flower brought Thunder Cloud with her and Will. I didn't say anything to her, I just let her be. It worried me that little by little she seemed to be losing her appetite. When I come in from riding one late afternoon, she was in the cooking room. I got me some coffee and sat down at the table, watching her. I reckon she didn't see me watching, because every so often I saw her move like she was in some kind of pain in her belly.

I didn't ride the next day. I decided to have a palaver with my friend. After breakfast, Will went out to saddle up. Yellow Flower took little Thunder Cloud back to the crib Will had made. I was alone with Blue Humming Bird at the table. The hollow look was coming back to her cheeks.

"I'm worried about you," I said. "I want to know if you are sick. I want to know what is the matter."

"Do not worry about an old woman, Genevieve. I have a few aches, that is all."

"You are not the Blue Humming Bird I know."

We sat there across from each other for a few moments before she began to speak in a sad, painful voice.

"You are not Apache. You cannot know what it is to live without your people. I am empty without the man who was my husband. My spirit is out of balance. I am happy to see my daughter happy with my grandson. I am sad because the man who was my son cannot give me a grandson.

There is no medicine man to renew the balance of my spirit."

"Is there anything I can do to help my friend?"

"You have helped me more than you can know. I am grateful for your friendship. I will ask the gods to care for you. But even you cannot take the place of the People. I have been listening to an owl for nearly a moon. This is not good. It is the ghost of one who used to be. I have the 'darkness sickness.' "

She rose from her chair and went to her sleeping room. I sat there alone for a while, thinking over what my friend had said. I felt very sad, but no tears filled my eyes.

It was a little more than a week later when Will and I got back to the corral from checking the lower windmill, making sure the tank was keeping full. There was plenty of feed on the foothills, so I decided to hold off awhile before drifting the cows up to the high country for the summer. Besides, we had seen a bunch of cows what were looking like they'd have late calves.

I noticed the zebra dun wasn't hanging around with the other horses for their grain. I unsaddled the roan and turned him out. Will said he'd grain him for me, so I ambled down to the house for coffee and to see how Blue Humming Bird was feeling.

She wasn't in the house, so I got my coffee. It was cold. I looked in the stove, and there was just ashes in the firebox. I poured the coffee back in the pot and got the fire going. I reckoned Blue Humming Bird was up with Yellow Flower and Thunder Cloud.

When the coffee finally heated, I poured out a cup and sat down at the table. It suddenly dawned on me that supper wasn't even on the stove. I finished the coffee and decided to go up the the barn to find Blue Humming Bird.

I knocked on the door. Yellow Flower, with the baby in her arms, opened the door. Sadness was all over her face.

"Is your mother here?" I asked.

"She left during the morning. We must talk."

"Where did she go?" I continued.

"Let us go to your house to talk, Grandmother Genevieve."

We sat at the table. Yellow Flower had put the baby in the cradle board and placed it on the floor, next to her chair.

"My mother has left us. She has left for another world. This morning she told me before she rode off on the zebra dun mare. She has the sickness of darkness, and has gone home."

"Do you mean she has gone to the mountains to die?"

"Apache do not speak of that. We accept. I will not speak my mother's name again. She is now 'the woman who was my mother.' "

Yellow Flower didn't cry, but the sadness stayed on her face for days. Somehow, after she explained about her mother, I didn't cry either. But I missed my Apache friend. I would never forget my Blue Humming Bird who flew in a different direction than the others. The zebra dun was standing outside the corral gate the next morning. She still had the bridle on her head, with the reins tied over her neck.

Living alone in the house took a passel of time to get used to. Yellow Flower was there every day to make supper. I did breakfasts for the three of us. She never mentioned her mother again. Neither did Will.

* * *

John Duncklee

I could see a summer storm building to the south. It was toward the end of July, and there had been a few storms. I was out at the woodpile splitting stove wood before the storm hit. The dogs commenced to bark, so I looked up and saw a rider coming up the road. I went on splitting, because I was almost done. When I looked up again, I recognized Sara Smalley, riding a tall chestnut sorrel. I sunk the ax into the chopping log and went out to meet her.

She was riding one of those English flat saddles and was dressed up in the darndest outfit I ever saw. Her hat was a little round thing with hardly any brim to keep the sun out of her eyes. The britches she had on looked like elephant ears sticking out. The dark blue jacket had brass buttons, and her high-top boots had tiny little spurs on the heels. The horse had a half-scared look in his eyes as he watched me come up. The bridle had a green and white colored headband, and double reins.

"Hello, Genevieve," she said as she was dismounting.

"Hello, Sara. What brings you to the Quarter Circle L?"

"I just decided to take O'Malley for a good long ride."

I reckoned that O'Malley must be her horse's name.

"Well, tie him to the hitchrack. The coffee's hot. I'll be with you in a minute. I need to bring in some stove wood before the storm hits."

I went out to the woodpile, gathered up an armful of the split stove wood, and brought it into the house to the cooking room. Sara followed me through the door.

"Sit down at the table. I'll bring the coffee."

I brought our coffee out to the table and sat down with her.

"That's quite a horse you're riding," I remarked, starting the conversation.

"O'Malley's a dear. His granddaddy won the Irish

248

Sweepstakes. O'Malley's an Irish Bred. I had Father send him out here last month. I missed him so. I used to go to our farm in Sudbury almost every weekend to ride."

"How's he do working cattle?"

"I don't know. O'Malley's a jumper. It's just nice to have him with me again. It's very lonely at the ranch."

"I get lonely once in a while, but there's enough to keep me busy near every minute."

"I really admire you, Genevieve. Most widows would have sold out and moved to town. Tom has told me a lot about you."

"I tried my best, is all."

"Tom is trying his best to establish himself as a cattle rancher. I guess that's why I get so lonely at times."

"Why don't you ride with him?"

"Oh, I do when he's home. But he spends a great deal of time in Tucson. Colonel Hooker and Colin Cameron are friends of his. They meet at the Stockman's Club to talk about cattle. I don't understand how men can talk about cattle all the time."

"Doesn't Tom take you to Tucson with him?"

"Occasionally, but there is very little for me to do in Tucson. There are practically no shops where I like to go. Tom's always with his friends. I would like to go to the music group's concerts, but Tom says he has to do business at the Stockman's Club."

"That seems like a long way to go to do business."

"That's where Colonel Hooker advised him to build the fences to keep his Durham bulls with his cows. He was going to drill some wells after the driller was through with yours, but he said the driller was charging too much money."

"I think Kenny Waddell was reasonable with me."

"I have an inkling that Tom made Mr. Waddell angry, trying to bargain with him."

"Tom's got his fences, anyways."

"And he has his precious Durham cattle."

A thunderclap interrupted our palavering. Sara jumped up from her chair to look out the door.

"It looks like a storm is upon us, Genevieve. I should put O'Malley in a stall. Do you have an empty one?"

"The best I can do is the corral," I answered, getting up from my chair. "You can put that saddle in the barn. I'll go up there with you."

She untied the reins from the hitchrack and led the horse to the corral. She hurried getting him unsaddled, and I took the pancake thing into the barn. Yellow Flower come to her door. I introduced her to Sara before beating it back to the house. The raindrops had started sprinkling.

After I poured out more coffee, we sat down again. Sara seemed to have something else on her mind. I just sat there sipping coffee, waiting for her to talk.

"Tom told me that you had Apache Indians living with you. Yellow Flower is a pretty girl."

"She's married to Will, my cowboy. I've known her quite a spell. Her father and mother were good friends with Custis and me."

"Where are her parents?"

"The Mexican Army killed her father and brother. Her mother brought her back here. Her mother isn't with us anymore."

"Tom told me the Apaches were savages and stole horses and cattle from Americans."

"I know how Tom feels. We had a big fight about that

once. He just doesn't understand Apaches are people just like us. They just live a different kind of life."

The storm hunkered in and commenced to rain hard. I had some beans and stew on the stove, so I put it in some bowls. I didn't know if Sara would eat such common food, but it was all I had to offer. She liked the stew especially.

"I don't do much cooking at the ranch. Ophelia, my Mexican maid, does most of it. Sometimes she gets a bit carried away with the chili. But I don't speak Spanish, and she doesn't do well with English. I try to teach her, but she doesn't learn very quickly."

"Do you try to learn Spanish?"

"Heavens, no. I had a terrible time with French at Radcliffe."

The storm passed. Sara wanted to start home before another cloud started spilling rain. I went to the barn with her and watched her saddle O'Malley for her trip home. She tried to dry him off with a grain sack as best she could before putting that dinky little saddle on. I could see she knew what she was doing.

I was glad Sara had ridden over. We didn't have much in common, but she seemed nice enough to palaver with once in a while. She invited me to ride over to the Slash Diamond anytime. I said I would, but I knew I probably wouldn't. There was always enough work to do to keep me busy. I couldn't help wondering how Tom and her really got along together. But it sure enough wasn't any of my business.

Sara rode over about once every two weeks after that. I reckon I was her only friend. Sometimes I was at headquarters, sometimes I was out riding. If I wasn't home, she'd wait. Eventually I learned a lot from Sara. She told me not only about what was going on at the Slash Diamond, but also happenings at other ranches in southern Arizona.

After fall roundup she told me that Tom had bought more Durhams, both bulls and heifers. I also learned that Tom was trading his Texas cows to Hooker for Durhams. From the numbers she talked about, I reckoned Colonel Hooker was a lot better trader than Tom Smalley.

She seemed to miss her life in Boston, because she told me all about all the things she used to do. I gathered that her family had more money than they could count. It was interesting that her father was in the same kind of business as Tom's, only Sally's father worked out of Boston instead of New York. Both men had known each other for years, being how they was in the same kind of business. I also found out that Sara had known Tom since they were both kids, and that their families had always reckoned the two would get married.

Sara had also known Tom's brother Hiram since they were kids. But Tom, with his independent nature, attracted Sara. She didn't like Hiram, and it was her wish and her father's money that made Tom buy Hiram's interest in the ranch.

She became quite fond of Thunder Cloud, and told me she wanted a baby. I asked her why she didn't go ahead and have one. She said that Tom didn't want children. That commenced me to wondering why he had paid so much attention to Roland on his visits. Time after time, Sally's comments led me to believe that Tom Smalley was a twenty-four-carat phony.

I reckon the next couple of years were as good as I'd seen on the Quarter Circle L. The heavy winter rains of 1888 and '89 filled the represos, and the spring feed on the foothills looked like a meadow. The mother cows, calves, and weaners slicked off and got fat. I noticed that more and more cows had calves and raised them to weaning age. My idea of getting rid of old and barren cows was paying off. It sure didn't make sense to keep cows that ate grass but didn't have calves. There was still a lot of ranchers what run steers. That was too risky a business for me. I knew a mother cow, come rain or drought, would pay for herself eventually.

The market held up real well too. I always got a mite less for my leggy devils, but they were better at rustling for feed than Tom Smalley's Durhams. But there's something about this country what a cowman can always count on. Drought will hit sooner or later. And it sure enough come in '92.

I could never remember working so hard in my life as I did then. Everything was dry as powder. During May and June the represos commenced drying up. I rode up to Skeleton Tank one day and found a young cow stuck in the mud at the bottom. Her calf was close to her, bawling for milk. I managed to throw my rope around her horns, and me and the horse dragged her out of the mud. I don't know how long she'd been mired like that, but once we got her on dry ground, she wouldn't get up. She just laid there. One thing about cows, when they decide to give up, there's not a thing you can do. I waited around for quite a spell, but this gal had taken it into her head to die.

The calf was too big and feisty to carry on my saddle, so I got my rope on him. By the time we reached the corral, I had that rascal broke to lead. There was others what died, but Will had most of them drifted to the high country. The springs were still running, but the streams had all dried up.

John Duncklee

Eighteen ninety-three was the year I'd like to forget ever happened. Beef prices had sunk so low, it wouldn't have paid to drive them to Willcox if there had been a buyer there. Cattle buyers were as scarce as rain, because nobody wants cattle in a drought. I watched a lot of cows die in spite of all Will, Yellow Flower, and I did to try and bring them through the dry times.

We drifted the entire cow herd up to the mountains earlier than usual the spring of '93. The grass on the foothills was ate off down to nubbins. The represos was just full of cracked, dried mud. The lower well was still strong, but with no grass and little browse for the cows to eat, there was only one place to go, the high country. But with the streams plumb dry and the springs beginning to slow down, we had a real problem to solve.

I took Will up to the high country to show him the "water trees" what Hiding Fox had showed me years before. Besides our camp gear, we packed in our shovels and a crowbar. We made our base camp where I reckoned it was about in the middle of the high country. Will went out hunting the first evening and brought back a yearling buck deer for our camp meat. We both saw that the drought had taken a toll on the wild game as well as the cattle. The buck was skinny, and we both figured that he would have starved to death if Will hadn't taken him.

We were up and around early the next morning. The nearest "water tree" was close enough to walk to, so we set out before sunrise after a breakfast of venison liver. I reckoned we'd walked less than a mile, following a dry streambed, when we come to the bent-trunked sycamore tree. I explained all this to Will before we started out, so he recognized it right off.

Right in the dry creek bed, opposite the bent tree trunk,

we commenced digging. It was sandy ground with just a few rocks we had to pry loose with the crowbar. After we dug down three feet, water started seeping into the hole. Will got excited seeing that and commenced making the hole longer. I dug opposite Will. It wasn't long before we had an eight-foot trench started. We kept on digging down. The water kept seeping into our trench until it was plumb full. Then it dribbled over the sides of where we had piled the sand we had dug out.

It was a pretty sight. We walked back to camp, caught the hobbled horses, and saddled them. First off, we rode to the seep to give the horses a drink, then went looking to find some cows to drive to the new source of water. Another of the springs was a half mile up the slope. We rode there first and found over thirty head standing by the slow-running spring, waiting for it to give out enough water. Will and I got around the cattle and started them toward our new bent-trunk seep.

By the time they were within a couple hundred yards of the water, the cattle smelled it and moved out at a trot. They drank the water out of the trench, but it filled up again after the cattle drifted off looking for something to eat.

I took Will to the next bent-trunk "water tree" next to another dry streambed. We commenced digging again. The water started seeping in at two feet. Again we rode out to gather cattle and drive them to that seep.

We spent three nights and four days in the mountains, digging seeps where I knew there was "water trees." I couldn't help think about Hiding Fox. What a wonderful parting gift he had given me.

The seeps by the water trees took the pressure off the dwindling springs. It also scattered the cattle over the high country more so they had less miles to walk to feed and water. We continued riding the high country, carrying our shovels to clean out the seeps so they would keep giving the cattle a supply of drinking water. Although the feed was scant, I knew most of them would survive the drought as long as they had water.

I was considering driving some of the cattle down from the mountain so they would water at headquarters and at the lower well. Those we could locate at headquarters could range some up into the high country. The cattle watering at the lower well would browse on the mesquite and catclaw. I had spent a bunch of my savings, but I thought about buying hay from the Mormon farmers in St. David.

Sara had ridden over while we were in the mountains. Yellow Flower told me about her visit when we got back. Yellow Flower said Sara seemed upset that I wasn't home. A week later she showed up again, right when Will and me were coming back from cleaning seeps. We went to the house after I got unsaddled.

"How are you surviving the drought over your way?" I asked her.

"Genevieve, I can't believe all the cows that are dying. It's so sad that I don't like riding in the pastures and seeing all the carcasses. And what a smell! Those redheaded buzzards are so ugly, too."

"I've got them here. Sometimes the sky is black with them. They're only doing what they're meant to do, clean up the dead."

"I came over earlier, but Yellow Flower told me you were in the mountains."

"She said that you seemed upset. Is everything all right?"

"Oh, I was probably upset not to see you. It's quite a ride over here."

"I'm sorry I haven't been over to visit, Sara. This drought keeps us busy near all the time."

"How I know that. Tom is really worried, and I don't see much of him. He's either riding or in Tucson. He's very upset about this drought and all the cattle dying. The tanks are all dry. Most of the springs up high are either dry or running very little water. The only water we can count on is from the well at headquarters."

"Too bad he didn't have Kenny Waddell drill a couple of wells when he was in the country."

"He realizes that now. He wanted me to ask if you would furnish water from your lower well for his cattle. He noticed you don't have many down there."

"I'm starting to drift more of the cows down to that well. There's scant feed, and they'll have to browse the mesquite and catclaw. His cattle in there would be too much for the browse."

"Tom said that Colonel Hooker is watering his neighbor's cattle for twenty-five cents a head. Tom will pay you thirty."

"It just won't work, Sara. I don't have the feed. Besides, my bulls would get to his cows. He built the fence to keep that from happening."

"Then I don't know what he's going to do."

"Has he thought about hauling water?"

"He says that's too expensive."

"Drought is always expensive. Cattle without water die. That's more expensive than hauling water. Maybe he could find Kenny Waddell and have him drill a couple of wells."

"I don't know about that. I suggested that, but he didn't answer."

"Sara, I'm real sorry I can't be more help. I'm busting my britches to get as many cows through this thing as I can."

"Tom's losing a lot of the Durhams. I think he wants to sell out, but there are no buyers."

"Nobody wants a cow ranch during a drought, Sara."

"Genevieve, you seem to be my only friend around here. I'm still trying to get used to living in the West. I have to admit that I'm almost ready to go back to Boston."

"What would happen to the ranch?"

"Frankly, that's the only thing keeping me here. Tom had me ask Father for more money, but he said no. And if I left, all the money Father has already sent would be lost. I can't help wonder about all the time Tom spends in Tucson. It seems to me he should be at the ranch during such terrible times."

"I'm afraid all that's something you have to figure out for yourself."

"Oh, I know that, Genevieve. It's just that I needed someone to talk to."

"I don't seem to be much help."

"You're more help than you realize."

Chapter Seventeen

We commenced moving the cattle. It was no big roundup, just a few every day. We drove some to headquarters, where we wanted them to get used to watering and then go back to grazing what they could find toward the high country. I reckoned the lower foothills could carry a hundred head or so. The lower well could take care of many more than that, but I knew the feed was mostly browse.

It took a lot of riding to make sure the cow herd was spread around. We also kept the seeps cleaned out. I thought about going to town to hire someone to tend the seeps alone, so the rest of us could take care of keeping the cattle drifted.

One day, riding the lower country to check on how the browse was holding up, I got to the lower well around midmorning when I knew the cattle would be in for water. That way I could check their condition without riding out into the brush where they'd go in the afternoon. As I rode up, the first thing I noticed was two of Tom's Durham bulls drinking from the wooden water trough Will had built. I rode through the cattle lying around the water hole and found fourteen head of Tom's cows with Durham-cross calves. I wondered how they could have gotten through the fence.

I thought my cows were thin, but those poor devils was even worse off than my older cows. In a way, I hated to move them. I thought about how they'd probably die back at the Slash Diamond. But it was no time to be sentimental if I was going to keep my own cattle alive, so I commenced getting them together. I was able to work them slow and cut my cows away from Tom's. In a little bit I had them headed out away from the water hole. They knew where they had come from, and headed straight toward one of the gates in the fence.

When they were within a couple hundred yards of the gate, I circled around them and loped my horse to the gate. I looked at the tracks before opening the gate. It was just like someone had painted a picture. I saw cattle tracks coming right through the gate. On top of those, there was horse tracks going back into Slash Diamond country. I could even see where whoever it was dismounted and closed the gate behind him. I reckoned Tom Smalley was getting desperate to do something like that.

I circled around behind the cattle again and drove them through the gate. I got off my horse, closed the gate, and mounted up again on the Slash Diamond side. I wanted to make sure those cattle got back to Tom's headquarters, and while I was there, I thought I'd visit Sara.

Jonas was working in the big corral when I pushed the cattle I was driving through the gate to the water trough.

"Hello, Jonas," I said when I rode up next to him. "I found these Slash Diamond cattle at my lower windmill. By the tracks through the gate in the fence, it looks to me like they was driven there. Where's Tom?"

"It's nice to see you, Missus Ames. Mista Smalley headed out for Tucson this morning early. Said he was going to get a well driller."

"Is Sara home?"

"No, Missus Ames, Missus Smalley done went to Boston, I believes. Took her Thoroughbred horse with her. That's all I knows."

"Are things pretty bad over here?"

"Missus Ames, I never in my life seen so many dead cows. They don't have no feed, and the only water's here at the headquarters. Mista Smalley's in a heap of trouble with this drought."

"We're having a time too. Tell Tom I'd appreciate him not driving his cows to my water hole."

"I'll do the best I can, Missus Ames."

"Thank you, Jonas. I best be getting back to my riding."

"Before you goes, Missus Ames, I'd like to ask you something."

"What is it, Jonas?"

"I don't hardly know how long Mista Smalley's gonna want me to work here. And I'd like to know if you got work for me?"

"I expect I could use your help most any time, Jonas."

"Thank you, Missus Ames. I'd be proud to work for you all."

I rode back thinking about Jonas. Tom would be a fool to let him go, but I reckoned that was his business. I got to thinking about Sara, too. From what she said to me, I reckoned she had decided she'd had enough of Tom Smalley

261

and the drought. I could understand why she felt lonely. I also wondered about Tom's Tucson visits. That wasn't my business either, but I was still curious.

I told Will about the Slash Diamond cattle at our water hole. He wasn't surprised, but thought we should make sure it didn't happen again. From then on, we rode by there at least twice a week.

Yellow Flower, with child again, quit riding with us, so Will and me had it all to do. The biggest job was cleaning the seeps. We kept most of the cattle in the high country that winter of '93. They seemed to be able to make a living on the feed up there.

I became a midwife when Yellow Flower birthed her second baby boy. Will was real happy, and they named their son Cougar Man, because Will had shot a cougar the day he was born. The cougar had killed a calf, and Will rode up on the big cat as it was having its meal.

I wished that Blue Humming Bird could have seen her grandson. Once in a while I hankered to ride to the old clearing to see what had happened to my friend. I knew she was gone, but somehow I wanted to go there.

A winter storm came from nowhere. I woke up one morning in February to see the clouds hunkered in over the valley, and then they commenced to cover headquarters. I reckon I was as happy as anyone could be to see those clouds, and then to feel the gentle rain. Will and me stood out in the rain and got soaked.

The storm stayed around for three days. I wondered if that meant the drought had broken. It had been so long since the ground was wet, it felt funny to walk on it.

The sky cleared to its usual blue without a cloud in the sky. The March wind arrived, drying everything out again, but the browse in the lower country commenced to sprout its new green leaves. The drought wasn't over in my mind. More of the older cows were getting poor, and some of them ended up as buzzard bait. I got to where I hated seeing those big birds circling overhead because I knew they'd found a dead animal. I was getting hard, too. I started taking dead cows for granted; no sorrow, just realizing there wasn't anything more I could do for them.

I rode down to Saint David to talk to the Mormon farmers about buying hay. They was sure a strange bunch. They asked a bunch of questions as to why I wanted hay and what I was fixing to feed it to. Then they'd tell me they didn't have any hay for sale. Strange clannish folks.

Come June, we spent most of the time at the seeps. I reckon if it hadn't been for those seeps and the few springs what kept running, I'd have lost a lot more cows than I did. It was a lot of work keeping those seeps cleaned out. Around the twenty-fourth I kept watching for those white clouds what should be coming in from the south. One day they commenced flying in high and fast. They were small for a while, but after the Fourth of July, they got bigger. Then they started coming in lower.

Will had ridden over to the seep I was cleaning.

"Look, Genevieve, the sky's getting dark. We may be in for a storm."

I stopped working with the shovel and looked up to the sky.

"You may be right, Will, but I believe it when I get wet through."

Neither one of us had been packing our slickers for ages. If that big black cloud did decide to give us its rain, we'd both get soaked, but neither one of us cared. I finished cleaning the seep and got back on my horse. By then the clouds had joined up, and all of a sudden lightning lit up the mountain and an earsplitting crash of thunder sent me to realizing we might be getting some rain.

It wasn't five minutes later when the rain commenced to pound down on us. I looked over at Will. He had a grin on his face like a quarter moon.

"I reckon we might as well ride on in," I said.

"Lead the way, Genevieve. I'm soaked, happy, and hoping this is the end of the drought."

I rode out to the trail off the mountain. We were back at the corral, but the storm hadn't quit. We didn't see a rivulet all the way down. The ground was real thirsty, soaking up every drop that storm gave out. We unsaddled, gave the horses some grain, and I walked down to the house. My boots was full of water so that it almost felt like I was slushing through a stream. I took the boots off, emptied out the water, and took them into the cooking room. I got some dry, uncooked beans and poured enough in my boots to fill the bottoms. Then I stood the boots against a wall. This way, the beans would soak up, swell, and my boots wouldn't shrink. Shrunk-up boots are worthless, because they sure don't fit again.

The next morning the clouds come in again. By midday they had built up into storms, and soon after, the rain commenced falling in buckets. Toward the end of that storm there was a little runoff in the barnyard. But that was hard packed from horses, so I figured the rangeland was still drinking the rain after so long a thirst.

It was almost like the clouds had been storing up water for two years and were finally so full they had to let it all fall. The storms came most every day. By August the ranch looked like paradise. All the represos had filled. The mountain streams were gurgling. The springs were back to normal, and the grass on the foothills was green and tall. The cattle what hadn't died looked fatter than I had seen them in a long time. I decided it was a good time for me to visit Paula in Tucson. I'd never been to Tucson, because I never had reason to. But I always wondered what it was like.

I didn't have any valises, so I packed a dress and a few other things in a clean flour sack. It was also the first time I had ever ridden on a railroad train. The steam engine blew a lot of black smoke out its chimney when we started out from Benson. There were some passengers what looked like they was used to trains. I got me a seat by the window and watched the countryside go by. It wasn't long before there was more of a desert than what we had in the Dragoons, and when we was getting fair close to Tucson, the country got flat and full of bushes with little dark green leaves on them.

At the Tucson station, I stood there for a while looking at the piece of paper with Paula's address she had given me. Out in front of the station I saw several buggies parked. I walked over to one with a man sitting on the driver's seat. He asked if I needed a ride somewhere, and I gave him the piece of paper.

"That'll be twenty-five cents," he said.

I reached in my pocket, took out a handful of change, and gave him the twenty-five cents. I got into the buggy, and we were off to Paula's house. We went through what seemed the center of town. There was stores selling this and that, people walking around, and horses tied to hitchracks in front of a few saloons. It looked a bunch tamer than Tombstone was when I first went there with Paula.

"Here you are, ma'am," the driver said as he reined in the horse.

"Thank you," I said, and stepped out of the buggy.

A small sign at the gate to the yard said, "Nathan Russell, Attorney-at-Law." I opened the gate, walked up to the front door, and used the big brass knocker. A young Mexican girl opened the door.

"I'm here for Mrs. Paula Russell," I announced.

"Come in. I will get the señora for you."

I stepped inside to a small room that led to a hallway. The girl went to the rear and disappeared. In a few minutes, I saw Paula walking toward me with a questioning look on her face. She suddenly turned all to smiles when she recognized me.

"Genevieve! What are you doing in Tucson? What a nice surprise!"

She was hugging me before I could say anything. I was sure glad to see her, and could feel the tears of happiness filling my eyes.

"I just came for a visit. The drought finally broke, so I left Will and Yellow Flower to take care of things at the ranch."

"I'm really happy to see you, Gen. Nathan is with a client at the courthouse right now, but he should be back soon. Let me show you to your room."

"This is quite a house you have here."

"I enjoy it. It's also Nathan's office."

"You're in a pretty fancy neighborhood."

"This is just next to the real rich neighborhood in Paseo Redondo. That's where Colin Cameron and Levi Manning have their mansions."

"I've heard tell of Cameron. He ranches out in the San Rafael Valley. He's one of the cowmen bringing in Herefords like Colonel Hooker's bringing in Durhams."

"Colin is one of Nathan's clients."

"I can see you're happy, Paula. That's wonderful."

"Remember, it was you who told me I should move to Tucson."

"And I'd never been here."

My room was nicely furnished with a carved wooden table, a soft upholstered chair, and a big bed. I put my few things in the chest of drawers and went back to the sitting room, where Paula said she'd have coffee for us. It was almost like being back at the parlor house in Tombstone where we'd had coffee so many times.

"Tell me about the ranch, Gen," Paula inquired as Alicia, the Mexican girl, brought in our coffee.

"It was a terrible drought. I lost a lot of cattle, but not as many as some. The high country and the seeps saved a bunch of them. I also had the two wells."

"How many did you lose?"

"When the drought commenced my tally book had me with seven hundred and thirty cows, fifty-three bulls, and five hundred weaner calves. The book now has me with five hundred and forty-seven cows, forty-three bulls and four hundred and twenty two-year-olds, two hundred and thirty yearlings, and some weaners."

"I've heard some ranchers say they lost seventy-five percent of their herds."

"I reckon Tom Smalley must be one of those."

"That's what I heard at the Stockman's Club. Why did he lose so many?"

"He run out of water except at the headquarters. He also lost a lot of those short-legged Durhams. I'm sure enough glad I stuck with my longhorns. What's the Stockman's Club like?"

"Nathan and I go there because of Nathan's clients. It's a nice place where ranchers gather to talk and drink. They also have a very nice dining room. I'll have Nathan take us to dinner there while you're here."

"I'd like that. Sara Smalley told me a little about it. She said that Tom spent a lot of time there."

"I suppose you've heard about Sara leaving Tom and going back to Boston."

"Jonas, one of their cowboys, told me Sara had taken her horse back there."

"It's still the talk of the town here. Sara went back to Boston for good. She caught Tom with another woman. Tom is trying to sell his ranches. Sally's father is taking Tom to court to recover the money he lent Tom to buy out his brother and buy his Durham cattle."

"I didn't know all that, and I'm his neighbor."

"All the talk seems to stay in Tucson, I guess. Nathan told me all about it. He's not involved with either of them, Tom or Sally's father, but he learns things from other lawyers."

"Sounds like Tom's in big trouble."

"According to Nathan, Tom Smalley has dug himself into a financial hole that's too deep for him to crawl out of. Most people in Tucson don't feel very sorry for him. Even the cowmen he calls his friends think he should spend more time on his ranch and less time trying to be a big shot in the Stockman's Club."

"I feel sorry for Sara. She used to ride over and visit. I was too busy cleaning seeps to go visiting. Sara seemed real lonely."

"She was well-liked the few times she came to town with Tom. She came to Tucson one time when Tom thought she was still on the ranch. Tom was coming out of the new hotel with some young girl on his arm when Sara saw him."

"She never told me about that."

"I heard that she went back to the ranch, packed her clothes, and made arrangements to ship her horse back to Boston. Tom never saw her leave."

"I must say, I had a good time with him while it lasted."

Nathan came in to join us. He seemed happy to see me, and we had a nice palaver. Paula asked him to take us to the Stockman's Club for supper.

"Genevieve is more of a stockman than a lot of those people who go there," she said. "And she's never been there."

"That sounds like an excellent idea," Nathan replied. "Colin will be there. I think he would enjoy talking cattle with Genevieve."

The Stockman's Club was the fanciest place I'd ever been to. The bar and lounge part was full of red leather chairs, shiny dark brown tables, and brass gaslights. Ladies were not allowed at the bar. Nathan led us into the lounge and introduced me to Colin Cameron, who owned the San Rafael de Zanja on the border, forty-odd miles from the Quarter Circle L.

"How did you fare the drought, Mrs. Ames?" Cameron asked in his Scottish accent.

"I reckon I lost twenty-five percent, so it was a pretty grim time."

"You, Mrs. Ames, are among the fortunate. I understand that your neighbor, Tom Smalley, lost over seventy-five percent of his herd."

"I haven't seen Tom to talk to him about the drought."

"He will probably come here in a while. I understand he's spending most of his time in Tucson these days."

"Like I said, I've had too much work to do at the ranch to go neighboring much."

"Smalley has mentioned you. I remember him saying

that he was unsuccessful in convincing you to crossbreed with Durhams."

"He tried. He even built a boundary fence to keep my bulls away from his cows."

"I believe he mentioned that the fence was a great expense, but worth it."

"It's none of my business, but I reckoned at the time he should've drilled some wells. The drought wouldn't have been so tough on his cattle."

"I expect you're correct, Mrs. Ames. I had to move a lot of cattle to California."

"Colin," Nathan interrupted. "Genevieve has been managing her ranch alone for some time. I think we should drink a toast to her determination."

"I should say that is an excellent idea. Here, let me have a round brought."

Cameron motioned to a waiter, who came over to the table for the order. We all told him what we wanted. In a few minutes he was back with a tray full of drinks. Cameron lifted his glass for his toast.

"To a very determined lady, Genevieve Ames, who successfully defies drought and the United States Cavalry."

"How in the world did you hear about that, Mr. Cameron?"

"Perhaps, Mrs. Ames, you are more well-known, and I must say respected, than you realize."

I reckon I was a mite embarrassed, because I felt my face get flushed. Here I was in Tucson for the first time in my life, and one of the most well-known cattlemen in the territory knows about me kneeing Lieutenant Holmes.

"I reckon I never gave that much thought," I replied.

"I understand that the lieutenant was transferred to Virginia. His troops spread the story of his impertinence to his superiors."

"I reckon I ought to come to town more often."

"Mrs. Ames, I know you will have nothing to do with Durhams to crossbreed to your longhorns, but have you ever considered Herefords?"

"They're just as short-legged as Durhams, Mr. Cameron. I want to keep the leg on my cows so's they can walk to water from more distance than a mile. I've seen my cows grazing four miles from the nearest water hole."

"That's an excellent point, but by developing water at closer intervals you might consider increasing the quality of your herd by crossbreeding to some of my Hereford bulls. I imported my original Hereford stock from Scotland."

"Well, Mr. Cameron, good luck selling your bulls. I might be old-fashioned, but I have to stick with what works for me."

Tom Smalley, with a young-looking woman on his arm, came into the lounge. He looked at Cameron but didn't see me sitting at the table. He walked over, leading the woman.

"Colin, how are things in Hereford heaven?"

"Jolly good, Tom, now that we have our grass back. I believe you know everyone here. It has been a pleasure to meet your neighbor, Mrs. Ames."

"Why, Genevieve, I didn't recognize you. How nice to see you. I would like all of you to meet Grace Holland."

Everyone said their howdies and all. Tom and Grace sat down to join in the palaver. Grace was a pretty girl, not more than twenty, I reckoned. She wore her light brown hair long, and she used a bunch of makeup like a lot of the girls did in the parlor houses in Tombstone. She didn't say much of anything, and sat there like she was supposed to

271

look pretty. Tom just about ignored her as he got into talking with Cameron.

"I understand you have your ranch up for sale, Tom," Cameron remarked.

"That's a fact, Colin. The drought killed me. I lost seventy-five percent of my cattle."

"I might have someone interested," Nathan said.

"That's better than I've heard so far."

"Why don't you come around to my office tomorrow and we can talk it over. Make it ten in the morning. I don't have a court date until Thursday."

"I'll be there," Tom replied.

"If nothing happens, I may have someone else," Cameron said.

Now I knew why the Stockman's Club was a popular place. I wondered how many head of cattle had been bought in the lounge, and how many ranches changed hands over a few drinks.

Tom avoided getting me into the palaver. I reckon Cameron was his target—always trying to be one of the important people, Tom was. Nathan excused us to go to the dining room. I was glad to leave the lounge and the one-sided palaver between Cameron and Tom Smalley.

When we got home, we had a brandy together in the sitting room.

"By the way that Tom Smalley talks, you wouldn't think he's about to lose everything," Paula remarked.

"He may think he can bluff, but this is no poker game he's playing," Nathan replied. "My client, who's interested in buying Smalley's ranch, is no amateur. He's wise to the market. He's wise to Tom Smalley. And he's been a cowman for forty-odd years."

"I reckon I'm about to get a new neighbor," I said.

"Genevieve, if my client gets Smalley's ranch, I think he will be a very good neighbor. He was smart enough to sell out his ranch near Globe just before the drought. He waited for the drought to break before looking around for another ranch."

"How much is Tom asking?"

"That's almost an irrelevant question. What's more pertinent is how much can he get. The market on ranches has not come back since the drought. People are too afraid of the risk."

"A bunch of work is what a ranch is," I replied. "But there's risk in getting out of bed in the morning."

"I'll keep you abreast of the situation as much as I can, since you live next to the Slash Diamond."

"Thanks, Nathan. I'm just curious as to who my neighbor will be. I haven't had the best of neighbors out there."

"There's another thing you may not know, Genevieve. There are all sorts of rumblings from the government about designating grazing leases on the public domain."

"I don't even know what you're talking about."

"There are just rumblings so far. If you want me to keep you informed on these matters, I will be glad to. To my knowledge, you are Paula's best friend."

"We have been best friends for a long time, Nathan, dear," Paula said.

"Would you be interested in buying out Tom Smalley, Genevieve?" Nathan asked.

"If I had the money, I wouldn't want to get any bigger. The Quarter Circle L is enough for me to handle."

"Suppose Paula and I bought Smalley's ranch. Would you be interested in becoming the manager? You could hire a foreman, he could hire the cowboys. You would make sure everything was running properly."

"Nathan, Paula, you know I would do just about anything for you two. But managing that ranch, trying to keep my outfit going, and having a little bit of time for myself wouldn't be a smart thing for Genevieve Ames. Besides, business and friendship make for an odd partnership."

"There are a lot of good ranches for sale right now. There are people who realize that they have overstocked the ranges. Some want to get out of the cattle business. Frankly, Genevieve, this is a good time to buy a ranch."

"I'm sure it is, but I have a ranch, and it's a good one to get my cows through the drought like it did. All this talk about restocking the ranches seems real stupid to me. The ranches had too many cattle before the drought. Comes the drought, and they lose half or more of their cows. Now they talk about restocking. Don't they learn anything?"

"Take Smalley's ranch, Genevieve. You, yourself, said he should have drilled wells instead of building fences. As a result, he lost most of his cattle. So a new owner comes in, drills some wells, and runs enough cattle so the place isn't overstocked. Doesn't that make sense?"

"A new owner coming in and drilling some wells makes more sense than me mortgaging everything I own to buy a ranch what would be too much for me to handle."

"Today's cattle business is based on volume, Genevieve."

"I'm getting by, and that's about all I really want and need, Nathan."

"If you two want to sit up and talk ranches, I think I'll go to bed," Paula remarked as she rose from her chair and yawned.

Chapter Eighteen

After three days in Tucson, the train wheels clickity-clicking over the rails almost put me asleep on the way to Benson. I couldn't help think about how Paula's life had changed so much since she left Tombstone. She and Nathan respected each other and enjoyed living together. They had a nice house and lots to do around Tucson. Nathan seemed to know everything that was going on, even in the cow business.

Meeting Colin Cameron and hearing about other prominent cowmen at the Stockman's Club got me to thinking how a few big shots had a lot of influence with their money, but the drought was something even they couldn't control. At least everyone realized that there had been too many cattle on the range. So why were some talking about restocking? I made up my mind to keep what cattle I had

John Duncklee

after the losses. Also, I thought about selling off some, because another drought was bound to hit sometime.

In spite of Cameron and Manning trying to push their ideas of crossbreeding to Herefords, along with Colonel Hooker and Tom Smalley singing praises to their Durhams, I still reckoned my longhorned cattle would be just fine for me.

Tom's trouble sounded serious. I couldn't understand how a man who was about to lose everything could strut into the Stockman's Club like he owned half the territory free and clear. I couldn't help wonder if he would be able to sell out before his father-in-law took over the ranch.

I'd been away for only a short while, but I was glad to get home to see Will and his family. I told them about what I'd seen, heard, and done in Tucson. Will asked a bunch of questions about what was happening with Tom Smalley. Jonas come over while I was gone. He told Will that he was thinking of quitting the Slash Diamond. Before he left, he said he'd be back in a week or two.

We commenced rounding up the high country a week after I got back. I had seen Frank Soldner in Tucson, and he wanted to contract the weaners and older animals what I had held over. The prices were better than what they had been for two years, so I told Frank he could come out and look at what I had for sale. When we had the yearlings, twos, and weaners gathered and down in the foothills, Frank came out to look.

"There's a bunch of feedlots springing up in the Salt River Valley," Frank said. "Your cattle will fit a couple of my orders."

"I've been selling to you for a long time, Frank. You've always been honest and fair with me. What do you think about the fellers who are crossbreeding with Herefords and Durhams?"

"I'll tell you what I've been hearing in the feedlots. The crossbreds fatten quicker and easier than your old longhorn cattle. Those old boys in the feedlots are paying a dollar or two more for the crosses."

"I've heard the same thing, but look what happened to Tom Smalley during the drought. He lost seventy-five percent of his cattle."

"Genevieve, you have to realize that Tom Smalley is no cowman. He'd have lost seventy-five percent no matter what kind of cattle he had."

"I just hate to think of breeding my leggy cows to short-legged bulls what can't walk more than a mile and a half to water."

"You have a good point, but the market's going to leave you behind."

"But the market changes all the time. I have a notion that it won't be too many years before leggy critters will be popular again."

"I'm no cowman, Genevieve. I'm a buyer. I never buy a cow brute unless I have it sold. You folks have to think about what's best over the long pull. I'm just telling you what I hear around the country. You've done well with what you have as far as raising calves. You might be satisfied with a lower price as long as your cattle suit you."

"I've long said that I don't want Durhams or Herefords messing with my cows. I just wanted to hear what you might have to say."

"Like I said, Genevieve, you've done right well with what you have. Another thing, you're ahead of the game, always have been. In this part of the country there's a fast trend from running steers to cows and calves like you've been doing. Luther Breeland isn't the only steer man to lose his hind end."

"We'll have these critters at Willcox in a month. I'll take your offer as long as you incude the hundred dry cows."

"Genevieve, you have a deal. Let me write you a deposit draft."

Two days later, Jonas rode in early. Will and me was saddled and ready to start gathering to cut out the dry cows. We waited for Jonas to ride into the barnyard.

"Morning, Missus Ames, Will. I'd like to hire on if'n you'll have me."

"What happened at the Slash Diamond?" I asked.

"Mista Smalley come in and told us that we is to have a new boss. He brought this new boss with him. The man looks like a cowman, and talks like one. He probably be a good boss, but he look at me wrong. I figures to leave before he tells me to."

"Are you ready to start today?"

"Soon as I take this horse back to the ranch."

"Take one of mine. There's four in the corral. You can put your gear in the barn when you get back. We'll be working the high country, looking for dry cows. While you're back there, tell the new owner we're gathering, and he's welcome to come over for his strays."

"Thank you, Missus Ames. I'll get back as soon as I can."

"Just get yourself settled in. You can start tomorrow morning."

Will rode one circle while I rode another. I saw where the seeps had all sanded in, but the bent "water trees" were still standing like they were, waiting to tell us where to dig again if we needed to. I wondered what my new neighbor was like. So far, the Slash Diamond neighbors hadn't been the best. Tom Smalley was a whole lot better than Dobbs, but he was still a coyote. There was lots of two-legged coyotes in the cow business.

Jonas was back when we rode down from the day's work. He had put his few belongings in the barn and seemed happy to be with us.

"The new owner said he'd be over in a few days," Jonas said. "He's too busy getting settled. I told him we'd probably be working the lower well country."

We got everything gathered from the high country, and were starting to cut out the cattle for the trail drive to Willcox, when the Slash Diamond's new owner rode up to the lower well and introduced himself.

"Mrs. Ames, I'm Vernon Loomis, your new neighbor."

By the way he sat his saddle I could tell he was not a tall man, but stockily built. His face was real round, with beady eyes and a reddish flat nose. I could see his hair was steely gray beneath his hat. He sure wasn't what I'd call handsome, but he wasn't plumb ugly either.

"Mr. Loomis, it's a pleasure meeting you. Welcome to the neighborhood. We found three of your yearlings the other day, and I had Will drive them toward your headquarters."

"Thank you. I'll do the same for you when we round up. I'm still trying to get acquainted with what's left of Smalley's herd."

Will had ridden up, so I introduced him to Loomis. Jonas kept his distance riding around the cattle.

"Mrs. Ames, I understand that one of my cowboys quit me to go to work for you."

"That's right. Jonas has been wanting a change for quite a while."

"In Colorado, where I come from, there's a code

279

between ranchers when it comes to hiring someone else's cowhands."

"I understand that, Mr. Loomis, but Jonas came over looking for work before you bought the Slash Diamond."

"To tell you the truth, Mrs. Ames, I probably would have let him go anyway. I just don't cotton to his kind working my cows."

"Then I reckon you're just jawing at me."

"Now, I didn't come over here for a fight, Mrs. Ames."

"Then I reckon you best respect my feelings about who works the Quarter Circle L."

"Why is it you women, who figure you can run a ranch as good as a man, always get your dander up so easy?"

"I reckon it's because you men don't give us any credit for brains."

"Well, let me know if you need help on your drive. I'll send someone over."

"Thank you, Mr. Loomis. We'll be starting the drive in two days unless something boogers these critters and we have to gather again."

Loomis left, and we continued our work. Two days later, we said good-bye to Yellow Flower and the children and headed the sale cattle toward Willcox. Loomis sent a man over to help, so it was easy to start the trail herd. I went on ahead with the pack mule to set up camp. I couldn't help wonder about that Loomis feller. I hoped he wouldn't cause trouble, even though he talked big for a newcomer. Maybe all newcomers had to talk big to try and impress their neighbors.

We got the cattle to Willcox without any problems. Most years we had to keep strays away from the trail herd, but this time the range was mostly empty along the route.

Frank settled up with me, and we headed back as soon as we loaded the cattle on the railroad cars.

It felt good having the dry cows out of the herd. I was still worried about the calf crop, since it had been so dry for two years. A lot of cattle don't breed well during drought. I had fifty two-year-old heifers what looked bred, but I really wouldn't know where I stood with the calf crop until we gathered in the spring to brand.

The winter storms helped the high country with several heavy snows. That high country was always important with the springs and streams. Small mesquite, catclaw, and white thorn had commenced growing with the foothill grasses. It looked like the brush was marching up the hillsides from the arroyos.

Loomis commenced buying Durhams and Durham crosses to restock the two ranches he had bought. I didn't see much of him, because he never rode over to my place. The only times I rode to the Slash Diamond was to drive the odd stray of his that we picked up. I was glad he didn't try moving any of his cattle through the fence into my country, but there was something about Loomis that gave me an uncomfortable feeling toward him. I reckon it stemmed from the first time we had palavered about stealing Jonas.

Jonas turned out to be a good cowboy. He was a lot like Will, because he went about his work without someone having to tell him what to do all the time. Will and Jonas got along good, too. Yellow Flower had Will speaking a lot of Apache, and was teaching Jonas, too. Of course, she had learned a bunch of English. The children spoke in Apache and English.

Ever since my visit with Paula and Nathan, I kept thinking about how happy they were in Tucson. I had gotten over the mess with Tom Smalley, and sometimes I wondered what it would be like to find a good man to love and be loved by. Whenever I'd get those lonesome moods, I'd saddle up a horse and ride the high country.

I took another trip to visit Paula and Nathan after the spring roundup was over. They were glad to see me, and I enjoyed the visit. I learned a lot about what was going on. Nathan told me what the government was doing about setting up grazing leases, homesteads, and things. I told him I didn't trust my new neighbor, Loomis. Nathan agreed to keep a lookout on anything that might affect my ranch. He was a land lawyer, mostly, so he kept track of things what I never heard about.

I had a long palaver with Paula about my lonesome feelings. She said I should come to Tucson more often, that there was a bunch of good single men looking for women to marry up with. I was pushing thirty-three years old, and told her I wasn't hankering to become somebody's wife in Tucson. If I was to hook up with a man, he'd have to move to my place. We had a good time palavering, and some laughs together. I promised her I'd visit more often.

The cow business prospered. The dry years of 1899 and 1900 didn't hurt the market any. Frank Soldner bought my yearlings for eighteen dollars. The crossbred cattle were bringing a few dollars more, but I was satisfied with the prices I got for my Texas leggy devils. Some ranchers complained about the drought, but I was lucky to get some summer storms and a few winter snows in the high country.

Vernon Loomis had Kenny Waddell drill six wells. Kenny stopped by to tell me what was going on. He also checked our two windmills. I decided another well would be good insurance, and my cows would be able to graze more of the foothill country. I had Will file for a homestead where the well was to be, and Kenny pulled his rig in when he had finished with the Loomis jobs.

Nathan had told me that he would write me about anything going on in my neighborhood. I checked at the post office every time I went to town for supplies. One day I got a letter from Nathan telling me I'd better get to Tucson and see him. The letter said that Loomis had put in for a grazing permit from the Department of Interior in the high country.

I packed a few things when I got back to the ranch, and left for town again. When I got to Nathan's office, he went through a pile of maps on a table. He pulled one out and spread it out.

"Where have you been grazing your cattle on the mountains?" he asked.

I'd never seen many maps, so I had a hard time figuring what was what. Pretty soon, I located my high-country pasture by seeing where the springs was.

"According to Loomis's application, he claims to be running two thousand head in the mountains."

"If he is, I don't ever see but a few strays."

"How many head do you run up there?"

"Since the drought of ninety-three, I cut down to somewhere around four hundred fifty mother cows, forty-five bulls, and fifty replacement heifers. Then there's the odd yearlings."

"You need to get busy and get your grazing permit established, or you won't be grazing any cattle on the mountain country."

"I've been grazing that country since we bought the ranch."

"Times have changed, Genevieve. The old ways of grazing are over. The government has taken charge of everything except deeded land."

"Can you do all that stuff for me? I don't even know where to go."

"I'll see what I can do. But I think your neighbor is pulling a fast one, and he seems to be in a strong position with the people from the Department of Interior."

Paula and Nathan took me to the Stockman's Club for dinner. Nathan pointed out Loomis's lawyer and told me about the man's reputation for being on the shady side.

I met General Levi Manning, who owned the Hacienda de la Canoa, an old Spanish land grant, and a bunch of land from the Santa Rita Mountains to the Baboquivaris. Nathan introduced me to him.

"Mrs. Ames, it would be a pleasure for me to show you Scotch Farms, where I raise my purebred Herefords. They are fine animals, imported from Scotland. I even brought the herdsman with the cattle."

"Thank you for the invitation, General. Everybody seems to be wanting to sell me bulls I don't want."

"I wouldn't think of selling you bulls you don't want, Mrs. Ames. In fact, I use most of the bulls on the Canoa cows. I just thought you might like to come out and look around."

"Maybe the next time I'm in Tucson, General."

Manning was a handsome man who certainly carried himself like a general. When we were alone again, I asked Nathan more about him.

"He was Surveyor General for the Territory. That's why everyone calls him 'General.' He made money in oil out in California. I guess you might say he's one of the most important men in Tucson."

"How big is the Canoa?"

"Manning has around four hundred sections, either deeded or under lease. They say he employs twenty-five to thirty cowboys. He also has a lot of business interests in Tucson."

As we were palavering, I saw Vernon Loomis come in and sit down with his lawyer. I wished Nathan could have heard what was going on.

"Genevieve, I think you should stay in town for a while," Nathan said. "I'll get an appointment with the regional director of Interior, and I'll need you with me to tell your side of the story."

"Whatever it takes. Will and Jonas can take care of everything on the ranch."

The next day, Paula took me around town while Nathan went to the Department of Interior office to set up a meeting. Paula enjoyed our outing, especially the picnic she packed. We had our lunch at the Elysian Grove. Then she drove the buggy out to Scotch Farms to show me Manning's Hereford cattle grazing on irrigated pastures. I must admit they looked nice in the green fields, but I still didn't think they would do well on my country. When we got back, Nathan said we had an appointment the next morning.

The Department of Interior office was in an old adobe house. We walked in at ten o'clock for our appointment with Harold Wamsley, the regional director. The walls were covered by maps. There was a few photographs here and there, but mostly maps. Wamsley's desk was a large oak table, and the top was covered with all sorts of papers. There were three pieces of furniture he called filing cabinets, also made of oak, behind the desk, and filled with important papers.

"Nathan, nice to see you," Wamsley said as we walked into the room.

"Harold, this is Mrs. Genevieve Ames."

"A pleasure, Mrs. Ames."

"Mrs. Ames owns the Quarter Circle L, in the Dragoon Mountain area. She would like to understand what you are doing in regard to grazing permits in the mountains there."

"Actually, I have never been in that area, but we have an application from Vernon Loomis for a grazing permit, Mrs. Ames."

"For how many head, Harold?" Nathan asked.

"He's applying for two thousand head. He claims that's the number he's been running. Of course, this is a seasonal permit in the higher elevations."

"Mr. Wamsley," I said. "If Loomis puts two thousand head on that mountain there won't be a blade of grass for anyone else. Besides, Smalley and Breeland didn't run that many in the high country, because most of the springs are where I summer my herd."

"We are charged with organizing rangeland into equitable use patterns to avoid much of the past trouble on the public domain," Wamsley said. "I suggest you apply for a grazing permit, as Mr. Loomis has done, based on your prior and present use."

"Before 1892 I had thirty-five percent more mother cows than I have now. That drought told me that I had too many for what my country would carry. Tom Smalley lost seventy-five percent of his, and now Loomis has restocked to more than what Smalley had."

"Mr. Loomis is buying some very fine Durham cattle, Mrs. Ames."

"The breed of cattle a man chooses should be no basis for preferential treatment, Harold," Nathan added.

"Like I said, Mrs. Ames should apply for a grazing permit."

I went back to Nathan's office with him. He had picked up some forms to fill out, and he helped me with the words.

"I can't guarantee I can do anything with this situation," he said. "Loomis's lawyer may have gotten in on the ground floor with Harold Wamsley. All I can do is try to convince Harold that he'll have a lawsuit on his hands if he deprives you of your summer range."

"This whole thing sounds like the governments can do just about what they hanker to."

"I'll follow up on this after I get your application filed. From what you tell me, Loomis has little if any prior use on the permit area he's applying for."

All that stuff stuck in my mind on the way back to the ranch. It was a gloomy train ride for me, and the glooms didn't go away after I was home. I felt like going over and telling Loomis he was a liar. But Nathan told me not to say anything about all this to Loomis. Nathan said he'd handle everything.

I told Will what was going on. He had the same feelings toward Loomis what I had. We decided to ride through the high country to see if Loomis had put any cattle where they didn't belong.

When we rode up to the spring farthest to the north and saw the fence cut, I was mad enough to chew nails. All Will did was sit on his horse and cuss out Vernon Loomis. The fence was cut on every side. We didn't have any extra wire to patch the fence with, so we rode back to the ranch. I reckoned this wasn't no matter for Nathan. He was in Tucson, and I was at the ranch. The cut fence was part of my ranch, as far as I was concerned.

The next morning, I sent Will and Jonas up the mountain with some wire and fence tools. I saddled up and rode to the Slash Diamond. The ranch dogs ran out barking as I rode into the barnyard. Loomis and two cowboys was working some cattle in the big corral. I rode up to the outside and sat there on my horse to wait for them to finish what they was doing.

Loomis finally rode up on the inside of the corral to where I was.

"What can I do for you, Mrs. Ames?"

"If you don't mind, I'd have a word with you about the fence you cut around my spring."

"Well, Mrs. Ames, that spring ain't yours, and the fence ain't legal."

"I built that fence before you even come to this country. I'm fixing what you done, and I'm telling you to leave it be."

"Now, Mrs. Ames, no woman is going to tell me what I'm to do or not to do. I think you better be heading back to your place."

"I'm not here because I want to be, Mr. Loomis. I don't want to find you cutting any more of my fence."

"You know, I've paddled women for a whole lot less."

"Mr. Loomis, don't you ever think I'm anything like the women you've known before."

I reined my horse around and rode out of the Slash Diamond barnyard without looking back. I had a feeling Loomis would go back to cutting my fences, but I'd have to wait and see when. Gollies, I was madder than a wounded she-bear, and it lasted all the way back home.

I commenced wondering if I should go back to Nathan and tell him what was happening. All this government stuff was way over my head, and then this sorry neighbor, Vernon Loomis, was making trouble what could turn into something I might not be able to handle. I'd seen enough of men killing each other over matters what could have been settled by talking things out. Will was completely faithful to me and the ranch. I was afraid Loomis might get Will mad to the point where they both resorted to their carbines. I wasn't afraid of what Loomis might do to me, but I sure enough didn't want something happening to Will.

We sat down after supper to have us a palaver about the situation. I could tell Will was upset with Loomis cutting the fence. Jonas said he was afraid Loomis might get mean with him. Yellow Flower, as usual, didn't have much to say except she thought Loomis might be like Dobbs, the man her father killed to revenge Custis's murder. I reckoned she might be close to right about that.

I decided to go back to Tucson, have a palaver with Nathan, and see what could be done to avoid any trouble with Vernon Loomis. I packed up my traveling things to be ready to leave in the morning.

The train ride commenced on time, but we stopped at Cienaga Wash for a while to wait for a trail herd to finish crossing the tracks. It was late afternoon when we pulled into Tucson. I went directly to Paula's house. She was surprised to see me back so soon. Nathan was at the courthouse, so we sat down in the sitting room with some coffee.

"I'm afraid that Vernon Loomis will cause a bunch of trouble and Will won't be able to hold on to his temper," I said.

I told her about the fence cutting and the talk what went on between me and Loomis at his corral.

"I may be a woman running a cow ranch, but I can't see why there's some men what can't seem to understand that I'm just as good at it as they are," I continued.

"Genevieve, there are few women who would have taken over like you did after Custis was killed. Most would have sold out and moved to town. I remember that's what I advised you to do. I think that men like your neighbor Loomis are afraid."

"Afraid of me?"

"Not exactly afraid of you. When they see a strong woman like you, doing the work that's normally a man's work, they're afraid for their own masculinity."

"What I do shouldn't affect them none."

"It shouldn't, but it does. What you told me about Loomis saying to you that no woman is going to tell him what to do or what not to do proves my point."

"I expect you're right, Paula. You ran your establishment in Tombstone dealing with all kinds of men for quite a while."

"When I met Nathan, I could tell that he was a good man and a real man. He isn't a man who struts around like a rooster showing off his feathers. He knows himself. He's as strong a man as I am a strong woman. You're a strong woman, Genevieve. I've told you that many times."

"I know I'm strong, but there's sometimes when I don't want to be."

"It's difficult to be a strong woman in a man's world."

"I reckon you're right about that."

Nathan was late getting back to his office, so we went to the Stockman's Club for supper. Some of the people who were there I'd seen before. Some I had met were missing. Loomis's lawyer, Leonard Ridgeway, was with two men wearing eastern-looking clothes. Nathan told us they were here looking to buy a ranch. He had talked to them when they first arrived in Tucson. Now Ridgeway was trying hard to make a sale for one of his clients. Ridgeway specialized in land the same as Nathan, but as he had mentioned before, Nathan didn't trust the way the man did business.

I told Nathan what had happened with Loomis and the fence.

"In this case, you have prior use of the spring. You built the fence. However, Genevieve, the government is tightening its control over the public domain. It has passed laws against building fences around watering places on public land."

"So the fences around my springs are illegal?"

"They may be, but the fact that you have been using those springs before the law went into effect is in your favor. I don't know what would happen if the question came up in court."

"What do I do if Loomis keeps cutting my fences?"

"My best advice at this point is to avoid any confrontation with him. Just bite your lip, and rebuild the fences until I can get the matter settled. I'll try to reason with Wamsley first, then I may have to take Loomis to court."

"Why is the government all of a sudden trying to control cattle ranchers?"

"The government is concerned about conserving the land. The cattlemen have overgrazed the ranges in the past, so the government wants to put a stop to it on public lands."

"The drought of '92 and '93 taught me a good lesson. I've cut back my cattle numbers. Now, with this grazing permit stuff, and Loomis wanting the whole mountain, I'm getting punished for trying to do the right thing. It don't seem fair, Nathan."

"I agree with you. That's one reason I'm trying to protect your interests. However, you must realize that government policy tends to generalize. It doesn't consider the individual as much as it should. The Department of Interior claims it's doing all this to be equitable. Yet this application from Loomis is based on his lies. Neither Wamsley nor anyone else from Interior has even been to your ranch."

"What should I do?"

"Like I said before, Genevieve, try not to worry yourself about these matters. I will do the best I can for you. Just go out and run your ranch the way you always have."

"The trouble is, with all this stuff going on, I can't run the ranch like I always have."

"Just do the best you can under the circumstances."

Chapter Nineteen

All the business wore me plumb out. Since I was already there, I decided to spend a few more days in Tucson. Paula was glad to have my company, and I was always happy to be with her. The next day she drove me out to Fort Lowell in her buggy. We made what the Mexicans call a *pasear*, meaning just a pass around. The fort didn't seem too active, but it was interesting to see the adobe buildings. I was more interested in the countryside. There was a bunch of farms scattered here and there, and along Rillito Creek there was bosquets of mesquite where some of the trees had trunks what looked to be four foot in diameter.

That night we had supper again at the Stockman's Club, because Nathan had invited a horseman and cattle buyer from Wyoming who was interested in moving to Tucson to get away from the cold winters in the north. Teddy Carpenter had supper with us. He was a tall, lanky man, with a full head of black hair with a few streaks of gray in it. His eyes were dark green, and his nose was thin and hawklike. I found out he was part Crow Indian.

Teddy was looking for a place to run his band of broodmares and his stud horse. He had been in Tucson for a month, but had not been able to deal with anyone who might have had pasture for his horses.

"Mrs. Ames, Nathan tells me you have a cow ranch around Tombstone," Teddy said once all the small talk was over with.

"It's a ways from Tombstone, in the Dragoon Mountains. I've got foothill grass and mountain country."

"Would you consider leasing pasture for my broodmares?"

"I never gave that any thought, because I run a cow herd."

"I've got fifteen Thoroughbred mares and a stallion. I raise mostly polo ponies, but once in a while I pick out a racehorse prospect."

"My ranch is all range country, set up for raising cows and calves. I run longhorns, originally from Texas."

"I don't think my horses would get in your way. The only time I'd need to use any of your corrals would be when I wean and halter-break the colts and fillies. Then I would take the youngsters to Tucson when I can find a place here."

"I'd have to think about having a bunch of horses on pasture. Why don't you come to the ranch to see if it would suit you?"

"You name the day, and I'll be there. Nathan, here, has told me about your ranch, and it sounds like a good place for my mares."

"I'll be going back in two days. If you'd like, we could

ride the train together. I've got my mules and buckboard at the livery in Tombstone. I'll take you around the ranch."

"In the meantime, I would enjoy having supper with you tomorrow."

"I believe that would be fine, Mr. Carpenter."

"I'll be around to Nathan's house at six."

I suddenly realized I had made a supper date with a man who was almost a complete stranger. We finished supper, and I noticed that Nathan didn't seem to have much business to talk over with Teddy. I commenced suspecting that Nathan and Paula had set me up.

Nathan had gone into his office after breakfast the next morning when Paula suggested we go shopping for a new dress for me.

"Paula," I said, tilting my head and twinkling my eyes. "You and Nathan aren't trying to match me up with Teddy Carpenter, are you?"

"Why, Genevieve, what ever gave you that idea?"

"I reckon I'm old enough to figure some things out. Thanks."

That brought on the giggles from both of us.

We went out in the buggy, and Paula took me to a store what sold dresses. She plumb took over the dress-buying, telling me which looked the best on me. The dress she picked out as being her favorite was green. I went into the dressing room and put it on. When I looked in the mirror, I reckoned it showed off my figure pretty strong.

"This outfit sure does show off my bosoms," I whispered.

"That's what it's supposed to do," Paula whispered back. "You have a beautiful pair, so why not show them off?"

"It's been a long time since I thought about stuff like that."

John Duncklee

"Well, it's time you did again. You're still a beautiful woman, Genevieve."

Paula wanted to pay for the dress, but I wouldn't hear of that. We went back to the buggy, and Paula took me to a restaurant for some Mexican food. We did have a good time together, palavering about Teddy Carpenter and a bunch of other stuff.

I was ready just before six o'clock. Teddy drove up in a hansom cab and we went to a small place that was almost out of town. There were a few people sitting at the tables when we walked in. A well-dressed Mexican man came over to us as we waited by the entrance.

"Ah, Señor Carpenter, it is a pleasure. I have your table ready. Come with me, *por favor*."

The man led us to a small table in an alcove. When we were seated, Teddy asked the man to bring us a small bottle of his best mescal.

"Well, Genevieve, and I hope you don't mind me calling you by your first name, this is a pleasure."

"I reckon I'll have to call you Teddy. I like that better than Mr. Carpenter. Where are your mares?"

"They're on a ranch near Sheridan, Wyoming. A friend of mine is looking after them."

"Is there a market for Thoroughbreds in Arizona?"

"From what I can gather, there are a few people here in Tucson who enjoy polo. Also, I noticed that horse races are popular here. I don't depend on the horses for a living. I order buy cattle for ranchers in Wyoming and Colorado. I came to Arizona to buy Colin Cameron's and Levi Manning's yearlings and two-year-olds. I do enjoy the horse business, though."

"You'll have to forgive me, because I don't know much about the horse business."

"But I know, from talking with Nathan and Paula, you're a smart cattle rancher."

"I was kind of forced into the cow business when my husband was killed and left me with a baby son. Now he's gone, too."

"Paula told me."

"What about you, Teddy. Are you married?"

"I was married quite a long time ago."

"What happened?"

"She was a wild filly. She wanted more excitement out of life than I could give her. We were married when I was twenty. She ran off with a gambler a year after we married. I haven't seen her since. I did get a letter from her a year after she left, asking me for a divorce. She told me that she was pregnant. I signed all the papers and sent them back."

"It sounds like it was tough on you."

"It was for a while. I had a lot of dreams shattered, and I've been a bit gun-shy of women since."

"Are you gun-shy of me?"

"Not yet, but it might be fun to try."

When the mescal came, we drank a toast to Nathan and Paula for introducing us. I felt comfortable with Teddy. He didn't brag or try to impress me. He was polite, listened to whatever I had to say, and the more I looked at him, the more I saw that he was handsome. Leastways, I thought so. Someone else might have found him different.

Teddy ordered a *carne asada* for each of us. The steak, broiled over mesquite coals, was delicious with the fresh *salsa chili verde*. We had three brandies after supper. With the mescal during the meal, and the brandy afterward, I felt a mite light-headed. When we reached Paula's, Teddy saw me to the door. I reckon the brandy had really sent me into some sort of mood, because I just lifted up my face and let him kiss me.

We met at the railroad station for the trip to the ranch. Teddy had his saddle and war bag with him. It was nice sitting next to him as the train wheels clickity-clacked along the rails. We didn't say much. He asked a few questions about the country near the railroad. I didn't know much more than he did, because I'd never been out in it.

When we got to Tombstone, he tossed his saddle and warbag into the back of the buckboard. We harnessed the mules and hitched them up. I paid the bill and headed for the ranch. I commenced telling Teddy about the lower range as we passed through it.

We reached headquarters late in the afternoon. Yellow Flower was in the cooking room, getting supper ready for Will, Jonas, and the children. I introduced her to Teddy, then took him outside to show him the well. Will and Jonas rode in while we were watching the windmill. By the look on Will's face, I think he was a mite surprised to see me with Teddy, but he didn't say anything to indicate it.

Supper was Yellow Flower's venison stew with beans and biscuits. Teddy told her he enjoyed the meal, making her smile. They left the house earlier than usual. Teddy and I sat at the table, and he told me about how he come to be part Crow Indian.

His grandmother, a full-blooded Crow, married a mountain man. They had two sons and a daughter. The daughter became Teddy's mother after she married a trader. Teddy had two married sisters, but his father had been killed in the Civil War. His mother, deeply saddened by her husband's death, had lost her reasoning. Teddy and his sister lost track of her.

I told him about my parents and what had happened to

them. He didn't seem horrified that I'd been raped and went with Paula to Tombstone to become a whore.

We were just palavering by the light of the coal-oil lamp when he took my hands in his.

"Genevieve, forgive my forwardness. I think you're a beautiful and wonderful woman. I admire your strength and steadfast survival efforts. I just had to tell you that."

"Thank you, Teddy. There's a bunch I like about you, too."

We palavered awhile, and then I went to my sleeping room. Teddy went to the back room, where Blue Humming Bird had stayed. I took my clothes off, got into bed, and stared at the ceiling. The coal-oil lamp made funny-looking shadows off the beams. I kept wondering about Teddy Carpenter until I felt myself trembling a little. I hadn't felt that way for a long time.

I got out of bed and went to the door of the room. For a moment, I stood there, then I eased it open and poked my head out into the hall.

"Teddy," I said.

"Yes, Genevieve."

"Would you come to my sleeping room?"

"I'll be right there, Genevieve."

I quickly returned to my bed. Teddy came in wearing his long johns.

"What is it?" he asked.

"Teddy, I hope you don't think badly of me. Please lie down with me."

He came to my bed and took me into his arms. I was tingling all over as he kissed me and I kissed him. I reached down to unbutton his long johns. He released me long enough to take them off, and we went back into each other's arms. I felt his tenderness as he caressed and kissed me. Then I knew I was a total woman again as we joined our passion for each other.

Yellow Flower getting the stove going in the morning brought me awake. I put my arms around sleeping Teddy and woke him with a kiss. I knew that if Yellow Flower hadn't been there, we would have thought about something else besides morning coffee.

We rode the foothill country all day. I showed Teddy the two wells with their windmills spinning in the breeze, and the boundary fence that Tom Smalley had built. We jumped a mule deer doe with a fawn as we rode up to Turkey Tank. It was a mite scary to watch the two jump the fence. The doe glided over it gracefully, but the fawn barely cleared the top strand of wire. Teddy agreed that fencing off the water holes was an excellent idea, not only to control the water holes but also as an easy way to gather cattle.

"We can't do that in my part of Wyoming, because there are too many streams coming down from the mountains," he explained.

During supper, and for a spell after, Will and Teddy talked horses. Jonas joined in with them, telling about the cavalry horses he had ridden. It was nice to see those three men get along so well. I brought the mescal jug from the cupboard and poured it into the small glasses. As we sipped the strong liquor, I felt like we were all a family.

It was another loving night with Teddy. I could feel myself give in completely, abandoning all other thoughts I may have had about men and the way they treated me. Teddy was a real man. I woke up in the middle of the night. The moon was peering through the window onto his sleeping body. I couldn't help watching him and wondering how come I was feeling so close to a man I had known less than two weeks.

I sat up leaning against the headboard, looking at him bathed in the moonlight. I reckon me moving made him wake up. I saw his eyes open and look up at me.

"What are you doing, beautiful lady?"

"Trying to see if you're real."

He leaned toward me, put his arms around my waist, and pulled me gently down next to him. He commenced kissing me, and again I gave myself to him as he gave himself to me. He was sure enough real.

After saddling our horses after breakfast, we rode up to the high country. The cattle grazed contentedly. They looked up as we rode along the trail, but went back to the grass as we passed by. Teddy commenced talking about crossbreeding, telling me how I could get more for my calves if they showed Durham or Hereford. He said his Wyoming customers preferred Herefords. I explained why I kept my leggy longhorns in spite of the lower price I was getting for their calves. We didn't argue, and he didn't say I was just a stubborn woman like some men had.

I showed him the Apache water trees. He was real interested in them. Then we palavered about the differences between Apaches and Crows. Teddy seemed to know a lot about the Crows and Cheyennes. He told me that me having Apache friends and the way I felt about different people made him feel closer to me than any woman he had ever known.

When I saw a bunch of Loomis's Durham heifers, I felt myself get tensed up. Then we rode up to the far spring, and there was Loomis and one of his cowboys cutting the fence again. We reined in our horses, and I crossed my wrists over the saddle horn.

"Well, Mr. Loomis," I said as calmly as possible. "I see you're cutting my fences again."

Loomis pulled a folded envelope from his shirt pocket and waved it at me.

"This here's my grazing permit, Mrs. Ames. Thanks to your lawyer, I only got a temporary permit for five hundred head."

"Well, Mr. Loomis, thanks to me they've got some grass to eat. For your sake, I hope you've got those heifers of yours bred to your Durham bulls."

"Why are you saying that?"

"Because my leggy longhorns will run those short-legged runts of yours plumb off this mountain. Good day, Mr. Loomis."

We reined our horses around without another word. When we got well out of earshot, Teddy rode up beside me and took my hand in his.

"You are one amazing woman, Genevieve."

"What are you talking about?"

"You put that jasper in his place in seconds."

"I just do what I have to do, Teddy."

After supper I got to thinking about all the government stuff. I was glad they didn't give Loomis a permit for two thousand head, but I felt up in the air about what was to become of my cattle. I talked it all over with Teddy.

"If I had my druthers, I'd just stay here with you," he said.

"I wish I didn't have to go anywhere. Gollies, the cow business is getting too complicated. Here I've been trying to take care of my range the best I can, and now the government's giving my sorry neighbor my grass."

"I think we should get back to Tucson to see Nathan. He's the best one to answer your questions."

"I know you're right, Teddy. I would just like to stay

302

here with you forever. And, by the way, do you think this country will be good for your mares?"

"It's perfect, my dear, but with Loomis crowding you on the mountain, you might need all the grass for your cows."

"I'll sell enough cows to make room for your mares."

"Let's forget about all this until morning. I want to feel you next to me in bed."

We wrangled in the mules after breakfast and got everything ready for the trip into Tucson. Teddy took away the worries about my ranch just by sitting next to me on the seat of the buckboard. We stepped off the train in Tucson late in the afternoon. I waited in the cab while Teddy took his war bag into his hotel room. He had left his saddle in the barn at the ranch. Then we went to see Nathan and Paula.

"I'm glad you came to town," Nathan said as he showed us into his office. "We have a lot of things to talk about."

I told him about Loomis cutting the fence and waving his temporary grazing permit at me.

"I can't figure out why he didn't get angry at what I said to him," I said.

"I have a good idea," Nathan said, and smiled. "Your friend, Loomis, has made an offer to buy your ranch."

"I wouldn't sell the Quarter Circle L to that coyote if I was starving."

"I certainly wouldn't advise you to take his offer. Your ranch is worth a lot more."

"What's going on with all this grazing-permit stuff?"

"I went to see Wamsley yesterday. He sees no complications, but you probably won't get the numbers you applied for because of Loomis."

"Loomis doesn't deserve a permit."

"You and I know that, but convincing the Department of

Interior is something else again. I have an idea I'd like to toss out to you, Genevieve."

"I reckon I'll listen to anything at this point."

"Do you remember the two eastern men who were talking to Loomis's lawyer in the Stockman's Club?"

"They're the men who had talked to you first about buying a ranch."

"Right. They came back to me the day you and Teddy left. They're not happy with Leonard Ridgeway. These men are livestock men from Virginia, where they raise Aberdeen Angus cattle. They're looking for a ranch where they can cross Angus with other, coarser breeds. I told them about the Quarter Circle L, and they seemed very interested."

"Does this mean you're advising me to sell out, Nathan?"

"I think you should consider it. Between Loomis and the government eating away at your independence, the inevitable droughts, and the fickle cattle market, I think you should, at least, think about selling for a good price."

"How much are they willing to pay?"

"I told them I would have to discuss this entire matter with you before I could give them a price to consider. Also, I told them that I would arrange an appointment with you to show the ranch."

"If I sold the ranch, Teddy wouldn't have a place for his mares."

"Don't let my mares interfere with that kind of decision, Genevieve," Teddy said. "If necessary, I can leave those babies in Wyoming."

"What in the world would I do if I sold the ranch?"

"Don't worry about that, Genevieve. We're both still young," Teddy said.

"Well, it sounds to me like you two are getting along very well," Nathan said, and grinned.

"You and Paula started it all. Where is Paula, by the way?"

"She should be back any minute. If you two don't have any other plans, why don't we all go to the club for supper?"

"As long as you let me pay the bill," Teddy said.

Paula came back from shopping and saw us in Nathan's office.

"Hello, you two. How did you like the ranch, Teddy?"

"Wonderful. The owner is wonderful, too."

"We thought you would think so."

"Teddy is taking us to the club for supper, Paula," Nathan said. "I think we should talk some more before we go there. You have a few things you wanted to discuss with Genevieve, I believe."

We palavered for an hour. Paula told me she thought I should sell the ranch and get away from my sorry neighbor and the government stuff. It didn't take her long to figure out that Teddy and me were happy together. She had a smile on her face like the owner of a racehorse what just come in first in a derby.

The two eastern Angus breeders were sitting at a table when we arrived at the Stockman's Club. After we ordered drinks, Nathan went over to their table. When he came back, he told us that the men would join us for a brandy after supper.

The Angus men turned out to be brothers, Dan and David Drummond. They were pleasant, but all business. Nathan had already described the ranch to them. I told them about the cattle, and they wanted to know the history of them. I told them all I knew, and we made arrangements to go to the ranch the next day. I had begun to think I was spending more time on the train than I was anywhere else.

Teddy went with me to Paula's to get my things. Paula gave me a big grin as I come out of the guest room.

"Why don't you two stay here?" she asked.

"We don't want to keep you and Nathan awake," I answered, and returned her grin.

The Drummond brothers met Teddy and me at the Tucson railroad station the next morning. During the trip, they told us what they were trying to do, and they asked Teddy all sorts of questions about buyers for their crossbreds. Teddy showed me that he knew a bunch about cattle markets.

The brothers spent three days at the ranch. Teddy rode with us as I showed them around. They spent a lot of time looking at the cattle whenever we come across them. The third evening, they wanted to talk to Will and Jonas. Dan was the one what did most of the talking.

"Neither of our wives would consider living out here in the West," Dan said. "Therefore, if we are able to come to terms on the ranch, we would like you both to continue to work here. We will make several trips a year to see how our breeding program is coming along. But, you men will be essential to us in caring for the cattle. We're willing to continue your salaries plus a substantial bonus when the calves are sold. Do you have any questions?"

"It's up to Genevieve," Will said. "If she wants me to stay. I'll stay. If she wants me to go to work for her somewhere else, I'll stay with her."

"I feel the same as Will," Jonas said.

"I don't know what I'll be doing if these fellers buy the Quarter Circle L. I think you men should stay here if I do sell out. I know that both of you know the country and the cattle better than anyone coming in new. I appreciate your loyalty. After all, you're like my family."

"If you don't mind, I'd like to talk with my wife before I say yes or no to staying," Will said, and went to the barn.

"Mrs. Ames, we would like to know your asking price for the ranch and the cattle, except for the bulls. We will be bringing in Angus bulls from our Virginia farm."

"You fellers are going to have to talk with Nathan after I get a chance to talk to him when we get back to Tucson."

"When will you be going back to Tucson, Mrs. Ames?"

I looked at Teddy. He made a face what said anytime.

"I reckon I can go back on the same train as you fellers."

Things was happening too fast. I was glad when Teddy slipped into bed next to me. With him there, all my nervousness about selling the ranch, or not selling the ranch, disappeared.

In the morning, before we climbed onto the buckboard for the trip to Tombstone, I took the Drummond brothers out under the mesquite tree and showed them the two graves.

"If I do sell the ranch to you, I'll keep this plot of ground. These are the graves of my husband and son."

"We would find nothing wrong with that exclusion, Mrs. Ames," David Drummond said.

"I'll have an iron fence put up around it."

I suddenly felt strange, and the feeling stayed with me for a while. I never thought about leaving those graves before. One part of me said, "You can't leave Custis and Roland out here alone." The other part said, "It's all right, Teddy is with you now." I don't know why Teddy made me feel free of the past, but he did.

When I was unhitching the mules at the livery stable, I took Teddy by the hand and led him into the barn. I stopped and faced him with both his hands in mine.

"Teddy, I got to tell you this right now. I know you said you were gun-shy when it comes to hooking up with a woman. I have to take this chance. I don't want to be away from you. I want to be with you, and live with you. I love you, Teddy."

"Genevieve, I was done being gun-shy the night I took you to supper in your new green dress. I feel the same way as you do. I love you too."

He bent down, and we kissed for a long time, until the livery stableman cleared his throat at the door of the barn.

We went to Paula's and Nathan's after we left our things in Teddy's room in the hotel. Paula met us at the door and went with us into Nathan's office.

"Well, how did it go? Did the Drummonds like the ranch?"

"They said they want to buy the ranch and the cattle, except for the bulls," I answered. "They wanted to know how much I was asking, and I had no idea what to tell them. I just told them that they could see you after you and me had talked."

"That was a good answer. I know they were looking at a larger ranch than yours out by Colonel Hooker's Sierra Bonita Ranch. The ranch runs eight hundred head, and the owner was asking a hundred thousand. They didn't like the cattle because the cow herd was second-generation Durham crosses."

"How much do you think they want to pay?"

"Genevieve, we won't know that until they make an agreement. Let me do some figuring. You said you're running about four hundred fifty cows since the drought. You have about forty-five bulls, so that's close to five hundred head. You have three excellent wells, and the house and barn. I would say you should ask seventy thousand for the ranch and the cattle. That would include your horses, mules, and buckboard."

"Whatever you say, Nathan. That sounds like a big pile of money to me."

"Let's give it a try. We can always come down, but once you price a ranch—or anything else, for that matter—it's difficult to raise your price."

"I'm leaving everything up to you, Nathan."

"Fine. Let's have supper at the club. The Drummonds are there every evening."

"Sounds good," Teddy replied.

Teddy took me back to the hotel so I could change into my green dress. We was a little late getting to the Stockman's Club.

We walked in and found the Drummonds sitting with Nathan and Paula. The men stood up as we approached the table. Teddy pulled one of the chairs out for me, and he took the other. Nathan winked one eye at me when I had sat down.

"Genevieve, these gentlemen want to buy the Quarter Circle L. I told them your price with the cattle, including your bulls. They have offered sixty-five thousand, without the bulls."

"What am I going to do with bulls if I don't have any cows?"

Nathan winked at me again.

"I think it's a good offer. I would accept it if I were you."

"Like I said, Nathan, it's up to you."

"Well, gentlemen, you have bought yourselves a ranch with a herd of unmarried cows. If you'll initial the changes on the contract and pass it to Mrs. Ames for her signature, I will start the procedure in the morning. Include your deposit draft with the contract, if you will, please."

I almost fell off my chair. In minutes I had sold the ranch for more money than I thought it would ever bring. Our drinks came, and I took a big swallow. Then I signed the contract where Nathan had put an *X*. Gollies, I was nervous.

The Drummonds were all smiles. They said they would have their bulls shipped in sixty days. That would give me plenty of time to gather and sell my bulls. We ordered our supper just as Leonard Ridgeway and Vernon Loomis came in and sat down to a table. Leonard got up from his chair as soon as he saw who was at our table.

"I hope I'm not intruding," he said. "But I saw Dan and Dave here. I just wondered if you were ready to accept the Deering Ranch's counteroffer."

"Leonard, if you don't mind," Nathan said. "The Drummonds have just purchased the Quarter Circle L."

Ridgeway scowled momentarily, then congratulated the brothers.

"I thought I gave you an offer on that place from Vernon Loomis, Nathan."

"You did, Leonard. It was refused."

Ridgeway quickly turned around went back to his table, and sat opposite Vernon Loomis. I watched out of the corner of my eye as he leaned toward Loomis to say something. As he leaned back again, Loomis looked our way, glaring. I reckoned I had won another battle. But I sure enough felt sorry for the brothers from Virginia having such a coyote for a neighbor.

Two days later, Teddy found a buyer for the bulls. I was glad to have that off my mind so we could get back to the ranch. I went to the blacksmith in Tombstone and ordered the iron fence for around the graves. Then we drove the buckboard back to the ranch. Will and Jonas were still riding. Yellow Flower and the children were in the house, getting supper ready. I told her about selling the ranch. She was sad at first, but she brightened up when I said that the Drummond brothers wanted Will, her, and the children to move into the house. Then Teddy come in to tell me Will and Jonas were unsaddling their horses.

We went up to the corral and waited for them to tend their horses. Then I broke the news.

"Genevieve, I'm glad for you. I sure enough hate to see you leave, but I've not seen you this happy since I hired on here," Will said.

"I got to say the same," Jonas drawled. "I just wish I'da come here earlier."

"Tomorrow we start gathering all the bulls. It'll be a tough job getting them away from their sweethearts, so we should probably gather some cows with them."

We were saddled up and ready to ride before daylight. I was hoping to gather the bulls without disturbing the cows too much. By the time we reached the high country, the sun was up. The cattle were spread out and grazing. Loomis's cattle were mixed with ours, making it difficult to separate our bulls. It felt strange riding through that beautiful mountain country for the last time. It was tough country to work cattle in, but it had been good to me, especially during the drought years. Teddy sensed my feelings and didn't say much as we rode.

Separating our bulls and cows from Loomis's cattle proved to be more chousing than it was worth, so I decided not to worry how many Loomis cows got in with ours coming down off the mountain. I showed Teddy where that old maverick bull broke his horn killing the cougar. I showed him other special places, too.

"You really love this high country, don't you, Genevieve?"

"It's been good to me, and I did my best to be good to it. But with all this government stuff, and Loomis getting set to put those short-legged Durhams up here, it's taken away the wild charm it once had."

"I think you made a smart move in selling out to the Drummonds."

"At least I stopped Vernon Loomis from building his empire."

It took us a week to get all the bulls gathered and separated from the Loomis cattle. All the work it took didn't seem worth what I was getting for them, but I had agreed to the deal. My word had always been good, and I was determined to keep it good as long as I lived.

The four of us drove forty-five longhorn bulls with a few cows to Willcox. Teddy took care of getting them shipped to the buyer in the Salt River Valley. We had to spend a night in town, waiting for the railroad to bring cars. Then we drove the cows back to the Quarter Circle L.

Once we got back to the ranch, we rested a day. It didn't take long to pack up the few things I wanted to take with us. I picked up the beaded eagle feather from the fireplace mantel and looked at it. I thought about giving it to Yellow Flower, but I couldn't part with it. Custis had brought it with him. It had been the sign from Hiding Fox that Custis was different than most other white men. I put the beaded eagle feather in my bag. When I settled in front of another fireplace, I would take it out and put it on that mantel.

The Tombstone blacksmith hauled out the sections of iron fence he had made. With Will and Jonas helping to dig the postholes, it didn't take long before the graveyard had a pretty fence around it. I had made a few cuttings from the big Tombstone rosebush and put them in a Mason jar full of water so they would grow roots. When they finished the fence and the blacksmith had left for town, I planted the cuttings at each of the four corners in the fence. Yellow Flower promised she'd keep them watered.

Saying my good-byes turned out to be tougher than I had thought, especially when I whispered my love to Custis and Roland. Will drove Teddy and me into Tombstone in the buckboard. I even cried when I kissed the noses of the mules. Teddy was wonderful. He put his arm around my shoulder until I got over it all. Before Will pulled away with the buckboard, I saw the tears streaming down his cheeks.

Two weeks later, Paula was helping me get dressed in her guest room. Teddy wanted me to wear my green dress, so I put it on. Paula had taken me out shopping and I bought a new pair of fancy shoes. I reckoned I was ready, but Paula pulled that beautiful pearl necklace out of her handbag what was setting on the dresser. It was the same necklace she was wearing when we were on the stage from Downing. She put it over my head and arranged it so it hung down between my bosoms.

"There," she said, looking at me as she tilted her head and smiled. "I think you are ready to become Mrs. Carpenter."

We held each other for a long while.

"Paula, my dearest friend," I said finally. "We've sure enough come a long ways since you was a madam and I was a Tombstone whore."

Epilogue

Genevieve Carpenter was alive and well the last time we sat down to chat over a cup of her delicious coffee. She seemed very happy with Teddy, but when we talked about the Quarter Circle L Ranch, she had what you might call a faraway look in her eyes. The idea of doing another story didn't bother her, except she said that her life in Tucson wasn't particularly exciting. Of course, I disagreed with her.

I know that I will continue to visit Genevieve and Teddy. I am very fond of both of them. In spite of Teddy's success at the racetrack, I wouldn't be surprised if one day they told me that they had bought another ranch and gone back into the cow business.

Soon, I expect I'll go to the old ranch to see how Will and his family and Jonas are getting along with the Drummond brothers from Virginia.

MOVING ON
JANE CANDIA
COLEMAN

Jane Candia Coleman is a magical storyteller who spins brilliant tales of human survival, hope, and courage on the American frontier, and nowhere is her marvelous talent more in evidence than in this acclaimed collection of her finest work. From a haunting story of the night Billy the Kid died, to a dramatic account of a breathtaking horse race, including two stories that won the prestigious Spur Award, here is a collection that reveals the passion and fortitude of its characters, and also the power of a wonderful writer.

___4545-1 $4.99 US/$5.99 CAN

INCIDENT at BUFFALO CROSSING

ROBERT J. CONLEY

The Sacred Hill. It rose above the land, drawing men to it like a beacon. But the men who came each had their own dreams. There is Zeno Bond, the settler who dreams of land and empire. There is Mat McDonald, captain of the steamship *John Hart*, heading the looming war between the Spanish and the Americans. And there is Walker, the Cherokee warrior called by a vision he cannot deny—a vision of life, death...and destiny.

___4396-3 $4.50 US/$5.50 CAN

THE ACTOR

ROBERT J. CONLEY

Bluford Steele had always been an outsider until he found his calling as an actor. Instead of being just another half-breed Cherokee with a white man's education, he can be whomever he chooses. But when the traveling acting troupe he is with arrives in the wild, lawless town of West Riddle, the man who rules the town with an iron fist forces them to perform. Then he steals all the proceeds. Steele is determined to get the money back, even if it means playing the most dangerous role of his life—a cold-blooded gunslinger ready to face down any man who gets in his way.

___4498-6 $4.50 US/$5.50 CAN

WILL HENRY

ALIAS BUTCH CASSIDY

No one would make a more unlikely outlaw than young George LeRoy Parker, grandson of a Mormon bishop. But at sixteen Parker throws in with Mike Cassidy, a shrewd old bandit who sees something in the boy nobody else does—the courage of a cougar and the heart of a renegade. Old Mike teaches the kid everything he knows, and before he is done there is no outlaw more feared, hunted, or idolized than George LeRoy Parker. . . .

___4516-8 $4.50 US/$5.50 CAN

THE HUNTING OF TOM HORN

WILL HENRY

Lively, action-packed, exciting, this is a collection of short masterpieces by one of the West's greatest storytellers. The characters in these tales—be they cowboy or bounty hunter, preacher or killer—are living, breathing people, people whose stories could be told only by a master like Will Henry.
___4484-6 $5.50 US/$6.50 CAN